Albatross II

Autodestruction

JOHN TRETHEWEY

authorHOUSE®

AuthorHouse™ UK
1663 Liberty Drive
Bloomington, IN 47403 USA
www.authorhouse.co.uk
Phone: 0800.197.4150

Published by AuthorHouse 04/11/2017

ISBN: 978-1-5246-7981-1 (sc)
ISBN: 978-1-5246-7984-2 (e)

Contents

Contents

Technical notes

1. **Technology**

In 1987, before the arrival of the IBM Desktop Computer in Europe in 1988, and then WINDOWS, all data collection and communication was on paper, transmission by post. Even the Fax machine was in its infancy, and in 1987 short messages were sent by Telex, a "Text-Telephone". Large institutions such as national police forces had primitive main-frame computers, but there was no networking, no Internet. The Soviet Union was still a closed, Communist state, and President Gorbachev's Glasnost and Perestroika only became newsworthy a year later. Practically the only technological contact between the USSR and the outside world was in the domain of Air Traffic Control, ensuring that commercial flights from anywhere in the world could transit Soviet airspace in safety.

2. **Air Traffic Control (ATC)**

A major element of this novel concerns civil aviation.
All Air Traffic Control procedures described or mentioned for the Geneva TMA and for Approach to and Departure from Geneva Airport are correct as implemented in 1987. The systems in place now differ in some respects.

3. **CB Radio (Cititzens' Band)**

Not only were there no PCs in 1987, there were no mobile phones. In Britain, trawlermen out at sea for days on end communicated with family back home by RT, Radio Telephone. The frequencies used were legally approved. But that was the extent of civilian mobile communication. Only the Police, the Fire Brigade, the Ambulance Service, Taxi cabs and ATC had legitimate radio communication.

In the USA, the long-distance truckers found a new means of communication: Citizens' Band Radio. CB radio was a VHF walkie-talkie radio for one-to-one communication, or even Conference-calls where several drivers participated on the same frequency. CB became a short-lived phenomenon in Europe in the early 1980s, ranging from hand-held models to desk-top bedroom sets. But the VHF frequencies used were neither officially allocated nor legal.

The illegality in itself was a thorny problem for the authorities, just as catching a mobile phone user at the wheel of a car is difficult today. But it had to be tackled; use of a CB radio in a built-up area interfered severely with TV reception in the neighbourhood. As all TV transmissions were terrestrial, decades before the advent of cable and satellite communication, numerous households had their viewing ruined by a selfish few. As the law began to bite, CB radio gradually died out.

Prologue

Rolle, Switzerland
1988

February 1988

There isn't a lot left of my family, just the few photographs in fact. It was on a night like this, staring at those faded enlargements and half-hearing their voices in the silence that decided me. The last thing in my mind then was writing anything. I intended action. God knows, if good intentions brought good rewards I would be a happy man. Yet today, a year later, after months in search of justice, I am not.

This is not a story about Charlotte, but it is for Charlotte's sake that I am setting it out. I thought of writing about Charlotte, but I am too close, even after all these years, and I can see in my mind's eye the trivial paper-back cover in airport departure lounges: "Charlotte's Story". No. But for her sake and in her memory, I have another, a cautionary tale. For they are out there, and they are everywhere. They have a hundred different names, a thousand salesmen, but a single fanatical aim: the acquisition of money and of souls. Freed of the joint nuisance of matter and mind, the enlightened victims are reborn crusaders, sent out to hunt down more souls. And more money.

I am talking in general about the wave of pseudo-religious Cults and Exegesis Seminars and Residential "Self-Discovery" Courses that seems to grow daily, and in particular about ALBATROSS. The 'ALBA' bit is supposed to indicate white, standing for purity, and the 'TROSS' is an acronym for The Religious Order of the Suri Sect. You may more readily recognise the name given to them by the media, the 'Suri-Saints'.

- - - - - -

February 20ᵗʰ 1987

The wind had crept round to the North and the snow was flurrying in whirlpools on the drive. The dead embers of charred wood in the grate looked too much like hard work, and I remember I opened a bottle of rum rather than bother with a fire. It was at moments like this that my eye and my mind always fell on the pictures. Then I had to stop running away, and face a bilious nostalgia. Always the same questions. Why, why, why? Where had she gone to? And what could I ever have done about it? Or done about any of them?

The level in the bottle sank rapidly, and at some point during the evening the decision was made for me by an inner area of the mind quite beyond conscious control. By the time I staggered to bed, hours later, the letter was written - typed - on this same ancient machine, property of Geneva City Police, but I don't think they've missed it. When I woke up in the pre-dawn darkness, the car was under fifteen inches of snow and I was cut off from the outside world.

I'd intended driving to work early to hand in the letter and clear out my desk without any fuss and bother. Then I would get the hell out of the airport before my superiors arrived, making all the right noises with a minimum of meaning, but it wasn't to be. By the time I'd dug out the car and swallowed a few mouthfuls of scalding coffee, it was past eight. We used to start the morning shift at 7.15 in those days, before the first rush of early morning flights, and I knew as I drove to work that the crumpled envelope in my breast pocket would not be accepted quietly without lengthy and probably embarrassing explanations. The temptation to claw it out and chuck it into the snow was great, but the inner mind had won the battle, and it wasn't going to give in now. The envelope stayed in my jacket pocket.

It was a Friday, late in February, and the roads were bad that morning, the snow-ploughs hadn't yet moved North from the Lausanne-Geneva motorway to the back roads and the forest-covered slopes of the Jura where I lived. Even with snow tyres the Mitsubishi was all over the road.

I'll never know whether it was auto-suggestion or pure coincidence that suddenly sent the car slaloming across a snow-covered patch that was no better and no worse than the six miles I'd already driven. Whichever, I ended up with the boot of the car off the road, hard against the trunk of a massive pine, the front wheels facing across the carriageway.

Even before I got out to inspect the damage, I recognised where I was. The trunk of the tree was badly scarred, and the undergrowth was torn up all around, although the night's snowfall had filled in the gouged earth, disguising the uprooted bushes as shapeless white mounds. Her car, of course, had been towed away several days previously. I had rammed the same tree where only a week previously an airport employee, an Air Traffic Controller I had known and liked, had died in an almost identical accident. Almost identical. Maybe the Mitsubishi wasn't so bad after all, for unlike her car mine wasn't even dented. When the local police had been called out, the Friday before, they'd found the remnants of her red Volkswagen Golf squashed like a concertina, and her body in a terrible state still inside it.

It was a pure fluke that I hadn't discovered her myself that Friday morning. The weather had been atrocious for days, and for the Thursday night I'd used the camp-bed at Airport Administration rather than drive to and from home. Otherwise my route to work that Friday, only a week previously, would have taken me right past her car just after the crash. As it was that Friday, Friday 13th with a vengeance, I'd been at the airport all night when the crisis broke, and she never got to work at all.

I think it was then, standing there in the bitter February morning air under that damned tree, unwilling to recognise that I was touch and go for a hangover from the night's drinking, that I actually admitted to myself the letter in my pocket wasn't a dignified close to a career - God knows there had been nothing very distinguished in it anyway - but an excuse. It was an excuse to undertake a pilgrimage I had wanted to make since the death of my wife in '81. A pilgrimage of detection, to find Charlotte.

To my superiors such an obsession was understandable but unhealthy. What they'd never understood was the bitterness, the tacit irony, of my small block of visiting cards that had been staring me in the face every day for six years. The neat black print of 'Second Deputy to the Commissioner of Police, *Aéroport de Cointrin*' made a mockery of the would-be military professional stance I had obstinately tried to maintain. "Second Deputy". There was no First Deputy, never had been, only a Second Deputy. Myself. Suddenly faced with the inevitable onset of middle age, conscious of the greying hair starting to recede around the temples, I was a man crossing the meridian of fifty who knew in his heart that his career had been sidetracked into a backwater, almost from the very day Geneviève had died.

Swiss medical experts rank among the world's best, and the best of the best have assured me that people rarely die of a broken heart. Geneviève did. After Charlotte's disappearance in '79, it was a bare two years before Geneviève looked up from her hospital bed, whispered something inaudible and slipped away. The doctors said it was an unusual heart attack, takotsubo cardiomyopathy, the "broken heart infarction". In truth, Geneviève simply hadn't wanted to live any more, not without Charlotte. Although I had never entirely given up all hope, Geneviève finally had. And died of the medically impossible broken heart. No miracles.

Stupidly, at best naïvely, I had thought at first I was being given an easy time after her death. It had taken a while to sink in that I had been side-lined into a desk-job. "Second Deputy" was a paperwork sop, contact with the public minimal, investigative work limited pretty well to lost suitcases and stolen credit cards.

God knows that, in terms of police work, Geneva was quiet enough anyway. A relatively small airport back then, we had never known anything approaching a crime wave, but my work had rapidly become no more than the duties of Honorary Consul to the Administration, to the Swiss Customs Officers, and to the French Office of the *Police de l'Air et de la Mer* in their special enclave. I was treated with due deference, and made to feel useful, but if you stopped to add up what I'd achieved in a given week or month, it came to precious little.

There had been a time when my appointment to the Airport Police had actually seemed a great step forward. In retrospect, it was my fluency in English that had swung the balance. Most people automatically speak French and German here, but fluent English at that time was a rarity. My mother was English, and I'd been to a British school at the other end of the Lake. It wasn't just the languages, though. I later discovered that the Head of Section in Carouge, where I was working before the transfer, thought I wasn't pulling my weight. That had been in the early Seventies.

At first things hadn't been bad at all. With a decent legacy and a small mortgage Geneviève and I had bought the chalet above Rolle in the Jura mountains. Charlotte was only twelve then, and had been delighted with the space and freedom of the forests. I suppose that to any father his daughter will always be the most special and adorable girl that walked the earth, and Charlotte was all of that to me. It was a sheer cruelty of life that, at the time the girl most needed a family, her mother took it into her head to have an affair with a Basel chemicals company rep on long-term secondment to Geneva. For a long time I blamed her, Geneviève I mean, but I know now that isn't right. My own pre-occupations with work and promotion had led me to spending days and nights away from home, fruitless needless to say, for already then Paul de Savigny was something of a joke to his colleagues. The All-Night Hustler they called me. More fool me, I had taken it as a compliment.

Not that Geneviève's affair was solely responsible for Charlotte's alienation, but it coincided closely, seeming to happen almost overnight. One day she was a quiet, slow-speaking, rather lonely fourteen year old, the next day a vixen with a viper's tongue and all the wayward eccentricity of a rootless organism desperately challenging everything.

It's hard to be objective about one's own flesh and blood, but attempts at rational discussion were as useless as emotional appeals. The more we tried to make contact, the more we were made to feel we were alienating her. I suppose in retrospect we got a lot of things wrong, I've met some of these wishy-washy social workers in the line of business who half told me as much.

We were more than surprised when one day Charlotte came home rabbitting on about the miracle of Jesus and the Resurrection. Moreover she was word perfect, she knew more about the Gospels than Geneviève and myself put together. Suddenly the balance was all the wrong way round, overnight it went from us telling her what was right to her spouting pious clichés about our own Godless state. And it's very hard to fight quotations from the Bible. That first evening we might, I think, have managed to put a stop to it, but after that... Day after day, starting at breakfast, and perhaps (if we saw her at all) in the evenings, Charlotte was a fount of wisdom and faith in a corrupted and evil family. It was suddenly all too easy to blame Geneviève for her indiscretions - there had been more than one, and she had taken a snide pleasure in enumerating them to me.

Have you ever tried telling someone, especially someone inspired with the idealism of youth, that they are too Christian? It doesn't sound right, and the stronger the hint, the less effective it is. And when you don't know and can't find out where it's all coming from... Oh, I know more about these people now, about their networks of attraction and persuasion, and the warmth of their magnetism to youngsters alienated by uncomprehending parents. But at that time we were as much putty

xii

in their hands as Charlotte was. Whatever we said, whatever we did, was instantly interpreted as repression, dogmatism and inhumane anti-Christian materialism. The irony was that the repression, the dogma and the inhumanity came entirely from her so-called religious mentors. But you couldn't expect her to see that. Very soon, nothing we said was right, and almost everything we did, from the way we blew our noses to the way we cut the grass, was sinful. I'll never know now how intelligent Charlotte was. Not, I suspect, a great mind, she was carried away as easily as a blade of cut grass in a hurricane, I defy anyone to have persuaded her that she was going in a wrong direction. And suddenly, one day, it was too late to persuade her of anything. She was gone.

This is not Charlotte's story, I said, but it was the initial blow of her departure that galvanised me from a pretty unspectacular career into an obsessive exploration of all that I could discover about ALBATROSS ; the media's name of "Suri Saints" always stuck in my gullet. Then a surprise discovery turned the obsession into a mania that was to destroy any career chances that I had left. This was, in fact, not connected with ALBATROSS, it was the discovery of how many such groups there were, and how many people like me and Geneviève. I was soon in contact with parents as far apart as Cape Town and Stockholm, Adelaide and Vancouver. The only part of the world that seemed immune from the assault of quasi-religious crusaders was the Soviet Bloc, and that probably because even the established Church was at the time itself firmly suppressed. Quite soon I was spending as much time on my correspondence as I was on police work. Luckily, as I've said, Geneva Airport never had much of a workload for the Constabulary, but I must have been blind not to have seen that my superiors were becoming less and less happy with the way I was moving. Blind, too, not to have realised that Geneviève was not well. I suppose I was so absorbed with my witch-hunt that literally everything else ceased to matter. I have to admit as well that I still found myself blaming her in large part for the entire situation. And then she too was gone.

With Geneviève's death I lost all appetite for the mania that had gripped me for nearly two years, I began a wearisome routine that consisted largely of getting up, putting in the requisite hours at the airport for duty, and then returning to the chalet. It was neither wholesome nor fruitful, and if it hadn't been for the Lakey affair, I am certain I should have been quietly released from duties and given early retirement last year. As it was, the Lakey thing pre-empted official action, and so I gave in my resignation and quit. But the Lakey affair would never have mattered half so much, if I hadn't received that damned dossier from Caracas...

Well, I've found the elusive first line, and quite a lot more. Now it's up to the truth and the word to have their say. I'll never write Charlotte's Story because I'll never know what happened to her, but this is something I do know about, because I have paid it in full: The Price of Enlightenment. As have so many others...

I said that I had lost all interest in pursuing my obsessive goal, the eradication of these manic groups and their mind-bending techniques. Until that day in November, when, with the snow falling and the sky darkening, a courier van drew up, yet another dreadful delivery which I no longer had any enthusiasm to plough through. However, what set this dossier apart was that it was entirely written by hand, and with several contributors.

A glimmer of the detective in me pushed me to glance at the first page. I was still reading in the early hours of the morning. Of the scores of dossiers gathering dust on my office shelves, it was the worst. By far.

I knew, as I closed that dreadful collection of little notebooks, that reading it at all had been a mistake. If my mania to find Charlotte had dwindled, it was now volcanically rekindled. Yet another mistake, as if I hadn't made enough already. It had reawakened my detestation, my loathing of everything these criminals wreak on their victims, driving them blindly insane. The forces that it unleashed in me were to be the final nail in the coffin of my career.

Chapter One

Friday the 13ᵗʰ 1987 - Black Friday

For me it started before dawn, as I happened to be in the airport already. Things didn't start to piece together until after seven o' clock Swiss time, but by then it was past nine in Moscow, and Lakey just leaving Sheremetyevo on the delayed morning flight to Zürich. Suddenly the phone lines were humming between Zürich Kloten and Geneva Cointrin, Air Traffic Control was up in arms about the whole thing, and there were high-ups I'd never heard of in Berne sending me urgent Telexes. But it wasn't until the Telex came in from Moscow, with my name on top, that I realised how important this thing was.

It may seem strange that an experienced officer should have been so slow in the uptake, but you have to remember that not only my body but also my brain had been sedentary for several years. The urgency of the Lakey affair was still not apparent to me when Zürich ATC telexed to say they were diverting flights, and could we take their midday Moscow arrival? I authorised the reply, and that was that. Geneva ATC held the morning DC10 to Delhi for Lakey, on the pretext that he was a VITP, Very Important Transit Passenger, and I thought we were over the worst of it. It wasn't until the pilot had been given clearance to join the localiser and descend on the Instrument Landing System that things really went haywire.

I got to know Captain Martin Fonjallaz fairly well in the days between the Lakey case blowing up and my resignation. He was a quiet, thoughtful man in his mid-forties, compact and competent. He sported a little sandy moustache, and his left hand was for ever reaching up as if to make sure it was still there. Most striking, however, was his strangely mixed personality - perhaps because he is mixed-bred Swiss with a Swiss German father and a Suisse Romande mother, I don't know, but it was evident that he had found the Moscow end of the business at the same time fascinating and repugnant.

In the end, Fonjallaz provided three reports for me. The first was so dry as to be no more than an amplified log of times and movements of his aircraft. The second, which he drew up in the ensuing days, again exemplified his dual nature. If the log was dry and factual, the personal report was full of imagery and detail, quite at odds with his curt, intellectual nature. And he later sent me a cassette recording in which he did his best to draw a clearer picture of events.

When I suggested I should also approach his co-pilot, Hans-Peter Mueller, he dissuaded me strongly. 'Mueller's a book man, a young man, his whole mind on career. I'm not, my career's established. But Mueller, no, whatever goes into the record that isn't orthodox... well, he'll either clam up as if it never happened, the Nixon technique, or he'll angle things in a way I don't think you could use. No. My advice is leave Mueller out of it.'

Of course, I met Mueller, interviewed him, I had to as investigating officer. Fonjallaz may have been right, for Mueller was an unimaginative and dour interviewee, and his responses were so reticent as to make me feel a very poor questioner.

From Fonjallaz's reports it is clear that he was as baffled by events at the Moscow end of the affair as I was in Geneva.

The first detail that was out of the ordinary was so unremarkable as to have been seemingly irrelevant. Then, with the flight fifteen miles out from Geneva on the ILS, it had suddenly taken on considerable significance. He and Mueller had piloted the evening Zürich-Moscow flight on the Thursday, and would make the return flight early on the Friday morning.

Normally the Swissair flight SR 496 would have used one of the recently-purchased stretched DC9-81 aircraft, an aircraft which Swissair was finding it increasingly difficult to fill on the evening Moscow flight, and equally difficult to fill on the return. As an experiment, and on that Thursday for the first time, the Swissair schedulers had replaced the 137-seater stretched DC9 with an extremely early model that must have been reaching the end of its useful life. The aircraft they put into service for the Moscow flight was a short, stubby DC9 Series 30, built in 1968. You can appreciate something of the difference if you consider that the modern variant can seat over 140, whereas the now prehistoric Series 30 seated around 80 passengers and was over 30 feet shorter. Fonjallaz explained the significance of this change of aircraft as follows:

"During my early years with Swissair," he wrote, "the DC9-30 was the aircraft on which I grew up, totalling many thousands of flying hours. It was an aircraft that I came to know inside out. Its successor, the Series 80, is in a different class. The re-training of experienced pilots to newer models may seem automatic to the public, but when I first flew the Series 80, it took me a considerable time to get used to the different flying characteristics of the much longer and more sedately powerful aircraft.

"First Officer Mueller, on the other hand, finds himself in exactly the opposite situation. He has been brought up on the stretched, quiet jets of the eighties. For him, the Series 30 is something out of the dark ages. When Mueller is flying the shorter aircraft, any experienced pilot beside him is going to know at once that Mueller is consciously suppressing his expectations of what the aircraft should do, that is, what a Series 80 would do. In some respects, he finds the machine's properties alien. This is no way detracts from his airmanship, on the contrary, First Officer Mueller is a first rate pilot." I had wondered, and still do, whether this wasn't a piece of professional niceness to water down the bad bits.

"What happened on our approach to Geneva," Fonjallaz concluded, "needed a pilot thoroughly acquainted with the capacity of the aircraft to withstand manoeuvres that would normally be illegitimate. There is no doubt in my mind that only long experience on that aircraft type made it possible to avert disaster, and had First Officer Mueller been in the left-hand seat, I am not certain what the outcome would have been."

The fact he mentions it at all seems to me to imply very clearly what the outcome would have been. And you can see from the way he mixes the Thursday evening aircraft substitution with its significance on the return that getting any sort of order into the events is difficult. Everything knocks on to affect everything else. However, from his very detailed cassette recording, I managed to piece together a fairly reliable sketch of the bits that mattered most that morning in Moscow. It's clear now that a department within a department was stretching its wings under the new rules of Perestroika, and seeing how far it could go. It was pure chance that they picked on Suri and ALBATROSS to do it. According to Fonjallaz, he and Mueller were settling down to the pre-flight check list when they had to break the list. Now we have a clear picture of what happened that morning in Moscow, but I can understand Fonjallaz's bafflement at the time. This is his version of those events...

'Swissair 493, do you copy?' The Moscow Ground-Controller's voice rasped tinnily in Fonjallaz's earphones. He drew a pencil line under check-point 33.

'Hold the list,' he said to Mueller, then in English into his microphone, 'Swissair 493, go ahead.'

'We have a problem.' The Moscow Controller was terse, 'A car is coming. Wait, please.'

Fonjallaz double-clicked his microphone switch to indicate 'message received', and stood up. 'Break the list. We'll have to start again, later.'

'Much later, probably.' Mueller nodded moodily.

A yellow airport car sped over the snow with reckless regard for the baggage trains and machinery in its path. It slewed to a halt so close to the boarding steps that the running-board - it was a very old car indeed - scraped the bottom step. A slight figure in a bearskin hat and shapeless coat skipped up the steps and past a heavy curtain which afforded some protection from the bitter cold outside.

Fonjallaz met her courteously, and they sat down in the First class section. The official - he never discovered her name - took a bulky folder from an attaché case, and opened it.

'Your flight will be delayed, Captain.' She spoke English with a Doctor Zhivago accent. 'An hour, perhaps two. We are the victims, Aeroflot and the Soviet Union, of an unacceptable state of affairs. A solution of sorts has been reached, one requiring your airline's assistance. Since the visit of President Aubert to Chairman Gorbachev last year, you understand, facilities for such co-operation have developed greatly.'

She looked at him unblinkingly from a distance of only inches. Fonjallaz recognised official bilge when he heard it and smiled politely. Mueller called him from the cockpit:

'I have Zürich on the radio. What do I tell 'em?'

'Nothing... no, wait. Monitor the Company frequency for now. Answer any questions with "Awaiting new clearance." And put the gust locks in on the stabiliser. Got that?'

'Checks aborted 7.19, gust locks in, Monitor Company frequency... How can I answer any questions?' Mueller's responses were overlaid by a tone of irritation. 'When I don't know anything.'

Fonjallaz turned to the young woman and prepared to listen to their "problem".

'We have a man in the airport,' began the official, 'in a most troublesome situation. He is a resident of Switzerland but holds a British passport. A director of television advertisements, his name is Benjamin Lakey. Do you recognise that name at all, Captain?'

Fonjallaz found time to wonder at the Russian woman's command of English even while he started on a rapid search through his memory.

'British? Lakey....' Fonjallaz shook his head, then hunched his shoulders, bringing his head forward sharply. 'Yes. Yes I do. If it's the same man, I do. A trial? Some television documentary he made... If I remember, he lost. I...'

He paused as Mueller brought coffee and several slabs of Swiss chocolate.

'You remember the Lakey case, Hans-Peter? Meridian Medicaments wasn't it, they sued him in 1984... or '85. It was a big thing. He lost, I think?'

Mueller shrugged.

'Never heard of him. I was seconded to American in California for all of 1985. Why?'

'It is like this.' The official sipped her coffee and broke off a piece of Mueller's chocolate. 'In the terminal we have twelve V.I.P.s, not Soviets, nor Swiss, checked-in on our Aeroflot flight 419 to Kathmandu. Nepal.' she added. 'Also in the airport, but in custody, is this man Lakey. They have all spent the last nine days together, travelling from Japan on the Trans-Siberian railway. You follow so far?' She paused.

'Nothing sinister in all this.' commented Fonjallaz, glancing at his watch.

'No. But the man Lakey is appealing to Soviet law to allow him to bring certain charges against the leader of this group, who in turn is pressing counter-charges against Lakey. Defamation. And felony.'

'Defamation again?' Fonjallaz stroked his jaw pensively. 'What's he supposed to have said this time?'

The Russian official sighed.

'It was unravelling that that took us half the night, Captain. You might like to ask Mr. Lakey himself.'

'Lakey is to travel on our flight?' Fonjallaz showed surprise for the first time. 'You're letting him go? Or expelling him? Who's paying his ticket?'

'One thing at a time, please, Captain.' The Russian wiped her eyes wearily with the back of her hand. 'Mr. Lakey is not being expelled from the Soviet Union, but it must *look* as if he is. If I tell you that his opponent in these counter-actions is the Indian Maharaj Suri, does that mean anything to you?'

'Suri?' Mueller spoke with sudden interest. 'The Suri of the Suri-Sect? You know him, Captain? I mean, you know who he is?'

Mueller, it turned out, had spent several years in the States, mostly California, and it had been there that he had come across ALBATROSS. Promising Heaven on earth to his "Golden State People", Suri had persuaded thousands of young people, over the years, to leave home and join him, if...

Invisibly, at first, and later all too visibly, he began to mint in the millions, no-one seemed too sure how, and the monolithic U.S. Tax Department had proved unwilling to delve too deeply. Only after the 1978 Jones-town massacre in Guyana did the full extent of the price paid for the liberties guaranteed by the US Constitution became apparent. But there are some lessons that the country that lost a thousand lives in the Guyana massacre seems incapable of learning. Suri had stepped in and effectively filled the gap that Jim Jones had left behind. But that morning in Moscow Fonjallaz was not yet clear where all this was leading.

'I know of him.' he said carefully. 'I think I begin to see. Yes. If Suri has people with him, they are probably converts? Perhaps Lakey has said some harsh things about ALBATROSS, and Suri? In public?' He lifted his hands and turned to face the young woman. 'I think I have it. On the Trans-Siberian, you say, for nine days. Hans-Peter...' He turned to his co-pilot, 'I read somewhere that ALBATROSS experiments with brain-washing techniques, transactional mind-sharing, or some such nonsense. Closed environment, public disgrace, enforced nudity, and then long sessions in violent physical contact. With sexual liberties as a so-called reward? That's the group we're talking about?'

Mueller nodded.

'That's only what the press dare print. When I was in California, there was a lot more being said. One thing certain, if I were a family man...'

'This Siberian journey?' Fonjallaz interrupted him. 'Am I right? It was a bunch of converts?'

'No. Is there any more coffee?' The nameless young woman was staring at the second slab of chocolate, then shuffled her papers again. 'When they left Nakhodka, there were no converts. Quite the opposite. Suri is travelling with his top ten people, from six different countries. What he calls his "Suri-Saints".' She sniffed angrily.

'With people like Suri proclaiming religion, do you wonder our authorities have had reservations about the power of an organised Church? Is it any wonder that "God" has been discouraged as a figurehead?'

Fonjallaz was momentarily astonished at this openness, until he remembered that, as far as the Soviets were concerned, this meeting was not officially taking place, the young woman did not exist, and Moscow would log his delayed departure as a "technical hitch."

He turned to an analysis of the situation, ticking off the queries on his fingers.

'Suri and his "Saints". What has Lakey done to harm them? What is this alleged "felony"? What has Suri done that Lakey wants to press criminal charges? Why should the Soviet Union want to be seen to expel Lakey? I'm sorry.' Fonjallaz lowered his hands helplessly. 'I'm lost.'

'You are not alone.' The woman stared bleakly out of the window to the terminal building in the gloom. 'Lakey also is convinced that he is lost. Suri is a powerful man, he will have observers, maybe even on your plane. As far as Switzerland, Lakey must be seen to be a man without hope, a man under arrest, handcuffed. It will be acutely uncomfortable for him... I thought he had suffered enough these past days.' She did not elaborate on this, but paused to sip with evident pleasure at her coffee. The second bar of chocolate was decorously unwrapped. She eyed it with restrained greed.

'It is said this Suri has a sixth sense for people who would move against him.' Unaware of her action, she sniffed aggressively. She wants some more chocolate, thought Fonjallaz charitably, and put her out of her misery. There was a very brief pause before she continued. 'I believe he calls it "God's Protection of the Blessed." If he even suspects that Lakey's story or charges are being investigated, he may change his plans. At all costs, the Soviet Authorities want Suri on flight 419 to Kathmandu, voluntarily, and today, and they want Lakey in Geneva by early afternoon.'

'Excuse me, stop there.' Fonjallaz laid a hand on her arm. 'Geneva? Surely... it may be naïve of me, but our flight plan is for Zürich.'

'You did not know?' She glanced at Mueller. 'Your flight has had to be diverted. By a pure coincidence, and one that has made things very much more difficult for us, one snow-plough has collided with another on Zürich's main runway. Zürich has three runways, but heavy snowfalls there had already necessitated diversions. Now there is the added complication of the immovable machinery...' She shrugged.

Fonjallaz was still maintaining an imperturbable front, but he began for the first time to feel a growing inadequacy. He did not really understand what was being asked of him.

'I see.' he said, realising as he said it that he did not. He looked at Mueller, who nodded.

'Zürich mentioned this.' he confirmed.

'So, Geneva it is. Lakey will be confined to his seat. No-one talks to him. No-one goes near him... no point in serving a meal to a man who can't lift his hands.' He paused momentarily. 'Come to think of it, will he be restrained? What Swiss law has he broken? Is he actually under arrest?'

Fonjallaz studied the slip of paper the woman produced, an arrest warrant in the name of Benjamin Lakey on behalf of American Express Card Services Headquarters in Brighton, England.

'This is genuine?' He handed it to Mueller. The Russian gave a perfunctory nod, as if it were a silly question.

'Lakey bought a first class ticket Zürich-Tokyo with a Charge Card already several thousand francs over the limit. It had, in fact, been cancelled, and Lakey knew it had. But he used it nevertheless. American Express dislikes prosecutions. Pressure was brought to bear by the Soviet government. Against their will, they have charged him. We all know the case will never come to court, but the warrant serves its purpose.'

'Geneva direct, handcuffed.' acquiesced Fonjallaz. 'What purpose? And what then?'

'He will be transferred to the terminal and disappear. Any observer will assume Lakey is in custody. He will, in reality, be driven in a closed van to another Swissair flight being held pending your arrival. This collision in Zürich has really made things very complicated.' She stared at the two men as if they personally could be held responsible, merely by being Swiss. 'None of this would have been necessary if...'

'Lakey is leaving Geneva?' Mueller was incredulous. 'Forgive me, but... Yes, of course. You have to be serious. The Swiss authorities condone all this? New passport as well, I suppose? False moustache perhaps?'

'None of that nonsense.' She yawned, evidently finding no sympathy for Mueller's silly questions. 'Lakey simply leaves.'

'Where will he go from Geneva?'

'Delhi.'

'I see. Of course.' Fonjallaz looked at the arrest warrant in his hand. 'Delhi. Where else? A destination for which he automatically has a visa, the necessary vaccination certificates, I presume?' His voice was deceptively mild. He expected her to explain, but she ignored them both, and continued as if neither had questioned the fact.

'Flight 419 to Kathmandu is routed via a stop in Delhi, but exceptionally, before Delhi, it will also land in Tashkent. An unscheduled stop. Such things are relatively common in my country.' She smiled wanly. 'The Soviet public is rather used to unannounced stops on Aeroflot long-haul flights. If you study this Notam for the next 24 hours for 419's destination, Kathmandu, Captain, you will see that two things will be achieved by the delay in Tashkent.'

She passed Fonjallaz a copy of the weather Notam - notice to airmen - for that area. He scrutinised it briefly, then looked up at her with a faint smile. Now he understood. His logical mind had no particular admiration for the plan, but a good deal for the speed with which it had been devised.

'One, Lakey will reach Delhi before Aeroflot 419 gets anywhere near India.' he began slowly. 'And two, by the time Aeroflot 419 *does* arrive in Delhi, Kathmandu will be closed - indefinitely I should say - by weather.' A smile crossed his face. 'Necessitating perhaps an overnight stop. In Delhi? Which would mean that Lakey and Suri will once again be in the same place, at the same time. And?'

She replaced the documents carefully in the attaché case and closed it.

'I think our problem will then be solved.' she said softly. 'Suri is disliked by the Indian authorities. He has never broken the law there, but...'

'But if Mr. Lakey is there waiting for Suri when he arrives?'

'The charges he will lay against Suri there will be sufficient to oblige Aeroflot to hand the Maharaj to the investigating authorities.'

First Officer Mueller had not yet grasped the situation with the same clarity as Fonjallaz.

'Why can't you just send Lakey direct to Delhi.' he demanded.

'I do not think you have been listening.' She sounded tetchy. 'Lakey is a Briton, but his official country of residence is Switzerland. Mistakenly, we tried the U.K. first of all, late last night, but the Foreign Office was unhelpful. Both Maharaj Suri and Lakey are British passport holders, I understand, and H.M. Government is not prepared...' She adopted a Foreign Office accent with accomplishment, '"to countenance a fight between Dieu", - they mean Suri - "et mon droit", - Lakey the common man.' she added. Surprisingly, she grinned briefly. 'If Lakey is not expelled from the Soviet Union very rapidly, Suri will insist on pressing charges here. Trumped-up charges maybe, but ones that defeat the Soviet interest.'

'And what charge is Lakey trying to bring against Suri?' Fonjallaz wondered what had been happening during nine days and nights on the Trans-Siberian railway.

'He alleges kidnapping.' The young woman paused. 'That is the legal definition. But the real charges against Suri can never be tried in a court of law. The Soviet Union has no interest in being, and cannot afford to be, involved in a trial of British citizens in Moscow, whether it be Suri, Lakey, or both. Either way, Suri would gain from it. Free publicity, greater coverage for his vile ALBATROSS. If Lakey prosecutes Suri, he is unlikely to win, but he would force a counter-suit. If Suri prosecutes Lakey, Suri seems certain to win. Our government would become a world-wide pariah for imprisoning Lakey and appearing to support ALBATROSS. At a time of international rapprochement such as we have now...' She shrugged and drained her coffee cup. 'You see our dilemma?'

'In Delhi things will be different?' Mueller sounded sceptical.

'The Soviet government is not responsible for what happens in Delhi.' She brushed her hair back impatiently in a tired gesture. 'Suri entered the Soviet Union with ten people. He is leaving with an eleventh, a young woman from Sweden. Lakey claims this young woman is leaving under duress. From what we know of Suri, this is quite possible, but we have no way of proving it, and no inclination to start the legal feud running. If we did not believe it, we would extradite Lakey to Zürich with Aeroflot, at our expense, and good riddance. Unfortunately, we cannot afford to prove him right or wrong. I have told you why. Perhaps now you understand that a trial in the Soviet Union is out of the question? The last thing we want.'

'What, exactly, do you want?' Fonjallaz could see the dawn growing in the sky through the window. A grey, foul haze seemed to rise from the very ground in the strengthening light. Through the mist he saw an Ilyushin 62 lift from the runway and seem to hover, nose high, as it struggled for height. He stood up to allow the woman to step into the aisle. She answered with the same refreshing directness that had marked the entire conversation.

'Until now we had no "want". ALBATROSS was a Western problem, an obscene one, but one that suited our propaganda machine very well. In the decadent West, Suri represented the dissolute fruits of Capitalism, bringing the well-deserved anguish of a dollar-rooted society in which true religion was conveniently - for our purposes - devalued. He was...' Surprisingly, she giggled. 'I was going to say, Captain, that he was a God-send to Communism as an ideal. Now he has come to us, and if ever we thought he was a God-send, we have learned differently.' She paused. In front of the distant terminal the red and blue flash of a police car could be seen. 'We accept Western currency readily enough, as your airline can testify, and Suri did not just buy eleven single tickets on the Trans-Siberian. His group reserved two whole Soft-class coaches and a restaurant car for themselves. What went on in there, Captain, defies the imagination, with Lakey and the Swedish woman the only witnesses.

'Captain, despite the Imperialist propaganda machine, we are not all Smersh square-heads hunting spies, and Imperialism and Capitalism are not our worst enemies. There are other, worse, forces in this world that we can do without. You ask me what we want now? We want to distance ourselves from ALBATROSS and whatever they have been doing here. You may find it odd, but we in the Soviet Union have a powerful feeling for natural justice, and we feel justice is on Lakey's side. In the old days, the Stalinist days, it was easy, so very easy. An aircraft went astray, crashed in some remote region. No survivors. No news reports. All finished.' She struggled into her heavy coat. 'Perestroika makes it all much more fun, don't you think?'

After an uncharacteristic hesitation, during which with a habit born of life-long watchfulness she glanced over her shoulder, she pulled out a plain envelope. 'Would you do something for me? Would you post this in Switzerland? It is nothing sinister, but people like me do not have friends "outside", certainly not in the country to which this is addressed. One day I shall be able to go to the Post Office, and stick a stamp on it, and send it off in the certain knowledge that it will pass through the system unopened and untouched. But that day...' She brushed her forehead again, '... is not just yet.'

'But soon, perhaps?' Fonjallaz thought he ought to feel surprise. The howl of the police siren was growing in the distance.

'My people are tired of "perhaps" as a postmark, Captain, and even Chairman Gorbachev cannot overturn seventy years' rule in a day. May I?' She held up a half-kilo slab of chocolate. Fonjallaz nodded silently. She slipped the envelope into his left hand, and brusquely turned her back on the two men. The siren was very close. 'They are bringing Lakey out now.' Her voice was steady again. 'His luggage has been impounded and will be sent on next week.' She was half way down the steps. 'Adieu.' she called, without looking back. The door of her car slammed, the yellow vehicle roared away to be replaced in seconds by a police car. Fonjallaz stood motionless in the doorway, aware that someone and something quite out of the ordinary had walked into his life and out again. Someone who was tired of "perhaps" as a postmark.

'Do I log all that?' murmured Mueller, perplexed.

'Log what?' asked Fonjallaz innocently. The crackle of the envelope in his pocket belied his attempt at a smile.

Chapter Two

I discovered from Fonjallaz's flight log that they took off from Moscow at 09.01, one minute past seven in Geneva. The Moscow Telex came in half an hour later, and it was that Telex that finally galvanised me into action.

In addition to the senior officers, we had two Sergeants detailed to the airport police. In the event of a real disaster, standing orders made it mandatory to call in a full team from the city centre, but on a normal night one senior officer or one Sergeant was deemed sufficient. There wasn't a Police Station as such at Cointrin, we were more of an on-call skeleton staff, the senior officers and a handful of routine staff.

The snow was so bad that Thursday afternoon that, as soon as I'd made up my mind to spend the night in the airport, I'd sent Sergeant Vinet home. He was a young officer with three children, and had been very involved on a fraud case that had kept him away from home for most of January. Besides, we hadn't had a busy night in the winter season for all the years I'd been at the airport.

The incident chart I pieced together later seems to give a stark clarity to the sequence of events; at the time, nothing was clear at all.

It started very early:

05.19 Woken by telephone call from Central Telex Office. Urgent message to collect

05.28 Arrived CTO. Found not one but three messages

Message 1. "BERNE, despatch time 05.00 Attention Night Duty Officer Cointrin. Zürich Kloten v. heavy snow, diversions Basel-Geneva-Bern likely. High probability excessive pax nos. Details to follow."

'Pax nos' was shorthand for numbers of passengers, referring to the diverted ski charter flights. The telex was signed *Polizeizentrale, Bern*, and was nothing more than an automatic warning of high passenger numbers. The next sheet was more unusual.

Message 2. "ZÜRICH, despatch time 05.04. Attention Paul de Savigny, Duty Officer Cointrin. Kloten has lost main runway, closed indefinitely. Following flights will divert Cointrin:"

There followed a list of a dozen flight numbers with their ETA's, and then:-

"Special attention SR 493 Moscow-Zürich diverted to Cointrin. ETA Geneva 12.25 CET. Pax Benjamin Lakey, UK passport, number unknown. Urgent you consult Berne Central Criminal Computer Records. Passenger Lakey deprived of liberty. Reason: arrest warrant *Strafanzeigezettelnummer 393/B* issued February 12th per American Express Card Services, Brighton UK. Await further instructions."

It was signed by the top man in Kloten Airport Police Department, a considerably more significant post than any that existed in Cointrin, if only because Zürich Airport is several times larger.

Then there was the third Telex, from Berne again.

"Personal attention Paul de Savigny, Deputy Police Commissioner Cointrin. Contact *Bern Polizeizentrale*. Urgent communication on line. Krug."

Manfred Krug was some backwoods man, buried deep in a little heard of political bureau that the *Bern Polizeizentrale* would rather I didn't talk about.

I hurried to my office and brought the computer on line. Text started pouring out of the damned thing.

I asked permission to reprint the text of that long message, but Berne adamantly refused, threatening dire actions if I went ahead regardless. The Swiss government doesn't make idle threats, but Fonjallaz encouraged me, particularly as some of the details struck us both as odd.

I was to send out two uniformed Security men but not, repeat underline not Federal Police Officers, to escort Lakey from the Moscow flight and have them bring him to my office. There I was to provide facilities for an instant wash and brush up, a change of clothing - my God, Berne practically had the man's collar size on record, no wonder we Swiss are considered meticulous - and a Swissair van to transfer him to the DC10 flight SR 196 for Delhi. That was odd enough, the insistence on the officials being Securitas men, not police officers.

This was the first thing that troubled Fonjallaz, that he'd carried a passenger "deprived of liberty" and the Swiss police hadn't wanted to be involved. When I told him that I doubted I could have found two Federal Police Officers in the entire airport anyway, he couldn't understand how a mini-city like Geneva Airport had such a small police presence. He hadn't appreciated until then the proliferation of security forces. Quite apart from the twin forces of Gendarmerie and Police, a special Army unit is responsible for airport security, you see them patrolling the terminal with machine guns and dogs. Securitas, a security company, more like a private army, covers baggage and personnel screening and cargo handling. Customs officers run their own business. There is a special drugs squad on call at Eaux Vives and an immigration team for aliens and the fairly frequent refugees. The real police were practically an anachronism, only called to cases detected 'in flagrante delicto'. All that changed after the Lakey business, when I quit. You'll find two or three police vehicles stationed outside the Arrivals building and a six man detail there now. Wise after the event. Until a year ago, things were very different.

The clothing matter was odd too. There is no shortage of shops, including clothing emporia, at Cointrin, and I could understand a man would need different clothes in Delhi than he did in Moscow, although I didn't see that was our responsibility. But what was really bizarre was that the clothes were to be bought in my name, categorically in my name on my own Charge card, with reimbursement at a later date. I was naïve enough at the time to suppose, in fact I thought I knew, that there was no suitable source of petty cash in the Police office. Now, of course, I know that the whole thing was a whitewash, in case things ever backfired. No police officers apart from myself would have been involved, I would have been seen to be acting - probably wrongly - in a private capacity. That alone makes me pretty bitter towards Cointrin Police and Berne, which is why I've taken Fonjallaz's advice and printed these details.

Finally, if the Moscow DC9 was delayed, Cointrin ATC would hold the DC10 for Lakey. That was it. No reason given, no further mention of the arrest warrant, or the rather quaintly worded "deprived of liberty".

By now it was nearly six in the morning, the shops wouldn't be open for another two hours, and I was hungry. Cointrin practically closes at night, but the air crew quarters have a self-service area for the early departures. I guessed that I would find a few of the Air Traffic Controllers there too, and I needed to see them about the Delhi flight.

"You went to *breakfast!*?"

I can still hear the Police Commissioner's angry bellow, God he had been angry, when he got back from holiday and read the preliminary report. As I've said, I hadn't really got tuned in to the urgency of the affair at that time. So yes, I had gone to breakfast. It was a strange feeling. The early aircrews were there, in their smart uniforms, tucking into croissants and coffee, unaware that, with one runway blocked by machinery and heavy snow falling, Zürich was under siege, unable to handle the first flush of incoming long haul flights, and that there would be growing disruption in the air all day.

The snow had stopped falling in Geneva, and the ploughs were out in force on the taxi-ways, their rotating yellow lights everywhere, reflecting off the snow. I got myself a large helping of Muesli and found a seat next to Michel Oron, Senior Air Traffic Controller.

Being an isolated and under-employed policeman didn't mean I had no friends in the airport. Michel Oron had got to hear of my hobby of aircraft spotting and it had become commonplace for me to spend off-duty hours with him in the Control Room, watching the coming and going of aircraft on the radar consoles. I was wondering how to tackle the Delhi flight problem, but he got in first.

'You'll know about 196.' He was cryptic, there was a barely suppressed anger in his voice. Oron was a dark swarthy man, lean and tall, with jet black hair swept straight back against the skull. His aquiline nose and strong features made him everyone's image of a French aristocrat, which was why he was affectionately called '*Le Comte*', 'The Count', by his colleagues. He had an aggressive sniff, almost a twitch, and this became most marked when he was under pressure handling many aircraft at once. It was in evidence that morning, too. 'What the hell's going on, Paul? I've got enough on my plate without Berne messing around with our slot times.' He sniffed again, and waved a lean hand towards the smoked plate glass windows beyond which there was just a hint of dawn in the darkness. 'Look at it. As fast as we sweep away the snow it's drifting back again. RVR is down to 500 feet.

'Those cretins in Zürich,' he snapped. 'Can you credit it? Two snow ploughs locked together on the concrete, and not enough machines left to clear the snow on the remaining runways. We have around twenty charter flights coming in, packed with moronic skiers, our own runway will barely cope with the normal traffic, let alone all the diverted flights. Lyon Airport across the frontier is closed, so they can't take any of the strain. One of my Controllers hasn't reported for work, she's probably stuck out in a snow drift, and now this.'

I had never seen Le Comte so worked up, he was dragging with his fingernails at some dry skin on the other hand, and his eyes were restless, glancing around the cafeteria. That was the first I heard about the absent Controller. It wasn't until much later in the day that we learnt she had been found in her crushed car beneath the tree.

'About that Delhi flight.' I said, trying to get down to something concrete. 'What time is it due out?'

'The 196? 11.10. And this man Lakey, diverting from Zürich, will arrive some time around one o'clock. But we're going to have a lot of congested air space around by then, all those damned charters going back empty, and that might mean putting SR 493 in a stack. Heaven knows when it'll touch down. What it all adds up to is, a major carrier delayed indefinitely, and no possibility even of giving the Delhi flight a slot-time until we have a definite ETA for the Moscow diversion. God, it makes me sick.'

He gulped at his coffee, and turned to face me. His face was strained, a tic working the muscle below one eye. I was horrified at the tensions that were building up in the normally unflappable Oron.

'Who is this Lakey, anyway?' he wanted to know. 'I've never heard of anything like it. They send him here under arrest, and next thing he's a VITP, en route to Delhi. Who is he?' he demanded aggressively. I was about to say I didn't know. Then I remembered the Telex recommending I urgently research Lakey.

'I'll find out for you.' I said, trying to placate him. I hadn't touched my food. 'Listen, I'll run the computer on him through Berne, and get back to you. You'll be in the Tower?'

'I shouldn't be, but I will.' He ran his hands wearily through his black hair and sniffed. 'Dominique Dantin should be here by now, you know her I think, she lives out near your place. Probably snowed in. I'll be standing in for her until she arrives.'

'Half an hour then.' I left him staring moodily into the sleet and the darkness and went back to the computer. Within minutes I had retrieved several pages of condensed reports about Benjamin Lakey.

He had had a chequered career, quite bizarre on occasion, but there was nothing in it to suggest why Moscow should now effectively be deporting him, nor why he should be freed on arrival and sent to Delhi. I wondered about Delhi, I wondered who was paying his fare. I could understand the Soviets deporting an undesirable at their own expense, but I didn't see where Delhi fitted in. And an arrest warrant issued on behalf of American Express implied he had defaulted on some financial arrangement to such an extent that he was worse than broke. A man in that situation doesn't just snap his fingers and fly half way round the world.

I fiddled around with the computer a bit, and when I couldn't find what I wanted I started telephoning. Swissair has a first class reputation for service, but the Inter-airline ticketing office on the Departure Level had a lousy record of bad manners. They were living up to it that morning. I could hear the chewing gum quite clearly when the man yawned. No, he didn't know who Lakey was, and he had no idea of who was paying the fare, and the computer wouldn't show it anyway. He rang off before I could put a supplementary question. This riled me a lot, and I didn't stop telephoning then until I'd found the answer, which meant asking almost the entire Swissair personnel in the airport the same stupid question.

The answer was a puzzler. Lakey's ticket had been paid for through Swissair ticketing in Moscow airport, so someone in Moscow had authorised his ticket Geneva-Delhi, but there was no trace of what currency had been paid or how much. I made a note of this and turned to the printout of Lakey's computer record. It was while I was browsing through this that the Moscow telex came in. It was headed with my name, and the full title of Second Deputy to the Commissioner, Cointrin Police. Someone in Moscow had extremely detailed records. The text was brief and within seconds of reading it I was on my way to the see Le Comte in the Tower. It read:

"Following message Moscow Sheremetyevo Security Office to Swissair Flight 493 Moscow-Zürich at 09.31, for immediate attention passenger Benjamin Lakey, copy to Geneva Cointrin. Maharaj Suri today has cancelled flight Kathmandu, has departed with entire group, repeat entire group, Helsinki, ETA 10.10 local time. Suggest you most urgently take measures appropriate, good luck, Sovenskaya."

Suri. The name was throbbing in time with my heart beat as I hurried across to the recently opened ATC department in the new black Tower building. Maharaj Suri. What was the connection between Lakey and Suri?

All the old aggression that had wound down since Genevieve's death sprang up again like a coiled spring. Suri. Lakey. Delhi. And now Suri flying to Helsinki? I had no way of knowing then that if Suri was in Helsinki, the last place Lakey would want to fly to would be Delhi.

I glanced at my watch, it was getting on for eight o' clock, so two hours later in Moscow - and Helsinki - which meant that Suri would land in Finland in less than an hour. I didn't begin to understand the significance of Kathmandu, or the "repeat entire group", there was a lot I didn't understand, and it frustrated me to have to wait for hours until Lakey landed to ask him. I stepped out of the lift into the upper level of the Control Tower, and looked around for Le Comte.

He was standing at a radar console, holding a mike and headset loosely in one hand against his head, and staring out through the smoked glass windows to the snow-covered airfield. He caught sight of me out of the corner of his eye, and gestured to me to take a seat, while speaking into the microphone.

'Swissair 720, line up behind the departing Airbus.' He flipped open a cigarette packet and tossed me one, deftly lighting his own with a flick of the wrist, never taking his eyes off the apron. 'Be about ten minutes,' he muttered to me, 'got to clear this backlog, and the charters are rolling in already. Can you wait?' I nodded, and settled down to watch.

Neither the panoramic view of the airport outside, nor the hypnotic sweep of blips on the radar screens and mutter of radio conversations, could take my mind off Suri. But I hadn't enough information, nor had enough practice in recent years in real detective work, my mind just churned fruitlessly over the few scraps I had.

The several years' inactivity was a handicap now. When I hadn't been chasing up lost luggage, I had found myself more than once called upon to calm semi-hysterical passengers who had ridden through thunder storms in bucketing aircraft on their descent to the airfield. I have never understood the blinkered attitude of the airlines - they are all the same. They spend a small fortune on passenger psychology, targeting advertising on wining and dining in recliner seats in the sky, providing 'Fear of Flying' classes, but never once giving attention to the obvious: the total ignorance of the general public about the most fundamental part of the operation - how air travel actually works.

Chapter Three

The actual mechanics of getting an aircraft from one point on the earth's surface to another probably represent one of man's greatest technological feats. There are those who argue that our overcrowded skies need a Pan-European Air Traffic Control Centre. And I admit that the congested airways, the growing reports of near-misses and overtired pilots, of Air Traffic Controllers' strikes and long delays to passengers don't look much like the jewel in the crown of man's technological mastery of his world. But, given the cracks in the joins, the system is still something special in that all nations work together, moderately fairly, to ensure the safe transport of people around the globe.

Until recently, when air traffic increased beyond all expectations, it seemed to me to be plain common sense for the airlines to inform the travelling public of some of the workings of the system. Now I think it is too late for the airlines to embark on such an information campaign. The system is starting to burst at the seams, and the public, far from being reassured by the information, might start peering out at aircraft passing uncomfortably close to one another over way-points, imagine near-misses every flight, and stop flying altogether.

As I have said, it was a combination of coincidences that led to my being in charge of the Lakey case. The fact that Suri was involved made it impossible for me to ignore it, but fundamental to these coincidences, too, was my knowledge of the way air transport works, especially at Geneva. Quite apart from the Suri angle, it rapidly became very much an air traffic case. As a result of this, it proved essential to know something about the system the airlines never talk about.

Commercial air transports follow much the same pattern of movement everywhere in the world. Before the flight starts, the pilot is given a 'slot-time' for take-off. A computer calculates the distance and flying time for all flights from departure airports over a set of radio transmitters used as way-points peppered across the ground en route, VOR beacons. The magic of navigation is thus reduced to little more than flying the aircraft to the next way-point - a VOR radio beacon - and the next, and the next, until the destination is reached. The slot-time is calculated to meet the often conflicting demands of the airline schedule and of other aircraft crossing the same airspace.

Also before take-off, every commercial aircraft is given a four-digit code number. In the cockpit the pilot punches this into a transmitter called a transponder: pilots call it the SQUAWK ident. After take-off, this number appears alongside the aircraft's blip on radar screens in ATC centres covering the airways. In the event of a potential conflict between two aircraft, the Air Traffic Controller monitoring the flights will direct pilots to deviate from their track to avoid. It may seem irrelevant, although it certainly wasn't that Friday 13th, that a Controller sometimes instructs a pilot to change to a new SQUAWK ident as an aircraft enters his control area. Apart from punching in the wrong number, there are several other unpleasant possibilities that can cause the system to malfunction. A computer breakdown, Controller fatigue, or pilot error in the altimeter setting are only a few. The crisis that developed on the 13th was not caused by any of these, and was altogether much nastier.

Air Traffic Control is not only divided into large sectors of European air space. Covering the airspace around each airfield, a number of different Controllers operate on different frequencies. As soon as an aircraft is approaching its destination, the pilot is handed over from the high-airways Controller to another, guiding aircraft down through the middle altitudes, and separating the flow of traffic approaching and leaving the airfield.

As the aircraft descends through an altitude of, say, twenty thousand feet, the pilot is again told to change frequency, this time to Geneva Approach. This Controller guides incoming aircraft at appropriate speeds and heights until they are on the glide to the runway, and perhaps ten miles out.

The busiest VOR in Western Europe is forty miles east of Geneva, at St. Prex. It is actually a man-made island planted on stilts in the lake itself.

Pilots landing at Geneva on the Approach from the East are instructed to cross St. Prex VOR at 7,000 feet or above. From here, the ILS guides the pilot's descent. During all of this, the Approach Controller separates incoming aircraft by four miles, more if the leading aircraft is a wide-bodied aircraft, for it causes wake turbulence that can actually throw a smaller aircraft following it too closely out of the sky.

Lastly, the pilot contacts the Tower Controller, the only one with a view of the outside world, who gives aircraft clearance to land and take off. On the Friday that Lakey flew in from Moscow the person scheduled as Tower Controller was Dominique Dantin, but her absence was unremarkable at first, given the appalling weather conditions, and it was normal that Michel Oron, Le Comte, should take her place.

Geneva airport is situated just North of the city, at the Western end of the crescent-shaped Lac Léman. To the North of the lake is the natural barrier of the Jura mountains, a six thousand foot high ridge, paralleling the lake's North shore. To the South are the French Savoy alps, with Mont Blanc visible on a fine day, its summit capped in snow the year round.

For the Approach from the East, aircraft cross St. Prex on a compass heading of 230°, i.e. facing West - to land on Runway 23. Conversely, for aircraft landing or taking off in the opposite direction on that same single runway, on compass heading 050° - facing East - it is called Runway 05. Thus the single runway can have two quite different names, and which is used often depends on wind direction – aircraft generally land and depart into the wind. Understandably, the one thing aircraft never do in busy periods, is to take off and land in opposing directions, one heading straight at the other.

For aircraft approaching Runway 05 over France from the West, the radar cover is hindered by a scattering of moderately high mountains that require a more winding approach than that over the lake. In fact, more than once when I was in the Tower the Approach Controller lost sight of a 'blip', and I recall one occasion, it was in 1986, that the Controller actually asked the pilot of a blip that disappeared, for his DME to the runway - that is, how far out he was. It was a British Airways 737, and the pilot was one of those suave Brits who drawl.

"Just comin' round the corner of the hill above Passeiry now". But on the radar screen he was completely hidden.

You can see that the whole system is as fool-proof as it can be made. At least, I always thought it was fool-proof, but I'd never come across a vandal like Thierry Scholl, and nor had Le Comte until that morning.

Oron was finally able to take a break at about eight o'clock. He fetched two coffees from a dispenser unit and led me to a quiet corner where a few armchairs were clustered around a low table. In the background the muted voices of the Ground Controller and the Tower Controller kept up a non-stop chatter.

'What have you found out?' He seemed to have calmed down, which I thought was very necessary, given the man's responsibility as Senior Controller. What could I tell him? I had no clear picture myself. I tried running through the events first from the Moscow end, then Geneva. I'd got as far as the Moscow Telex when he interrupted me.

'What you're saying is, you don't really know what's going on?' I shrugged. It didn't sound very good.

'No.' I admitted in the end. 'I haven't a clue.' I held up the Moscow Telex. 'I thought...'

'Can I see that?' Le Comte sniffed aggressively and held it to the window to read it. His face went dead-pan as he reached the Suri bit. 'I don't think the Commissioner is going to like you being on this, Paul.' He handed back the Telex. 'Not if Suri is involved.' Half his mind was visibly still listening to the Controllers behind him, I had the feeling that if any of them made a mistake he would overhear it and be on his way to their console. He was a very conscientious man.

'You think he'll stop me? Bring in someone else?' I was acutely aware that this was a strong possibility, and I wanted at all costs to avoid that. If Suri was involved.

'Has he any option?' Le Comte was pensive. 'With your... what shall I say... history?'

'But if I could wrap it up, today?' I was on my feet, the frustration at waiting for Lakey getting on top of me, the knowledge that this unknown Englishman was personally connected with Suri, that I was directly involved as the Officer in charge, only to have the whole thing perhaps taken away from me because of... because of Charlotte and Geneviève. And Suri's ALBATROSS.

'Wrap up what, for Heaven's sake?' Oron stood up to face me, one hand on my shoulder. 'Paul, I think that until Lakey arrives, there's nothing you can do. And what are you going to ask him when he gets here? Your orders are quite explicit, for whatever reason he's to be rushed through to the Delhi flight... Heaven knows why Delhi.' He scratched the black stubble on his chin. 'What's all this about Kathmandu, Finland, Helsinki? The "entire group"?' He handed back the Telex, and gestured that we sit down again. 'It looks to me as if you're going to have about eight minutes, maximum, to talk to Lakey between him getting off the DC9 and getting on the DC10. For which we still haven't got a damned slot-time.' he added sharply. 'What are you going to achieve in eight minutes, Paul? The way I see it, this isn't a case at all, it's just one of those bizarre things that crops up in the course of a day and never gets heard of again.' He looked at a clock on the wall. 'I ought to get back to work.' he said. 'Looks like we shan't be seeing Dominique today. You want to hang around here till this Lakey man comes in?' I shook my head.

'I can't. I'm on call in Admin. Also,' I added rather bitterly, 'I have to go and buy those clothes. Can I come back around midday? See the flight in, and pick up Lakey at the aircraft?'

'Sure.' Le Comte was already back at the console, studying the aircraft movements, picking up the picture for a few minutes before he took over the mike. 'See you then.'

I went back to the Administration Buildings and sat down to try to puzzle out what the hell was going on. It was half past eight.

Chapter Four

At half past eight, Thierry Scholl was just leaving the rough wooden building that acts as clubhouse to Bex airfield. Situated at the eastern end of Lake Geneva, it is a country flying club with a single grass landing strip. The length of the runway limits the size of aircraft that can land or take off there, and further limits are imposed by an horrendous network of high-voltage cables and pylons surrounding the airstrip and the nearby motorway. Although busy in summer, the airstrip is rarely used in winter, and the number of flights in February could be counted on the fingers of one hand, until Thierry Scholl started, unofficially, to live there. His plane, a converted Curtiss, was housed near the end of the runway in a barn hired out as hangar space by a local farmer. Scholl had intended sleeping in the aircraft, where he had installed bedroom, washroom and a sort of space-age salon. But it had been too damned cold, so he had made up a log fire in the deserted clubhouse and a bed on the sofa.

Thierry Scholl was a German, thirty years old and extremely fair, whose all-consuming interest was flying. Until recently he had had another consuming interest, but she had given him a very wintry and very definite brush-off. It was after that that he had started to live at the deserted airstrip. Practically every day since then he had vented a lot of his resentment and frustration beating up the skies over the lakeside towns of Montreux and Vevey in the elderly twin-engined Curtiss. He must have done other things during those two weeks, but the only one I managed to discover was a flight to Southern Germany and back.

An airline psychiatrist's report has suggested that, although each of his appallingly risky aerobatic flights worked some of the anger out of his system, Scholl began to find he needed to go one risk further on the next flight to get rid of the same amount of anger as on the last. He was a psychotic.

In hindsight I think that's a fair description. Any flight in winter here carries a strong risk of icing. Scholl had been up in his plane, and it wasn't a baby Cherokee or anything as light as that, nearly every day for fourteen days. Fonjallaz told me that the work needed before take-off to prevent icing on an aircraft that size is considerable, and Scholl had always done it himself. For a man to go to such lengths, practically daily, and then only fly dare-devil aerobatics for a couple of hours ten miles away, scaring the locals out of their minds before returning and landing, well I may be unimaginative, but it doesn't fit my idea of a sober and serious pilot who flies to get from A to B with minimum inconvenience, or of one who simply flies for the pleasure of it. This is not all surmise, for in the investigation into Dominique Dantin's death I came across some correspondence, and diaries, which told me a good deal about Scholl. She had been his lover, until she dropped him.

On the other hand, Scholl was an able pilot and had held a private pilot's licence for ten years. He had applied to more than one airline for further training, and every time had been instantly rejected. Airlines select their pilots not only on flying skill and ability, but also on the basis of extremely sophisticated psychological tests. A man as unbalanced as Thierry Scholl failed them almost as soon as he entered the room. Rumour had it that on the one occasion a minor South American company had allowed him to moonlight a flight of something probably illegitimate down in Uruguay, he had mismanaged the approach, and had to go round twice to get down at all. Rumour or not, this kind of thing had added to the grudge he felt towards the world in general and the flying community in particular. The final insult had been Dominique Dantin's rejection of him after a particularly unsavoury evening together. Separation from girl-friends was nothing new to Scholl, but never before had a girl got rid of him. It was a new and profoundly humiliating experience. And to come from a chit of a Trainee Air Traffic Controller of all people...

We know now that Scholl had never heard of Swissair flight 493, and did not know that either Maharaj Suri or Benjamin Lakey even existed when he took off from Bex that Friday morning, but Scholl had few friends and those who knew him mostly lived in the North of Germany or South America. At the time of the enquiry, given the circumstances, everything pointed to a connection between the three: Suri, Scholl and Lakey. And with Dominique Dantin dead, their relationship only came to light later. It was piecing all this together that made the whole thing such a nightmare. Nobody in the area seemed really to know Scholl, probably for two reasons: he travelled extensively and often, and the one thing all those who had been in contact with him agreed on was that he was an almost uniquely unlikeable and egocentric person.

Just before dawn on Friday 13th, fair-haired Scholl had made a phone call from the club house, and listened with a mixture of anger and disbelief to the man's voice that had answered, then slammed down the receiver.

It was two weeks since that terrible night when, screaming and crying, she had thrown him out, late at night and in the snow at that, and told him not to come back. This early morning phone call, designed to reach her before she left for work, had already been a climb-down for him that he had never believed possible. Now after a fortnight only, already another man was answering the telephone. At six in the morning, that could only mean...

Sitting on the edge of the sofa and staring into space, Scholl felt again the needles of jealousy pricking at his thoughts. He wondered if he was going mad. The very possibility aroused the anger in him again. If he were, it was her fault, the bitch, her fault. He stared at his flying gear, old leather, he had picked it up at an auction in aid of war veterans. Almost without thinking he climbed into the worn garments, and left the clubhouse. His mood altered rapidly, spirits lifting, he was going flying again, and flying always made him feel good, something that Mr. Everybody couldn't do. The cold morning air was filled with snowflakes, and the snow crunched underfoot as he made his way to the barn.

As he climbed a ladder with the de-icing spray, his head was ringing with different voices: there was his own inner voice, reminding him of the injustice and the humiliation; there was her voice, a beautiful face screaming invective; there was the voice of the man who had answered the telephone, a peasant's voice, rough and coarse. Scholl started the laborious anti-icing procedure.

Switzerland has more than its fair share of young and idle rich. Thierry Scholl was not a millionaire in the jet set class, but he had never worked in his life. He had been born in South America, his father and grandfather having fled from Germany as the Allies entered at the end of the war. South America was not known for its educational excellence, so Scholl had been sent to school in West Germany. To avoid military service there, he had moved to Switzerland in 1976 where, after the death of his parents, Scholl had inherited a fortune - in US dollars.

Whatever anyone else thought about him, he considered himself essentially a playboy, and wherever he stayed a while, South America or Europe, he sought two experiences at every opportunity: flying, and, if possible, a woman to sponge off. In 1986 he arrived in Montreux, a playboy's haven if ever there was one, he had immediately discovered the nearby airstrip at Bex. At about the same time he heard of a bargain in Friedrichshafen in West Germany. Armed with a suitcase full of cash as a deposit, he had been so determined that he would buy the plane that he had taken the train North, intent on flying his own aircraft back to Bex. He could never have afforded to buy a private jet, nor was he licensed to fly one. The aircraft he found suited him ideally. Having a West German passport facilitated the paper work, and within a few days a lawyer had drawn up the necessary documents. Scholl was the proud owner of what Fonjallaz described as a flying dinosaur.

The plane was an old Curtiss C-46, a remnant of the American occupation forces. Fonjallaz doubts whether there were many pilots in all of Europe who would know how to fly the thing - the few remaining models were all in America or Asia, which was one reason why it was going cheap. Such aircraft are still occasionally in service in some of the far-flung airstrips of South America, and Scholl had actually once taken a training course on one.

To look at, it closely resembled the DC3 Dakota which gained its reputation in the Berlin airlift. In fact, designed and produced as a competitor to the DC3, this particular model had left the production line in 1944.

For Scholl, possession of his own aircraft moved him from the status of rich playboy to the seat next to God. He had known the rattling old Curtiss would never meet the stringent Swiss registration requirements, and in one way this suited him very well. He re-registered it in West Germany, giving its base airfield as Friedrichshafen, and thus had the best of both worlds - a lower air registration fee than the Swiss demanded, and yet an aircraft technically insufficiently air-worthy for Swiss standards often stationed in Switzerland. With the plane, Scholl had also bought part of a hangar where the previous owner had accumulated a stock of spares, including two rebuilt Pratt and Whitney engines. Discovering all this required some of the most tedious police work I have ever encountered.

The Curtiss C-46 is not a light aircraft. Some were converted to high-density layouts to seat up to thirty passengers, even if they were squashed in like sardines. Others had sleeper accommodation installed, carrying a dozen wealthy passengers the length and breadth of America overnight, when commercial air travel was in its infancy. But those aircraft, although the maximum altitude was a paltry 23,000 feet, were pressurised. Scholl's "dinosaur" was not.

Its wing span, length and height make the Curtiss look like a small airliner, and, crucial to the events of that fateful Friday, its radar profile is indistinguishable from that of a small commercial jet. I discovered during the enquiry that Scholl had, in fact, no right to be flying an aircraft of that size without a co-pilot, certainly not in Switzerland, I don't know about South America, and that was yet another distraction. He probably never had flown with a co-pilot, and had falsified the log-book for the annual checks. Nor was there any precedent of a pilot converting his plane into a flying caravan and living in it. All this meant passing all the information that came in to the Civil Aviation Board, who would have prosecuted Scholl, except you can't prosecute a man who's dead.

It was still almost dark when Scholl climbed into the freezing aircraft and started up the two engines. I don't think he had any clearly formed idea in his mind of what he was going to do, other than to fly, to get up in the sky and be free. It may have crossed his mind, whimsically, to fly low over Rolle and her house, and see what this oaf with a gardener's voice looked like. But Rolle lies near the Western end of the lake and that was one certain way to lose his licence for good. The eastern end of Lake Geneva is free for military and private aircraft to come and go as they please. But from Lausanne Westwards, including the VOR at St. Prex, all airspace is controlled airspace, needing clearances, SQUAWK idents and flight plans that Scholl did not have.

It became clear from later investigations that Scholl was as good as mentally unhinged, and legally could not be held responsible for his actions. Even contemplating a take-off from a snow-covered grass runway in semi-darkness and surrounded by high tension cables and pylons was sheer madness, and only luck or great skill got him airborne. I think the nearest parallel I can find is the man Hinckley, who fired at and shot President Reagan. Hinckley's defence was that he simply did it to impress an actress he wanted to know better, and he ended up in a closed institution. If he was deranged, then so must Scholl have been. But at five past nine that morning, when Scholl finally lined up the old silver C-46 and took off into the sleet and the cloud, there were no witnesses to this event, and no one knew of his madness. We only know now because the flight recorder revealed the time of take-off, and his subsequent actions could only be those of an insane man.

All this sounds as if we might have done something about Thierry Scholl if we had only known he was there, but short of actually shooting the man out of the sky, I don't see even now what preventative measures anyone could have taken. And anyway, neither Oron nor I knew of Scholl's existence at the time he took off, and I doubt whether even Scholl himself had a clear intention.

One of the penalties paid by Fonjallaz and Mueller in flying an elderly DC9 was that not every item of equipment was in A1 working order. Before someone jumps on the phone to their lawyers at this calumny, I suggest he checks the facts. There are parts of aircraft that need to be working one hundred percent for the damned thing to fly at all, and other parts that need to be in moderately good order for everything to work properly. And there are a few items that will be logged by pilot after pilot as non-functioning and which are put off with equal regularity until the next overhaul, simply because they are of no significance to the air-worthiness, but their repair would take the aircraft out of service for an unacceptably long time or a spare part is not readily available. There was such a fault on the old DC9-30 that Fonjallaz and Mueller were flying. Under normal conditions it would have been trivial.

The tiny item that failed to function on their flight deck was a single red lamp. Precisely because the co-pilot is constantly changing frequencies for ATC messages that are of great importance to him - whether or not he is in conflict with another aircraft, for instance - less important messages from the Company on their own frequency cannot be heard immediately by the pilot.

The system is simple. When a message is to be transmitted on the Company frequency, the ground transmitter sends a signal that causes the light to flash on the flight deck. When the co-pilot eventually has time to answer the call, he selects the appropriate Company frequency, and the conversation goes ahead. But if the light fails to flash, as it did on the flight deck of 493, the pilot is quite simply unaware that a message is waiting for him. As a last resort, the Controller handling the flight can be telephoned and asked to tell the pilot to call the Company, but for reasons that I only recently discovered, the young woman in Moscow did not wish her superiors to know what she was doing, and calling up the Soviet ATC offices was therefore out of the question.

Using the name Sovenskaya, she tried repeatedly to contact Mueller on the Company frequency, and failed. As a last resort she sent the duplicate message to me in Cointrin, and went on trying for Mueller. Flight 493 never received her message. If it had, Fonjallaz would certainly have discussed it with Lakey, and probably have radioed ahead to let the Delhi flight go on time.

Much earlier than anticipated, about eleven Swiss time, Oron rang me from the Tower to say that 493 had started descent, and maybe they wouldn't have to hold the Delhi flight much beyond the half hour, he would aim for an 11.45 slot time. Did I want to join him to see Lakey in? I didn't hurry because an aircraft leaving the upper airways will take a good half hour before actually landing. I rang the Securitas offices to confirm that their men were ready and then checked the Swissair van was set to go. Then I rang the SR 196 departure lounge and told them that they could start boarding the flight as soon as their slot time was clear. They already knew we had a VITP coming in by van.

Then I made my way to the Tower, blithely unaware that every one of my meticulous preparations was a total and utter waste of time.

Chapter Five

When I got to the Tower everything looked exactly as it had three hours previously. There was Le Comte at the window, mike and headset still pressed to one side of his face, staring out through the darkened glass. A few yards away the Ground Controller sat on a high stool at his console, directing taxiing aircraft around the apron and taxiways. From the spiral staircase that led to the lower level where there were no windows, I could hear the muted voices of various Controllers working the Geneva Radar and Approach frequencies. As before, Oron caught sight of me and this time handed over the console immediately.

'Watch that MEA 707,' he told his assistant, 'he'll increase speed ten miles out in case of wind-shear, even when there isn't any, he always does, and you'll have either to get the Number One traffic to increase or tell the Arab to slow down.' With a violent sniff he joined me. 'Bloody murder in here again today.' he said, glancing at his watch. 'Your Moscow flight should be passing through 20,000 feet and contacting Approach any time now. You want to see?' Without waiting for an answer he ushered me to the spiral staircase and we went down to the next level. His nervous energy and brittle manner were in evidence again, the tic pulling at his eye.

'Over here.' He led me through an airy but dimly-lit room, it was crammed with computer machinery and glowing radar screens, half-seen figures hunched in front of them. Here and there huge sloping chart-tables were covered with differently coloured flight-progress strips, and now and then a computer in the corner, the "sausage-machine", belched out a newly-printed strip to join those already there.

We stopped behind a young woman seated at a large circular radar screen, with its myriad patterns of baffling fine lines, tiny printed numbers and blips a glowing fluorescent green on black.

'I have 493 at Flight Level 190 descending on course one-two-zero, sir.' She spoke to Oron through the side of her mouth, and went on speaking immediately into her mike in slightly accented English without stopping for breath, 'Air Europe 755 Alpha, turn right and leave the hold on heading two-three-zero, re-cleared 5,000 feet. What is your speed?'

The English pilot's voice echoed tinnily, but very quietly, in a loudspeaker above the console as Le Comte flicked a switch. '...speed 200, reducing, Air Europe 755 Alpha.'

'Another damned charter.' snapped Oron. 'The Alpha suffix means inbound Charter, Bravo homewards. That's the ninth from England this morning alone. And here...' he pointed to the screen, 'another Brit, scheduled BA Speedbird 622. We're holding all the incoming flights in the stack over St. Prex.' He pushed me gently back from the chair and stood directly behind the girl. 'I don't see 493.' he said, speaking to her.

'Iberia 555, turn left course zero-two-zero for the Sierra Papa Romeo hold, maintain speed two-sixty knots minimum, further descent in five miles.' The Spaniard repeated the message through what sounded like a mouthful of molasses. Still the girl gave no sign of having heard Oron's question, and he none of expecting an answer until she was ready.

'Geneva Approach, good morning, Speedbird 622 passing Flight Level 210, descending to Flight Level 140. Any speed restriction?' A very British voice spoke out of the loudspeaker.

'Speedbird 622, short delays in the St. Prex hold. Continue as advised to Localiser only, Runway 23.' Now the girl relaxed, pushing herself back from the console. She pointed to a small blip on the outside edge of the screen, the digits 4041 beside it. She spoke to Oron in French. 'That's 493. The SQUAWK ident will have to be changed.' she said. 'The French have a similar number over Lyon.' She shifted her chair closer and keyed the mike.

'Swissair 493, confirm you are squawking 4041.'

'Affirmative, Swissair 493.' Mueller replied instantaneously. The girl consulted a strip of paper beside her, one of the sausage-machine slips.

'Swissair 493, new squawk ident 4608, repeat 4608.'

'Swissair 493 squawking 4608.' Within seconds the tiny number beside the blip had changed.

'Break. Sabena 639, heavy Charlie Bravo at your twelve o' clock, ten miles. Do you require a new track?'

'Good girl,' muttered Le Comte. I was impressed that, even with all she had on her hands, she had seen the "Charlie Bravo", a storm cell of heavy cumulo-nimbus storm clouds threatening.

'Geneva Approach, Sabena 639. Affirmative. Request 10° degree to the right to avoid. For information, moderate turbulence at level one-six-zero.'

Above seven thousand feet heights are referred to as Flight Levels, in hundreds of feet, one-six-zero being 16,000 feet. The girl gave the Belgian a new heading to avoid the build-up of storm clouds, and Le Comte and I settled in to watch and wait for 493 to descend and enter the holding pattern. But by now the damage had been done, and nothing could avert the disaster that was only minutes away.

Perhaps if the Controller working Geneva Approach that morning hadn't been a girl, and young, perhaps then Thierry Scholl might not have acted as he did, we'll never know for certain. My theory, for what it's worth, is that, hearing a young woman on Geneva Approach, and flying as he was in the close vicinity... But another theory is that he flew too long above fifteen thousand feet, suffered oxygen starvation and the inevitable consequence of light headedness, which in addition to his already unstable state... Unfortunately there wasn't enough left of him for the doctors to examine with any usefulness.

In the enquiry that followed, however, I was obsessed with a quite different theory.

From the flight recorder, we know that Scholl headed first of all out over the eastern areas of Lake Geneva, as he had on many previous occasions. Cloud cover was on the deck that morning, with light sleet falling over Montreux. Being an all-time exhibitionist, and realising that aerial acrobatics would be unimpressive in such conditions, he must then have turned due South to the Rhône estuary. He was picked up seventy miles away to the South-east at 9.47 by Sion radar. Sion is a small airport that is trying hard to make national impact, but that isn't why they have top-level radar. Just down the valley of the Rhône are two strategic Air Force fighter strips, with the aircraft actually stationed in huge caverns hewn into the mountainside. Scholl wasn't doing anything wrong in the Rhône Valley, but every aircraft in the area is automatically challenged. He was last logged by Sion Radar as climbing and heading South over the Schwarzhorn, North of Zermatt.

Although the Curtiss C-46 has been widely used as a passenger transport with a pressurised airframe, Scholl's model did not have the advantage of a pressurised cabin, so he could not safely fly above about 15,000 feet without using oxygen. To fly any higher would inevitably cause the pilot disastrous oxygen starvation. This most insidious of medical states is particularly nasty in that the victim is not only unaware that anything is wrong, in its early stages he goes through a state of euphoria that convinces him of his razor-sharp facilities. By the time an oxygen-starved stupor sets in, brain damage is almost certain, and the victim in no better state than a junkie who has topped up with a full bottle of whisky.

Scholl's flight-recorder showed that he climbed to fly over the eight thousand foot Schwarzhorn, but realising that to continue South would bring him straight up against the much nastier obstacle of the Matterhorn shrouded in mist and snow, he turned right, Westwards, and headed towards Annecy. Within minutes he was in French air space, hidden from the Geneva radar by the Savoy alps South of the lake.

Dating from some earlier owner's commercial use, Scholl's aircraft also had a cockpit voice recorder, and a fair indication of his mental health is the frequency with which he voiced angry expletives to himself. Surprisingly, and to my extreme irritation, and later that of the Commissioner, during an hour of cockpit noises when Scholl spoke a great deal to himself, there was not a single clue as to why he did it.

At one point he was challenged by Chamonix Control, far to the South, and obediently punched a SQUAWK-ident into his transponder at their request, but he lied about his non-existent flight plan, saying he was diverting due to weather from Nyon, a smallish strip near Geneva, to some indistinguishable name he produced, supposedly near Fribourg. He left Chamonix control at ten thirty-seven, and seems to have flown in figures of eight over Annecy for a while. The next time he appeared on anyone's radar was at 11.21, over Passeiry, forty miles West of Geneva, at six thousand feet. He was squawking 4608, the identical number to Swissair 493, and presenting an identical radar profile. Incredibly, it was several minutes before the Controllers noticed him on their screens.

"We hadn't had as busy a day for nine months," Oron told me later, "but you can't make excuses to dead passengers, and there was no excuse for what happened."

I thought there had been every excuse, and said so, but he had refused to accept that.

"It was a cock-up, and I don't remember anything like it in all my years in the Tower." he said. He had even sent a formal written apology to British Airways, who sent a one line acknowledgement, which probably meant they thought it had been a "cock-up" as well. Oron wasn't referring to Scholl's illegal presence in the West, but to a near-miss conflict over St. Prex, which was the main reason no one had time to notice Scholl's rogue blip.

I still think he was much too hard on himself. In the first place, we didn't know Thierry Scholl was West of the airport because he had been flying in French air-space at only two thousand feet behind the loaf-shaped Salève mountain which lies South of Geneva. He had approached the Salève heading due North from Annecy, and turned West to fly the length of it rather than fly over it, where he would have been instantly visible to Geneva radar.

We know now that Scholl must have been listening in to Geneva Approach radio for a long time before he came round the shoulder of the Salève and turned east towards the airport. And because he had been listening, he had heard the new SQUAWK ident number for Swissair 493 being transmitted by the young female Controller. My view is that it was probably then that he flipped. He must have seen what to him was a God-sent opportunity to show Dominique Dantin once and for all what he was worth. If she had been alive to see it, he would certainly not have impressed her in the way he intended. Scholl of course could not know that not only was Dominique Dantin not in the Tower that morning, but that she was lying dead in her crushed Volkswagen out in the snowy wastes of the Jura.

It was while the Moscow flight was in the St. Prex holding pattern, awaiting its turn to approach and land, that the "cock-up" occurred. Nobody ever panics in ATC, but I was made abruptly aware of the responsibilities that were turning Le Comte into a prematurely old man. It happened like this.

The Iberia 555 had turned North to cross the lake and the Approach Controller had directed it on a radar vector towards St. Prex. There were already four aircraft circling there at one thousand feet height separations. It was a classic holding pattern, or stack. The synchronisation was remarkable. All four aircraft, carrying upwards of 600 passengers, all flying the identical oval pattern at identical speeds. One of them was 493.

As the Iberia closed on St. Prex, the Speedbird 622 from London was approaching the holding pattern from the North. The British plane had started its descent later than the Iberia flight, and was considerably higher. And, being closer, the Iberia blip would reach the stack over St. Prex before the Speedbird.

A sudden commotion in the Control room was caused by a middle-aged computer operator who lost his cool. I doubt whether he was a certificated Controller: the one thing a Controller never ever does is to disturb the concentration of his colleagues. For some reason, a computer snarl-up I think, this man blew his top and let out some ripe comments on the technological wonder that wasn't behaving wonderfully. Something like that. He was very loud.

The young woman controlling Approach Radar completed an instruction to the flight at the bottom of the stack to leave the holding pattern and peel off towards Geneva and the field, then between messages she turned to her neurotic colleague and told him in no uncertain terms to get lost.

Oron had left her station to investigate the man's sudden outburst; unlike the girl's response, he addressed colleague and machine with great tact. Even under those conditions, though, he had one ear tuned in to every word spoken in the room; the man's assumption of responsibility was incredible.

'Iberia 555.' The girl's voice was as steady as if she had been ordering an ice cream, but by the way she kept flicking the hair from her eyes and squinting at the screen it was evident she was feeling the strain. 'Fly radar heading 010 to join the hold at Flight Level 100.' The Spaniard acknowledged the instruction:

'Flight Level one-théró-théró.' and there was a short pause, with only the mumble of a Controller behind us handling the outbound traffic. In less than a minute she keyed the mike again.

'Speedbird 622, recleared Flight Level nine-zero..., correction Flight Level one hundred, repeat Flight Level one hundred, to join the hold.'

The British co-pilot repeated the instruction verbatim, ending with the words 're-cleared one-zero-zero for the hold, Speedbird 622.'

'No.' Suddenly Oron was standing behind her chair again. How he got there, how he had overheard all this, with his attention on some loose plug he was fiddling around with at the computer, I'll never know. Before he could explain, and the girl clearly hadn't cottoned on what was wrong, she was staring up at him in confusion, the Speedbird Captain himself came on the air again, a different voice, very calm, very dry, a Public School voice:

'Er, Geneva Approach, this is the Speedbird 622. You just cleared the Iberia 555 to ten thousand feet, I think.' He paused, then went on in a gentle drawl. 'Am I supposed to hit the bugger flying clockwise, or anti-clockwise?'

'Mon Dieu!' The girl froze, her thumb keyed the mike and she spoke with a sudden urgent clarity that was compelling. Her eyes scanned the screen, one hand was twisting compulsively at a lock of hair. 'Iberia 555, descend *immediately* to Flight Level nine-zero, repeat immediate descent Level nine-zero, turn left heading 180° for a 360 over the lake.' She flicked again at her fringe, her eyes shifting across the screen to check that there was no conflicting traffic over the lake. Even as the Spanish pilot confirmed he was descending, she spoke again. 'Speedbird 622, continue as cleared.'

There was a long pause, and when the British pilot did press his microphone key, he still didn't speak for some seconds. The strange sounds of air rushing past the flight-deck and the movements of the pilots echoed from the loudspeaker. Finally, in the same drawling voice:

'Rule Britannia!'

Oron grinned and squeezed the girl's shoulder. She breathed a sigh of relief, and looked up at him.

'Can I be relieved a moment?' He nodded, and as she slipped out of the chair he took her place.

It doesn't sound much of a conflict like that, but if you consider that both aircraft initially had accepted their instructions... If the Speedbird pilot hadn't been on the ball, they would have met head on over Lausanne. At ten thousand feet. And although Oron had grinned, I could see he was riled by the whole affair, his shoulders were hunched, and his aggressive sniff was going non-stop. He lit a cigarette, and slipped me one, as he had earlier.

'Next off the stack'll be the Lakey flight.' he said. 'I'll be handing it over to the Tower Controller, but you can watch it from here if you want?' I nodded.

'Michel? I have a conflict.' The man behind us handling Departures had been watching the St. Prex affair develop and die down on his own screen, which is probably why he hadn't spotted Thierry Scholl when he first appeared. 'Christ. What the hell's going on? Michel...' he called more urgently.

'What is it?' Oron slipped the earphones to the girl again. 'Why did Dominique have to choose today of all days...? Jesus!' He had moved to a position where he could view both Controllers' screens and looked momentarily shocked, then recovered. 'Well, I've never seen that before...'

'Do I tell 493 to continue approach?' The girl must have been unnerved by the earlier incident, her voice was uncertain and she didn't know what Oron and the Departures Controller were talking about.

I saw Oron nod, then, as he realised that with her back turned she couldn't have seen him:

'Yes, continue.' He studied the plot on the departure radar. 'That's the SAS, passing through 5,000, climbing out over Passeiry?' He pointed, it was a question. Two of the off-watch Controllers had gathered round now to see what was happening. The Departure Controller spoke into his microphone.

'SK 608, stop your climb immediately, descend to 5000 feet and turn...' He hesitated momentarily. Right lay the Jura, at six thousand feet. Left lay the French Alps and the radar blind spots. '... turn left, heading 190°. Further climb shortly.' he added hopefully. The Scandinavian pilot confirmed, as if such a manoeuvre was an everyday event, which it definitely was not. If he didn't get further climb very soon he'd be plastered all over a French mountainside.

'What is that idiot doing?' Oron spoke very slowly, very cool now, his face immobile, the twitch gone, 'Can you call him up?'

'I'll try. The odds are against him being on Departure frequency though.' The Departures Controller pressed the microphone switch. 'Calling unidentified aircraft squawking 4608, South of Passeiry. Identify aircraft type, aircraft registration and intentions.' There was no please and thank you in this.

Oron had picked up a telephone and was talking to the upper level, telling the Tower Controller to hold all departing aircraft. He covered the mouthpiece and sniffed violently, then called across to the Arrivals Controller:

'After 493 is down, get the others back to St. Prex. Turn them right to Pétal at 5,000 feet to the stack. Oh, and this may go on for some time, so check them all for fuel in case any have to divert. Antoine...' This to the Departures Controller who had spotted Scholl. 'Get that SAS out of here, give him a climb-out over Salève and across the lake for a Seven November departure. Call Henri and tell him to watch out and clear the SAS through the descending traffic.' He spoke into the phone again, his eyes fixed on the radar plot. 'This is looking very nasty. Do you have either of them on visual? Well, when you do, or if anything happens, I'll come up.'

'Swissair 493, 20 miles to run, contact now Tower on 118 decimal 7, good bye.' The girl handling Approach radar signed off the 493, and set about turning round the aircraft following it. She was amazing, never once losing her cool, even when one got stroppy, predictably an American. He was unwise enough to try to argue, asking why, wasting precious time.

'You do your job!' she snapped, 'And I'll do mine!'. But then there was nothing else she could say, none of us actually knew why.

'Has he answered yet?' Oron put down the phone and stared at the plot. 'Christ, what's he playing at? He's moving east, towards the field. And descending... Where's the 493?' The Departure Controller pointed to the blip slowly moving in from the right. Everyone's eyes were fixed on the centre of the screen, where the runway was marked as a thick white line. From the right the radar profile that was Swissair 493 was slowly getting closer and closer, its SQUAWK ident of 4608 clearly visible. And from the left, an identical radar profile at the same altitude was descending to the runway at the same speed, and it too had the SQUAWK ident of 4608. If both continued like that, in only a few minutes, the two identical blips would collide head on in the middle of the runway.

Chapter Six

'Try to raise him on any of the frequencies. Arrivals, Departures and Tower.' Le Comte was speaking in French, very rapidly but with extreme clarity. 'I want him identified, and I want to know what the hell he thinks... *Mais merde.*' He swore. 'I can't even tell from this,' he gestured at the radar blip on the left of the monitor, 'whether he can land on the grass runway - its under snow, but it's a last resort - or whether he needs the concrete. What's his height?' he demanded, but there was nobody free to answer him. Already the desynchronised sound of three different voices came from the consoles all around. The girl on Approach had the lead, followed by a new Controller working a spare radar on the Tower frequency.

'Unidentified aircraft squawking 4608 over Passeiry, identify and state your intentions.' All three were using exactly the same words, as if they automatically knew what to say, although I doubted that any training existed for an event such as this.

It was understandable that a mystified Mueller should respond, pointing out that he wasn't over Passeiry but over Pétal and the lake, that he wasn't unidentified and what the hell was going on? After all, he too was squawking 4608.

A telephone buzzed, it was the Tower Controller on the floor above, I could hear his voice echo down the staircase. He didn't know what to say to Mueller, who was eighteen miles out on final approach and he wanted Le Comte up there with him. It was as Oron went up the steps two at a time that he started me on what was be the wildest of all wild goose chases. He said:

'A bloody pain in the arse, this Suri-Lakey business of yours has turned out to be.' It didn't sink in consciously, but it was to colour all my thinking in the following enquiry, and led me in a totally wrong direction.

We stood at the plate glass windows looking over the misty airfield. It all looked normal enough at a glance. There was a light sleet falling, but you could see beyond the runway at each end, and the landing lights of 'Swissair 493 were clearly visible hanging in the sky to the East.

'Swissair 493 ten miles out.' murmured the Tower Controller. His eyes were fixed on his radar console, flicking from left to right and back again, interpreting the shadowy contours into hard fact. 'Unidentified aircraft leaving Passeiry, heading

050, speed one-five-zero. 493 has nine miles to run, height four thousand.' He paused. 'Passeiry aircraft eight miles to run, height three thousand.' Now he was sweating. Oron grabbed a pair of field glasses from a shelf, and stared to the West, trying to glimpse the rogue blip, to identify the unknown aircraft.

'What is the wind speed?' His voice was very distant, controlled.

'Two six-zero degrees, eleven knots gusting to eighteen.'

The knuckles of the Tower Controller were white as he gripped the arm of his chair. With his other hand he operated the microphone switch.

'Swissair 493, for information, we have unidentified traffic approaching the airfield from the West...' He read out the height and speed, and then gave the command that was to prove fatal. Fatal, at least, for Thierry Scholl. 'Continue approach. Call passing outer marker.'

'Swissair 493, continuing. Call you at the marker.' What Mueller was thinking of I have no idea. It is true that pilots on approach are perhaps more completely in the hands of Air Traffic Control than at any other time, and Geneva has a first-class ATC record. But he must have been hypnotised by the artificial calmness in the Controller's voice not to have seen the danger, and told Fonjallaz to initate a go-around. And Fonjallaz, he must bear some of the responsibility. Certainly he had his hands full and it was snowing hard at 2,000 feet as he brought the plane down, but even so...

'I see him.' Oron's voice was a shout. I moved over to join him at the window, and stared out into the grey mist and sleet. I couldn't see anything. 'Twin engine prop, looks like a DC3. Over the Outer marker West. German registration, write it down Paul... Delta Papa Charlie Echo Mike...' He made a snorting noise. 'Now at least we know what we're looking at.'

I scribbled the registration on a spare jotter. There is a sad irony that it had last been used by Dominique Dantin: if she had got to the airport that day, she would certainly have known instantly who we were looking at, for Scholl had more than once flown her to France and Italy in Delta-Echo-Mike. But the registration letters meant nothing to any of us.

I still couldn't make out anything in the milky sky. Le Comte lowered the glasses and looked at me blankly, he was actually visualising the scenario of the two aircraft trying to land simultaneously, in opposing directions.

'Good Christ.' He started muttering to himself and lifted the binoculars again. 'He's mad.'

He told me later he'd had nightmares in the days and nights that followed, always of an old aircraft with ice building up on the wing roots and engine cowlings, and nobody knowing until it crashed. Unlike Scholl, Le Comte could clearly see the accretion of ice. He was still muttering to himself.

'He'll never land a crate like that in these conditions. Tailwind eleven knots and heavy icing. What the bloody hell is he... Has nobody raised him on RT yet?' he called over his shoulder. I hadn't heard anyone call it RT for years, he was reverting to his early training with the stress. 'All right, that's it.' He seemed to make up his mind. '493 to break off the approach...' But it sounded indecisive, sotto voce, and when he turned to the Tower Controller who was staring at him, waiting for a firm order, he hesitated, and by then it was too late.

'Swissair 493 inside the outer marker. Clear to land?' Mueller's voice on the small loudspeaker sounded strained, the Tower was leaving landing clearance very late. The Tower Controller had no option but to act as he saw fit.

'Swissair 493 negative, repeat negative, execute immediate go-around procedure, repeat immediate...'

'No.' Oron's voice was a stifled groan, he dropped the glasses and leapt for the microphone to countermand the instruction, but it was too late. 'His landing gear's still up, he's not going to try to land, not into another aircraft, it's a stunt, it has to be.' His eyes were fixed now on the approaching DC 9, his fingers gripping the man's chair-back like pincers. 'Get the 493 down, man, and then we'll get this lunatic... Oh Christ...'

His voice tailed away, his face suddenly blank, but the tic was going like a trip-hammer under his left eye, and his upper lip gleamed with sweat. I glanced down at the radar, where the two blips were almost joined together, they were so close, and then literally had to drag my eyes from the plot, unwilling to identify them as real objects in the white mist outside.

It was a sight that imprinted itself on the mind's eye for all time as if frozen there, although the combined speed of the two aircraft was actually over 300 miles per hour.

Hanging in the air, as it seemed, over the eastern end of the runway, was the glaring triangle of the DC 9's spotlights surrounded by the red and white airframe. Black smoke was belching from its rear-mounted jets as Fonjallaz applied maximum thrust for the go-around. Above the other end of the runway the broad-winged Curtiss faced it like a squat insect, the propellors making eerie pools of rainbow-coloured light against the snow-filled sky. In the split second in which the eye identified all this, neither plane looked as if it was moving at all.

On the flight deck of the DC 9 Fonjallaz quite automatically went into the missed approach procedure, calling out each item even while doing it.

'Flaps 5, undercarriage up, full thrust. Keep calling the airspeed and height. Cut the ground proximity hooter, I can't hear myself think.'

Mueller winced at Fonjallaz's slow methodical speech. It irritated him, and the irritation irritated him even more. Fonjallaz repeated the order.

'Call airspeed and height.' Fonjallaz started to worry. He couldn't see the other aircraft, and the six seconds it took for the jets to wind up to maximum thrust felt like sixty, they were still dropping dammit, he'd forgotten how long the delay could seem in regaining thrust. Mueller started calling the altitude and speed.

'1,000 feet, speed 180 knots... flaps 5.' He stared ahead and below, but neither man could see the Curtiss. Mueller jabbed the 'Seat belts fastened' button three times, a signal to the Cabin Crew to keep their heads down. 'Rate of climb 1300. Height 1200. Speed 190. Landing gear fully retracted,' he added. At this moment the Tower Controller came on the air again.

When I asked Fonjallaz to describe what he and Mueller actually did, blow by blow, during the overshoot procedure, the first thing he did was to light his pipe, the second to take a deep draught of his beer, and then he said:

'I don't think I remember.' And as none of us ever knew what Scholl was actually doing during the conflict, the only view I'll ever have of what happened is what I saw from the Tower.

Very slowly, unbelievably slowly, the DC 9 started to climb, steeper and steeper, until it looked to be nearly vertical. The screaming jets left a stream of smoke like black lace hanging over the runway.

'Swissair 493, conflicting traffic one mile, your eleven o' clock, below you and climbing left. Have you the traffic in sight?' It was the Tower Controller. I don't think many men would have had the overwhelming presence of mind that he showed. Mueller made some sort of acknowledgement.

'Swissair 493, collision avoidance turn right immediately, and climb at full power...' Tower Controller realised that with the old Curtiss so close and beneath the DC 9, Fonjallaz couldn't see him.

At that moment the phones started ringing, and it was pandemonium, no one able to say what was happening and half the airport demanding to know.

I think it was his next manoeuvre that Fonjallaz was referring to when he afterwards used the word "illegitimate". Towering above him to his right were the Jura mountains, very close. To his left the Salève, high enough to be a danger. Beneath him and to all appearances about to ram him, the Curtiss. I can see what he meant about the outcome if Mueller had been in the driving seat.

From the Tower I had a clear view of the two aircraft. Fonjallaz had not, he had no option but to rely a hundred percent on the Tower Controller. But the plane Oron had mistakenly identified as a DC3 had a kind of self-destructive determination to stick like glue to the DC9.

Obediently Fonjallaz swung his jet sharply to the right, and he was already at a maximum rate of climb, passing through 4000 feet.

I don't think Scholl was actually homicidal, and Oron agrees. It was more probable that the heavy icing was affecting the controls, and that the plane's behaviour had nothing to do with his intentions. In any event, despite Fonjallaz's avoidance measures, the Curtiss/DC3 swung left and clawed its way back into the DC 9's path. The Tower Controller realised that from now on Fonjallaz must be better off flying purely on instinct and stopped transmitting. We clearly saw the wing flaps retracting, then the swing of the tail as Fonjallaz slammed his foot down on the pedal.

The jet reared round as if swung by a giant hand, and at the same time Fonjallaz must have pulled back on the stick. The aircraft went into a controlled stall, seeming to sit on its tail in the air, then the right wing dropped steeply. He told me later that such a manoeuvre wouldn't be so bad at 15,000 feet, you've got some room to play with, but at 4,000...

In an optical illusion the nose of the plane seemed to touch its own wingtip, and then he was round, the Curtiss had passed beneath the DC 9's tail, and was ahead of him at the same height, still pulling left away from the airfield towards the Jura.

Fonjallaz had four times the speed of the twin-engined relic, and a clear view of it as it headed away to his left. From the Tower, however, the DC9 seemed to be sinking tail-first straight into the ground. With a new flare of smoke from the jets it started to flatten out and a new voice, Fonjallaz himself, came on the radio.

'Tower, Swissair 493 requesting go-around clearances. Please.'

'Swissair 493, climb to 5,000 feet, radar heading 040°, turn right over Morges to join the Localiser. Will you require assistance on landing?'

The Tower Controller's face was pale, and the colour only started to return when he heard Mueller's very unprofessional reply.

It is incredible, but I have not been able to find anyone who actually saw the Curtiss fly out. I suppose we were all so stunned by events, and also staggered at Fonjallaz's handling of the DC 9. Everyone, though, once they realised the madman was no longer over the airfield, tried to locate the Curtiss. On account of the mist and the sleet, relatively few succeeded; I never saw the plane again. The Approach Radar Controller reported losing the blip some thirty miles North of the airport, high up in the Jura mountains. Scholl's aircraft had ploughed into trees on the mountainside at 5,000 feet in one of the most inaccessible spots imaginable, and on account of the weather could only be reached by helicopter.

Oron, who had stood motionless since the Tower Controller had given the order to 493 to break off the approach, was like a man carved from stone, his face very still, no tic or twitch or sniff to betray what he was thinking. Finally he came to life, speaking like an automaton. Every man and woman who worked on the upper level was standing, watching us, waiting for orders. They were waiting for me, but it was Oron who took control.

'Bring down 493. Send out the fire brigade for the landing. When it's down, have it parked out of the way in Sector Charlie.'

He glanced at me, but I was too shocked to understand why, or to see him pointing at a red telephone. On getting no response, he continued:

'Send out the Red Cross squad, Securitas, a baggage handling team, and the wide-bodied VIP coach. Call in the Deputy ATC Supervisor.' He glanced at the Controllers' duty roster, picked a name. 'Pierre, make a log of all movements,' - he meant the two aircraft - 'and backups of the control videotapes. There'll be an enquiry, of course.' he added, speaking to me.

As they got into action, he picked up a red telephone and began giving orders. The Red Cross Search and Rescue helicopter to locate the wreckage, the Conference centre to be opened up and made ready for SR 493's passengers, whom he euphemistically described as "probably a bit shaken up". He broke off in mid-conversation, apparently waiting for someone at the other end, picked up a grey phone and gave orders to the Departure radar to start getting aircraft airborne again. In the same breath he added some friendly remark to the girl on Arrivals, I forget what, but it sticks in my mind as typical of the man. Then he was back on the red phone, asking for a Russian interpreter if possible, and the Airport Chaplain, and drinks and refreshments, to be sent to the Conference centre. Free telephone calls to be laid on, access to a Telex, and more.

During the last part of all this he also handled a call on yet a third telephone, the Swissair Administrator asking what the hell was going on.

I suddenly felt sick and sat down on a stool beside him. The difference between the man's immense concentration and my own frankly ineffectual presence was suddenly very hard to swallow, He looked at me curiously over the two telephone receivers he was holding, one in each hand, a strange sadness in his eyes.

'Paul, I don't mind doing half your job, but you are in charge of logistics, you know? Get it together, hey?'

That really got to me. He was right, of course, I was the senior police officer in charge, and he had just done everything that I should have been doing. I felt strangely numb, I'd never actually had to admit to anyone else before that I was probably in quite the wrong job.

Through the windows I could see 493 coming in to land again. A red helicopter was just taking off and swinging low to the North, towards the spot where the unknown pilot had come down. I pulled the walkie-talkie from my belt, called up Sergeant Vinet and told him to meet me by the Swissair jet when it reached Sector Charlie. He wanted to know what about the Press, and a hundred other questions, but I cut him short and said the Airport authorities could handle that, there were enough of them and only two of us. My priority was Lakey. And now Suri. I wanted to find out from Lakey what made him such a threat that Suri should have sent a Kami-kaze pilot to kill him and all aboard his flight.

Chapter Seven

The notion that Suri was behind the whole thing wasn't that clearly identified in my mind as I took the lift down to ground level, but it was there all right, just waiting for any pointer at all to bring it out into the open. Now I can see how preposterous it was, but at the time it seemed so obvious as to be...

Sergeant Vinet was a better detective than I was. Rightly assuming that I had no transport at the Tower and wouldn't want to walk across half the airfield to get to Sector Charlie, he had entirely disregarded my order to meet me there, and was waiting for me in his police car at the foot of the Tower.

'Still snowing.' he said obliquely, letting in the clutch with a jolt. 'Thought you might need a lift.'

He seemed to be about to ask me something, but probably realising that I would know nothing anyway he changed his mind and we drove in silence across the snow-covered apron towards the red and white DC 9 that was slowly taxiing to Sector Charlie.

In seeming chaos, a dozen vehicles were vying for space around the Swissair jet. The mobile steps were just being positioned against the forward door as Vinet carved a track in the snow through the melée. The sleet was still falling, and the whole place was shrouded in a damp white mist. It was bitterly cold. I jumped out and made for the steps at the same moment that the door swung open and a uniformed air hostess appeared framed in the oval doorway. The radio at my hip bleeped, I made a switch. It was Oron in the Tower.

'I have a Federal Air Commissioner here,' he told me, his voice distorted and crackly. 'She wants to see you and all the aircrew as soon as maybe. What shall I tell her, Paul? Half an hour, perhaps, in the Fed. Bureau offices?' Oron was being over-protective, he thought I couldn't cope and was leading me by the hand. Stupidly I resented his initiative, I didn't think I was that useless.

'Who is it?' I demanded. He sighed audibly, and I knew I had done the wrong thing.

'I have the Federal Enquiry Agency President, Madame Simona Sentori, up here.' he said wearily. 'What shall I tell her?'

Sentori again. In a reflex of chagrin, I sucked in the freezing air through my teeth. Simona Sentori.

We had had a run-in nine months previously when a light aircraft, a Robin piloted by a young man with his parents as passengers, had misunderstood a command from the Tower. The consequences had been appalling, he had turned his aircraft to a premature landing in a thunder storm, come in too close behind a landing Jumbo 747 and been caught in the wake turbulence, with the result that his aircraft had capsized completely in the wash, and crashed. All three had been killed.

Sentori had been in charge of the Federal Commission of Enquiry, and had tried to make out it had been partly my fault. I had been in the Tower at the time, watching planes come and go.

Worse, some eleven or twelve years previously, Simona and I had had a brief but very intense affair; Geneviève hadn't been the only one to mess around. Even though the whole thing hadn't lasted more than a few months, Fate seemed determined to keep on throwing us together in unfriendly situations. I hadn't known that Oron knew, but judging by his efforts to smooth things along he probably did.

The hostess was staring at me as I climbed the steps, her face uncertain and shaken.

'Half an hour, Michel, as you say.' I signed off and hooked the radio to my belt again. My eye fell on the hostess' name badge. I shook her hand, using her name in greeting. She seemed pleased that for once someone had found the badge useful.

'What do you want me to tell the passengers, sir?' It was a long time since anyone had called me that, I supposed it was the seniority of the uniform that did it.

'Would you escort them to the VIP coach, please.' I said formally, 'The Conference Centre is being prepared to receive them, and Swissair personnel will be there to assist. I should like to meet the passenger Lakey, if I may?'

She sniffed meaningfully. 'That will be a little difficult for the moment. He is at the rear of the plane, and all the other passengers are already in the aisle, but...'

'The rear door.' intervened Vinet coldly. 'Please have it opened immediately. We shall only be in the way of passengers here.'

She gave the order on a wall telephone, and we walked around the aircraft to the rear, where an automatic stairway was descending from the belly of the aircraft.

'Who is this Lakey, anyway?' Vinet wanted to know.

Always the same question, and still no answers.

'I think he's the reason that all this happened.' I said. Unconsciously I was preparing myself for the probability that Suri had sent out a killer. 'But at present we... ahh. Come on. Now we'll see.'

We went up the rear steps two at a time, and were suddenly faced by a crowd of about a dozen passengers turning in their tracks and urgently pushing towards us. There was that indefinable quality of restrained panic in the air, you can smell it and you can feel it, but you can't actually describe it. The hostess came on the cabin loudspeakers, and the tide of passengers turned again and began to shuffle to the front, where the cabin crew were ushering them down to the waiting VIP coach. One man wasn't shuffling anywhere, although he wasn't handcuffed to his seat either, as Fonjallaz described him.

'Mr. Lakey?' The man turned his face from the window to stare up at me in surprise. My stomach twisted, and I knew as soon as I set eyes on him that here was a victim of the Suri Sect and not a Suri Saint. My correspondence and meetings with families who had lost people to the various pseudo-religious and Exegesis "Enlightenment" groups may not have done anything to improve my competence as a police officer, but being a dud in one job didn't make me a complete zero; I was strong on human nature and suffering. It was striking how all those who had suffered loss to one of those Sects bore remarkably similar scars. I was not imagining anything when I thought I identified the same hurt in this man, and from what he told me later it turned out I was right.

Nor had anything prepared me for the marked difference between the description on the Berne computer of a thirty-eight year old and the man in front of us, sitting squashed into the rear window seat. He would be about six foot when standing, a fit eighty kilos. His hair was fair and curly, and thick with grease as if he hadn't washed it for weeks. His cheeks might probably have once been full and even on the chubby side, but at that moment they were drawn in and almost emaciated. His blue eyes and the very fair eyebrows and eyelashes made me think of the kind of men you see in fashion magazine adverts, selling leather jackets or sunglasses.

And I understood why Moscow thought some new clothes might be a good idea, for his green cotton shirt and cheap cord trousers stank of travel and of sweat and all that goes with it. He wouldn't have sold many jackets like that, lines of fatigue etched on his face and his eyes all bloodshot and ringed with dark shadows. His wrists were smudged with grime, and his finger nails were black with it.

'You speak English?' He blinked very rapidly, his hands twisting a cat's-cradle in front of him as he spoke. He was very stressed. 'For God's sake, what's happening?' He made as if to stand up, but Vinet had him hemmed in. 'Listen, this Delhi flight? Am I still in time, is it on? You do know about it, I mean...'

'Delhi?' Vinet stared at me, perplexed. I remembered the Moscow Telex in my pocket, took it out and handed it to Lakey wordlessly. He was nearly at the end of his tether I thought, and also I wanted to watch his reactions. 'Helsinki?' His voice was a whisper, he brushed his eyes with the back of his hand in a gesture of disbelief. 'Helsinki.' he repeated, and turned his head to stare up at me. 'Why? Why Helsinki, of all places? And this...' he waved the Telex at me, 'this was sent three hours ago, to the pilots. Why didn't I get it before?' He screwed up his eyes and I thought for a moment he was about to burst into tears, but he caught himself and started muttering under his breath, staring blindly at the Telex. 'She's in Helsinki, I'm in Geneva, and I was going to go to Delhi to find... Helsinki. Oh Christ.' He started muttering a girl's name over and over again then, and I realised that the Soviets had been right to get rid of him as quickly as possible, he was well past breaking point, on the edge of complete nervous collapse. Vinet was staring at him, and waiting for me to do something. But what? Before I could make up my mind, Lakey shook his head violently, a purely animal movement, and looked at us. His eyes were bright and the pupils very small. 'O.k. So what happens now?'

How the hell was I supposed to know? Torn between conflicting duties and feelings I turned to Vinet.

'There are two Securitas men outside. Have them escort this man to my office, get him cleaned up - under supervision of course - and get him some food and drink. There are clean clothes for him there too.' I added. 'But no phone calls, no visits. I must see the Federal Commissioner about that madman in the other plane, and when I'm through there I'll interview Mr. Lakey.' Turning to Lakey I was about to translate the French for him, but he nodded jerkily.

'I understood that.' He swallowed. 'I'm under arrest, is that it?' He gave a kind of sickly laugh. 'Me, under arrest?' His mouth twisted with bitterness. 'That's just bloody, that is...'

'I don't know.' I glanced at Vinet. I didn't want to talk about that here and now, not with Vinet listening. Berne's instructions had been explicit, no police involvement other than myself. 'At the moment let us say you are *"gardé à vue"*, under observation.'

'For what?' Despite his exhaustion he was tough, and I wished to God he would shut up and do as he was told. 'I've broken no Swiss law. This American Express rubbish is a trumped up piece of nonsense by...'

'Please, Mr. Lakey, this is not the time or place!'

Thank God Vinet stopped Lakey when he did. I didn't want Vinet to know that Suri was involved in all this, and Lakey had been about to let it out. Ironically, Vinet's thin patience stopped him. I wondered, though, whether it was a clever idea for anyone to remain with the Englishman in my office for any length of time, as Lakey could at any moment let drop the name Suri in passing. And once any other police officer knew that Suri was in this affair, I knew Oron was right, I would never get another look in. I told Vinet to stand by in the Sergeant's office and let Securitas handle Lakey, we shouldn't leave the shop unattended I said. Fortunately he agreed.

Leaving Vinet to locate the Securitas team, I made my way forward through the now empty cabin and went onto the flight deck. Fonjallaz and Mueller were still strapped in, talking quietly. It was Fonjallaz who crystallised the question I had been putting off examining.

'Tricky one for you, Monsieur de Savigny.' Amazingly he was smiling. 'From our point of view, as we have just been discussing, we do not see what law has been broken here today... As far as we know, there is no actual law that denies a pilot the right to fly head on into another... Although there bloody well ought to be.' he added with a renewed grin. 'We did rather well, I thought.'

'"Well"?' Mueller looked at Fonjallaz as if he were mad, and made to unstrap himself. 'What in God's name was going on out there? Who was that madman, the Red Baron for God's sake? "Did well!?" If you hadn't been flying the plane, we'd all be plastered over the...'

'Ah, the exaggerations of youth.' Fonjallaz was sharper in tone than the words suggest, he was trying his best to stop Mueller doing himself a lot of harm. The cockpit voice recorder was still going, and it only required Mueller to admit openly that, had he been flying the plane there would have been catastrophe, for his career to take a very sudden downward turn. Fonjallaz's left hand reached up to test for the continued presence of his sandy moustache. 'I have to agree that it would be nice to know exactly what has been going on.' He was an incredibly mild man, pedantic in his seeming disinterest. 'Have they located the other aircraft? The pilot? Do they know why?'

'I'm afraid that for the moment, Captain, I am "they", and the answers are all negative.' It was so easy to fall into the trap of talking like Fonjallaz, it sounded almost like mimicry. We collected the remainder of the cabin crew and drove in convoy to the Federal Offices in the Administration block where Simona Sentori was waiting. Even as we went down the steps a team of engineers was arriving. The aircraft would be grounded indefinitely pending a full technical check.

Simona Sentori. I wished I hadn't got to meet her, to talk to her, not because of what happened at our last encounter, or years ago, but because I was desperate to get to Benjamin Lakey and tackle the Suri angle. And as I've said, the longer Vinet was even near Lakey, the more probable that the name Suri would come up. That was my major preoccupation, an unforgivable one for a senior detective, I readily admit. And it was deepening every minute.

There aren't many women in positions of authority in Switzerland, in fact in one canton women had only just been given the vote, so any woman who makes it to the top has extraordinary powers of survival in a man's world. Simona Sentori was one of them.

She was waiting in the miniature conference room. At one end was a computer terminal, an elderly Telex machine and a battery of telephones. In the centre of the room an oval table was already laid out with blotters and pens, and a trolley with coffee and soft drinks was being wheeled in as we arrived.

Simona hadn't changed at all as far as I could tell. In her early forties, she was a strikingly beautiful woman with short golden fair hair, green eyes and a stunning figure that left any normal man staring, and his wife fuming. This had been my exact situation twelve years' previously, and perhaps Geneviève's, if she had known. I was past the staring, but young Mueller hadn't met Simona before, and as she thoroughly enjoyed proving to herself that she still had the looks to make it happen, she did nothing to discourage him. Fonjallaz was seemingly oblivious of her presence, and the hostesses somewhat unnerved. As soon as we'd served ourselves, Simona

Sentori waved us to the table, and then sat down herself in the end seat. With an encompassing glance, she quelled the quiet conversations.

'Thank you for coming here so promptly after what I gather has been a rather harrowing experience.' She spoke in French, although I knew she could have handled Swiss German, Italian or English as capably. She went on formally. 'This is a preliminary hearing to determine the terms of reference for the coming enquiry. Everything that is recorded here today may be used as testimony for further investigation. I am here to explain to you the guidelines of that enquiry, and what it will seek to discover.'

Fonjallaz looked at his watch and covered an ostentatious yawn.

Oblivious to his hint, Madame Sentori went on at her own meticulously tedious pace.

'There is one line of enquiry only for the Federal Investigation Committee. That is, how the aircraft...' she consulted her notes, 'Delta Papa Charlie Echo Mike, identifying itself with a commercial aircraft's SQUAWK ident number, came to be on course to land on runway 05 at the same time that a commercial airliner legitimately SQUAWKing the same number was approaching to land on runway 23. Further, we shall seek to report on the flight pattern of the pilot of Delta-Echo-Mike prior to the event, immediately after the event, and how he came to crash on the Jura mountains. The pilot was killed in the crash. We have no positive identification of this person, but if he was the normal pilot of the Curtiss C-65 and its owner, then his name was...' The notes again. '...Thierry Scholl, 31, registered ownership in Friedrichshafen, Bodensee, in the Federal Republic of West Germany.' She looked up at me, her lower lip tucked pensively under her very white upper teeth.

'Deputy Commissioner de Savigny will need these details.' she said to the stenographer. 'Prepare a full dossier as soon as we're finished here. Will that be all right, Paul?' Sweetness and light, I didn't begin to understand her civility, quite at odds with our last few meetings. I nodded, nonplussed. 'Good. Now, you will all want to move on, so I shall try to keep this short. Captain Fonjallaz, First Officer Mueller, had you any further flights today?'

'I was to pilot the evening Copenhagen flight from Zürich.' muttered Mueller morosely, 'The Swissair coordinator met me on the way in. A replacement crew is taking it, I'm off-station.'

'I see. Captain?'

'Also off-station, no further flights today.' Fonjallaz was playing with his moustache again.

'Cabin crew?' She turned to a Swissair representative at the other end of the table. 'I suppose they too are off-station?' He nodded. Simona Sentori turned to me again.

'I shall shortly be asking the aircrew for a preliminary report of the events that occurred between the aircraft being handed over to Geneva Approach radar and touch down. I cannot see that this will in any way be of use to the police investigation. Nor can I see for the moment what police investigation there can usefully be, as the alleged miscreant is dead. We shall, however, need your full report into the antecedents and movements of the late Monsieur Scholl, and for this we shall be very grateful.' Again the smile flickered across the table at me. What the hell was she playing at? 'Will you be needing to interview any of the crew individually, Commissioner?'

Before I could reply, Fonjallaz cleared his throat.

'I believe I should speak with Monsieur de Savigny, regarding one of the passengers, and it might be instructive if he could speak later with Caroline Zbinden, who was attached to the said passenger for the duration of the flight.'

'May I ask why?' Simona Sentori brushed a wisp of fair hair from her eyelashes, and looked piercingly at Fonjallaz. She wasn't asking if she could ask, she was asking Why with a major question mark.

'This is a matter outwith the jurisdiction of the Federal Enquiry.' murmured Fonjallaz. 'A civil case.'

'Hm. Yes. I see. Very well.' She treated the entire room to the same penetrating glance, she was clearly dissatisfied with the reply. 'I shall have to assume, then, that the Scholl event and whatever Monsieur de Savigny's enquiries may touch on are quite separate from each other, and in no way connected? That is right? Captain?' She pressed him again. He nodded, said nothing.

Dammit, if she hadn't pinpointed the possibility of a link, the probability factor in my mind wouldn't have swung another ten points towards certainty. I was in a quandary with that question. I was convinced there was a link, and I was desperately keen to avoid all mention of Suri. And without mentioning Suri, I couldn't identify the link. I shook my head and said nothing.

'Very well.' She stood up. 'Please help yourselves to refreshments. I shall reconvene the meeting in five minutes.' Again the piercing look, this time directed at myself. 'Deputy Commissioner, a word before you go, if you please.' It was as neat a way of saying goodbye as you could have imagined, and I would have expected it to be frosty, but quite the reverse. She took me by the arm as we crossed to the door, her perfume was powerful as she paused, holding me close. So close that it touched a memory that I had thought long since buried. 'Paul,' Her voice was a murmur, 'You look dreadful, are you all right?' This hadn't occurred to me, that the strain of my obsessions was on public view, but I didn't see what else she could be referring to. If that was it, I didn't appreciate her concern.

'I'm all right.' I said. 'It was a bad do, bit of reaction perhaps.' I changed the subject quickly. 'What did you want to see me about?' I didn't really want to know, my mind was suddenly on things I hadn't thought about for years. Passion, and sex. I wished she would let go of me, not hold me that way. And then again, I didn't.

'Oh, that.' She made a wry face and looked over her shoulder at the cabin crew behind us. 'You remember that Robin case, last May?' I did indeed, she had tried to make public mincemeat of me then.

'What of it?'

'Don't be like that about it Paul.' She was tugging at my arm now, 'I was wrong, and I wanted to tell you myself, as soon as the opportunity arose.' Her eyes were playing with mine in a way I remembered all too well, that weird melting and wish-wanting effect that some women can achieve. I hadn't had a woman look at me like that for a very long time. When she went on talking her voice was slightly husky.

'I don't know why, I had this obsession with the idea, I suppose, that you were distracting the Tower Controller and, well... it seemed to fit. We're publishing the Final Report next week, and your name doesn't appear anywhere in it. That's what I wanted to tell you.' she said more formally. She had let go of my arm. 'You know how it is, sometimes obsessions like that make us fit selected facts to the theory, and not the other way round.'

She stopped. I thanked her, confused in more ways than one. Fool that I was, I didn't think of applying the lesson to myself, and by now the obsession that Scholl had been working for Suri was more than fifty percent in place.

Chapter Eight

It was nearly three in the afternoon when I finally reached the police offices to question the man Lakey. I was passing Vinet's room when he caught sight of me through the open door and called out to me to stop. Unwillingly, and worried that he might have caught on about Suri from Lakey, I stuck my head round the door.

'Well?' I could hardly have sounded more impatient.

'I have a call for you, from Martin Verre of the Rolle Police. Mr. Lakey is in your office, so I wondered if you would rather take the call in my...'

'Yes.' I took the receiver from him. 'de Savigny.' It was the Rolle Commissioner. I knew him well, despite my lack of career charisma, or because of it, we were good friends. We fairly often met socially. He sounded distressed.

'Been trying to reach you for hours, Paul. Too long over lunch, yes?'

This reminded me that not only had I had no lunch, I hadn't even finished breakfast either.

'Something like that.' I was trying to be friendly. 'Busy day. You?'

'Bad news I'm afraid, Paul.' He paused, then went on more rapidly. 'Dominique Dantin, you know her? I mean you knew her?' My heart lurched. When a policeman changes tense like that, well, we all mean the same thing.

'Go on.'

'I was saying, bad news, very bad. I'm afraid she's dead, Paul. Her mother has been in asking if you could call round, this evening I think. I gather you knew them fairly well?'

Poor Dominique Dantin, that was what I thought then anyway, poor little Dominique. Only twenty-four and...

'... hit a tree, complete wipe-out.' Martin Verre, the Rolle Commissioner, was still speaking. 'Really very ugly, took the firemen an hour to cut her... her remains free. I wonder Paul, will you tell the people at Air Traffic Control? I don't think her mother's in any fit state to do it.... Paul, you there?'

'I'm here.' I answered eventually. 'An accident? What's this about her mother?'

'Get it together Paul.' He sounded exasperated. 'If I remember, you live roughly half way between their places, up in the hills, no? Dominique's mother asked me to have you call her as soon as you've a moment. That's all. Have you got that now?'

'I'm not a complete idiot, Martin.' I snapped. 'We do have actual cases and crimes here too, you know, and I'm in the thick of one right now.'

'Sorry, sorry.' he mumbled. 'I'm never any good at these things, the telephoning bit I mean. You knew her well?'

'Dominique? Or her mother? Of course. When Geneviève was alive. Dominique was about Charlotte's age. We often had them round...'

'Hell, I'm sorry, Paul.'. There was a longer silence, then: 'Listen, can I have the mother call you? At the office?'

I said that would be fine, and rang off, depressed. I left Vinet to call the Tower and tell Oron, and at last made it all the way to my office, and Lakey. Only minutes before I'd been elated, eager to discover what it was about Lakey that might lead me - legally - into battle with Suri. Now the news of Dominique's death had left me deflated and not a little shocked.

I dismissed the Securitas men and waved Lakey to the chair in front of my desk. He sat down on the very edge of the chair, his gaze fixed on me strangely. He seemed to be sizing me up. His eyes were more strained than when I had met him on the plane, and his fingers were dancing a tune against his thumb. Clean clothes and a wash had done little to remove his stressed appearance.

'Have you had anything to eat?' I spoke in English, and he looked surprised at the lack of an accent.

'They gave me some biscuits. Stale ones.' he added.

'No lunch?' I guessed not, not on the plane. He shook his head.

'Am I under arrest?' he asked again, shifting to a more comfortable position. His tone and manner were aggressive. 'Because if not I'd like to...'

'Mister Lakey.' I stopped him. He looked as if he was about to burst into tears, his face working and his hands going like trip hammers. 'I think I can safely say that no legal proceedings will be pursued by this office. But there are matters that need clarification. Now, you have not eaten. I have not eaten. I suggest we rectify that.' I smiled thinly. 'Nothing in regulations says I can't interview someone over a meal...'

'I have no money.' he said wearily, as if that made it quite impossible to eat at all. 'And besides, I don't want to be seen...'

'Because of Suri?' I prompted. 'You're worried about him having another go?' Now it was out in the open, I was almost glad to have identified my belief that Suri was out to get Lakey. He was staring at me, suddenly upright in his chair.

'You know about Suri?' He was leaning far forward over my desk, his gaze fixed on mine, the formerly bloodshot eyes suddenly alert. 'How can you know? Has the Russian woman been in touch again? Is there any news of... of Miss Sorensen?... No.' He slumped back in the chair. 'There wouldn't be. Not with them in Helsinki, dammit.' His eyes met mine again. 'All right, if you're paying, let's have some food, and I'll answer your questions. For all the good it'll do...'

I stood up, and walked round the desk. The man reeked of hurt, of bitterness and all that these damned Sects can inflict on normal human beings by way of gratuitous punishment. I wanted to learn all about Sigrid Sorensen and Benjamin Lakey, and what had happened on the Trans-Siberian, and not just on their account. There was still Charlotte very much on my mind. Truth be told, I was already visualising myself, backed by the power of Interpol, in some international court, with the rat-like Suri, his hands chained, in the dock. That it never came to that and never will is perhaps understandable, given my record as a police officer. I was living on dreams and half-truths, a policeman's nightmare.

'Paul de Savigny.' I said by way of introduction. I missed out the Second Deputy bit. 'Before we leave here, there is something you should know. I am perhaps one of the best informed men in all of Europe...' it sounded pompous, but it was also true, '...on the activities and atrocities of ALBATROSS, the Suri Sect.'

Lakey stood looking at his new shoes for what seemed an eternity. Then he turned to me with a faint smile that transformed his fatigue into a boyish face.

'Well, well.' he said, very British. 'I rather thought I was. Paul.' I told Vinet where he could find us, and we left for the airport restaurant overlooking the apron and the aircraft.

The full story of what Benjamin Lakey went through between Japan and Moscow would be out of place here, and besides, only days later was I able to get a complete picture. It quickly became clear that Lakey had no money, nothing with him but a passport, and no means of getting all the way across the country to his house in Müstair, in Graubünden. He could hardly have had a place to live further from Geneva, it was at the extreme opposite end of Switzerland.

Over a belated lunch I managed to piece together the basics. Between leaving Japan and reaching Nakhodka, the Soviet port where the Trans-Siberian starts, the man Lakey had fallen in love with a Swedish girl, Sigrid Sorensen. In winter there is no connecting ferry service between Takaoka and Nakhodka, but both had managed to get tickets with an ALBATROSS group that had chartered a boat to connect with special reservations on the Trans-Siberian. Accommodation on the Trans-Siberian would be pretty spartan for these two, travelling out of season as they were, and they had readily accepted the invitation to spend much of the nine-day journey with the ALBATROSS group, who had reserved two first class coaches and a special dining car for their own use. During these days, both had been approached by the Suri group as possible targets for conversion. Lakey, who had a horror of such Sects that was quite equal to mine, had wanted nothing to do with it. The girl, according to Lakey, was singled out as an immediate target for conversion by none other than Suri himself, if only to spite Lakey for his resistance.

After nine days of battling wits and apparently some physical violence, the group arrived in Moscow where Lakey contacted the authorities and accused Suri of kidnapping Miss Sorensen. Suri counter-attacked. The subsequent manoeuvring on the part of the Soviet authorities has been covered by Fonjallaz.

Now Lakey touched on the trickiest part of the whole thing, for me. He asked yet again whether he was under arrest.

'I don't think you are.' I wasn't at all sure about this, at this point I hadn't heard Fonjallaz's version of the Moscow plan. I could have done without the additional distraction of Dominique Dantin's death. I wasn't prepared to admit it to myself but already I was suffering the Sentori syndrome of forcing facts to fit theories and not vice versa. In reality, of course, I had damn all facts to go on, and even had I had any, insufficient detective skills to interpret them. Looking back, my attitude was pitiful. At the time, though, I felt very much in control, a master chess player manipulating the chessboard of Fate. 'This American Express mandate is primarily a civil action, for the lawyers. Not a police matter at all. Surely there was no mention of police involvement...?'

'That's right.' He nodded. 'The Soviets proposed it as a last resort, to avoid a civil case in the Soviet courts.' He stared at me piercingly, willing me to take the decision. 'So I'm not under arrest?'

'No.' I made up my mind. 'But you are involved directly in today's business.' I decided not to mention again that I thought Suri wanted him dead. 'I personally am answerable for your continued presence until the enquiry is completed, and that won't be finished in a day or even in a week. But you...'

'A week?' He was horrified. 'I want to be out of here today, tomorrow at the latest. I have to find her, Paul, and the fact that they're in Helsinki now...'

'How are you going to find her, Mister Lakey?' I was impatient. 'By now they'll have left...'

'Ben,' he said, explaining how he hated Benjamin as a name.

'All right, Ben. How are you going to find her, and even if you do...' I shrugged. 'Remember, I've met or had contact with hundreds of families that have lost people to ALBATROSS or similar. Just finding the person doesn't bring them back...'

'So what the hell am I going to do?' He looked and sounded pathetic, suddenly deflated. His eyes were pinpoints again, and he was twisting the rim of the table cloth unseeingly. 'I have no money, no transport. All I know is that this bastard has control of Sigrid to the point where she has no way of knowing what she thinks herself...'

'And all I'm saying is that dashing off on your own will accomplish nothing.' I was tempted to ask him for his passport, as a security, and a few days later I was to wish I had done. The Wine Waiter caught my eye from the Caisse, pointing to the telephone. I stood up, suddenly acutely aware that I hadn't the first idea what to do with Lakey now that he was here. It was as I made my way through the nearly empty dining room that a still more disquieting thought struck me very forcibly. If I was right that Suri wanted Lakey silenced, and if he considered the need so pressing as to have sent out a killer with the intention of downing an airliner full of innocent passengers, then

Lakey was now a high-risk category witness, and entitled to full police protection. I put the thought on ice and took the phone from the waiter, keeping my eyes fixed on Lakey. The further thought he might abscond had just occurred to me.

It was the Airport Administrator. He had seen Oron, who had hedged like mad, and now the powers that be wanted some hard information, and they wanted it fast. They wanted to know who this Lakey was, who was Scholl, why the Curtiss had seemingly tried to ram the DC9, what was the significance of the Delhi flight - they didn't know about the Moscow connection, and nor did I at the time - and a dozen other unanswerable questions. I referred him to Simona Sentori, she was the one who had said there needn't be a police investigation. He didn't like it, so I told him curtly the alternative was to wait for the preliminary report, still several days away. I had no sooner put down the phone than the radio at my hip bleeped.

This would be Vinet, I thought, with another list of impossible requests. I acknowledged, but it wasn't Vinet, it was a radio link through our offices from Berne.

The unknown Manfred Krug announced himself frostily, it was a crackly line anyway which made him sound even less friendly. He too wanted a report on the situation, via the computer terminal, and he wanted it immediately. Dammit, the very fact that he contacted me personally and in that unusual way seemed to emphasise the importance of the affair. I thought that then, anyway. It was only afterwards that I realised he wanted the whole thing buried, and for Berne to distance government from anything to do with it. I promised something on line by five o'clock, and went back to Lakey. I was only just realising the mess I was getting into. Nor did it please me that just about everyone, Oron, Michel Verre in Rolle, the Airport Administrator, and now Manfred Krug in Berne, seemed to consider that for one thing I was semi-incompetent, for another probably a bit simple and to cap it all could be pushed around by just about anyone. It rankled.

Just looking at these lines now, a year later, up here in the chalet above Rolle, it is hard to credit that I could have been so incredibly obsessed as to believe that Suri really had sent out Scholl to down the Swissair flight. It not only sounds ludicrous, it's as mad a notion as I now know Scholl's to have been. I suppose if I believe in his insanity, and it seems beyond doubt, I have to accept my own. Not easy.

I collected Lakey from where he was sitting, and we returned to the police offices. I had suddenly had a brainwave, connected with police protection and also my need, my all-consuming and driving desire, to find out from him what made him so special that Suri wanted him dead, and through that, a way to confront Suri head on in the courts. I had decided to invite Lakey to stay at the chalet with me for the coming days.

If I had thought things were humming that morning, I hadn't even begun to appreciate what was to come. In my office I found Michel Oron, twitching like a tuning fork, and alongside him, but not with him, Captain Fonjallaz and the Stewardess

Caroline Zbinden. Vinet was hovering near the door with some papers for me, and as I entered the office and took all this in, the phone on my desk buzzed angrily. I hadn't faced anything like this for more years than I could remember.

Leaving Lakey in the corridor, I waved Vinet to answer the phone, and took the papers from him as he crossed the room. It was the dossier Simona Sentori had promised me.

'That's what I came to see you about.' Fonjallaz pointed to the papers I was holding, then looked at Oron. 'But I think the Air Traffic Controller's business is perhaps more urgent...?'

'No.' Oron flicked at his cigarette lighter nervily, with the cigarette the wrong way round between his lips, the filter about to catch the flame. Fonjallaz gently touched him on the shoulder, Oron stared blankly, then with a little grimace flipped the cigarette around and lit it deftly. 'Thank you, Captain. But no.' He drew deeply on the cigarette. 'No urgency.' I wondered what had happened to unnerve him so completely, but I should have guessed, it was Dominique Dantin. I didn't know it at the time, but he'd had an old man's crush on her, in his own quiet way.

'Switchboard have a Madame Dantin for you.' Vinet held out the receiver to me. 'Are you in?'

This was all I needed. Fonjallaz lined up with, I suspected, recriminations, and I supposed the Stewardess thought she had something worth saying about Lakey. Oron looking like death warmed up, and the other half of death, Dominique's mother, waiting on the telephone. I made a sudden decision.

'I'll call her back in ten minutes. My condolences, meeting I can't leave, you know the kind of thing. Mr. Lakey, would you...' I hesitated. Would he what? What could he do, where could he go, and I wanted Vinet out of the way before anybody started saying anything worth hearing. 'On second thoughts, Captain Fonjallaz, Mlle...' I stared at her name badge, 'Zbinden, Michel, Mister Lakey, there simply isn't enough space... I think we'll commandeer the Federal Enquiry Bureau for this investigation.' I glanced at Vinet. 'All right, was she?'

He nodded, he had never seen me actually take control of a situation before, and I think he was as surprised as I was that I could even do it.

In the next hour I achieved more by way of hard work than I could remember having had in a year. More than a year. Fonjallaz gave me a brief report on the log of his aircraft movements, and Caroline Zbinden filled me in on Lakey's behaviour en route, but neither was much help. Not then. It wasn't until much later that Fonjallaz came up with the full Moscow report. And Michel Oron... As he put it over a cigarette and a brandy, it wasn't every day that he watched his staff produce a near-miss over Lausanne, lived through a still nearer miss over the very airfield he supervised, and then heard that a person he had liked too much for his age to allow was... He was simply looking for a shoulder. Earlier that day, as more than once in recent years, I had used him for no less. But it all took time, and it wasn't until after five that I remembered I hadn't phoned Madame Dantin, and I hadn't sent my report to Krug. Worse, there was no compatible computer terminal in the Federal Enquiry Office so I had to trek all the way back to Police Offices. And all the time Lakey followed me around like some sort of faithful dog. This happened to suit me very well, but it must have looked odd to others.

I got a message off to Berne without Lakey seeing the contents, which was as well, for he would have taken little satisfaction from its ostensible contents. I had little time to worry about elegant wording.

"Lakey affair closed. Moscow flight diversion no police significance. de Savigny."

Nothing could have expressed more totally the opposite of the way my mind was working. For me the case was far from closed, and the diversion was of great significance. But I'd managed to figure out that if Berne had wanted minimum police involvement that morning, they'd be wanting none at all by now.

I didn't realise it, I should add "of course", by now it's clear that I was incapable of realising anything that was obvious, but the diversion was acutely significant in a different way. Suri could not have known that the flight would be diverted from Zürich, as he knew nothing of the runway collision there, and even if he had by some means known of it, he certainly could not have known whether the flight would divert to Basel, Berne or Geneva. Given this simple fact, Scholl could not possibly have been alerted by some Suri-Saint to "get Lakey". Unfortunately, I hadn't yet heard the full story from Fonjallaz, and didn't for some days, which left my imagination full rein, and reality way behind.

Vinet was packing up to go home, just briefing the replacement Sergeant who was coming on night duty. He broke off what he was saying as I came in from my office, this time without Lakey. Normally I'd have been angry or simply embarrassed; the little I had overheard before they caught sight of me hadn't been flattering, in the vein of the old days and the jibes about the 'All Night Hustler', working his ass off and achieving damn all. It happened that this time it suited me perfectly, if the Lakey thing could be downgraded and devalued as one of Paul de Savigny's day-dream cases, all the better. It would keep the Airport Administration out of the game, it would justify my message to Krug in Berne, and leave me time to pursue my enquiries without being answerable to my superiors. For now. Not in the long term, no, for I still had visions of facing Suri across some International Courtroom, but for now, if Vinet thought I'd been wasting my time on a wild goose chase, all well and good.

The Night Sergeant made all the right noises, none of them I felt sincere, and Vinet left. He had the weekend free and wouldn't be back until Monday, and that was fine by me as well. It meant that the weekend duty would be covered by an ever-changing sequence of officers, myself for much of the time, and little chance then of any one officer picking up anything of significance about Lakey. It didn't occur to me that this slender chance might also apply to myself, for I had other plans for Lakey.

'You staying the night, sir?' There was a hollow insolence that was not lost on me.

'No.' I turned towards my own office. 'Just tying up some loose ends.' Like Madame Dantin. I still hadn't called her. I wished I didn't have to. Under normal circumstances I'd have called round the same evening, but things were anything but normal. After a ten-minute conversation that was hardly sociable, I agreed to call on the Sunday morning to help her go over her daughter's affairs at Dominique's place. This was something else that hadn't occurred to me, that I was probably her closest friend qualified to help in such a formal yet so personal a task.

Now I closed the door on myself and Lakey, and sat down wearily behind my desk. He was still as restless as he had been since landing, realising I think the impossibility of his situation, the futility of fighting an invisible and distant enemy. And, despite the new clothes, it smelt as if he hadn't washed since he left Japan.

'Now what?' He was teasing at a torn nail on his left hand, his fingers constantly near his mouth. 'Down to the cells, is that it?' He gave an odd kind of laugh. 'I don't know anything about police work, but...'

There was a strange truculence about him that came and went: in private it seemed to return, only to vanish when there were others about.

'No arrest.' I interrupted him with uncommon harshness. 'You can go.' I leaned back and, feigning disinterest, stared blankly out through the window into the frosty evening light. It was savage, but it was all I had left. I'd used up my day's share of charity, first on Michel Oron, and now on Madame Dantin. I wanted, too, to shake Lakey into realising that he had few options open to him, in fact only the one, for the immediate future.

'Down to the cells after all, then.' he replied eventually, giving that little laugh again. 'You know I have no money, no transport, and not even the key to my own front door, even if I could get to it, which I can't, it's too far.'

I turned to face him again, wondering how to tackle this.

'I think we can do better than that.' I hadn't met very many of the people I'd been in touch with as a result of Suri and his ALBATROSS, most of my knowledge had been at second hand. It was sickening to see at close quarters what happened to a normal, decent person after Suri was through with his version of religion and so-called evangelism.

All the violent hatred of the Suri Sect and others like it welled up in me, I couldn't remember having felt this bitter edge of bile on my tongue, nor the strange involuntary quickened heartbeat, not since the days just after Charlotte had disappeared. Some strange paternal urge, perhaps, but I had to tell myself consciously that it didn't matter a damn what kind of strange parental urge I might be feeling, it was unreasonable to expect Lakey to understand it. To him I was just a senior Swiss Police Officer, doing a job in his own idiosyncratic way, and if I tried to blackmail him into the gratitude game with hospitality, he would identify the technique with those of Suri and run. A thousand miles.

'The Salvation Army hostel?' He was bitter. 'Or the transit lounge?' I spoke persuasively for about five minutes, not stopping to let him intervene. I remember I mentioned Charlotte a few times, and Geneviève as well. It was a psychological ploy, but a long remove from the ones Suri played, and by the time I finished speaking, I'd even managed to convince myself that I really needed him at my place in the fight against Suri. He would have had to be superhuman not to be convinced as well. Not for the first time that day I wondered what on earth had induced me to become a police officer.

We left the building, and crossed the frozen forecourt to the staff car park to locate the Mitsubishi. Light snow was falling again, and there was a bitter chill in the air, but I scarcely felt it. It was a long time since I had been so keen to return to the Chalet, I couldn't remember when I had last felt such urgency and animation. It was nothing to do with Lakey as a person, from what little I had learned of him he wasn't even a particularly likeable man. No, it was what he represented, suddenly he was Charlotte, and he was Geneviève, and the embodiment of the several hundred dossiers that lined the wall of my little office at home. He was the means to an end. Eight years of bottled-up hatred and of impotent anger had at last found an outlet. I didn't recognise the madness of it that night, of course, no, rather I identified myself as an avenging angel given the magic sword with which to take on and overwhelm the devil. Looking back, my obsessive desire for revenge was as bad as Suri's revolting thirst for souls. And for dollars. No wonder nothing came of it.

All along the snowy motorway, and then up through the wastes of the deserted vineyards, neither of us spoke, our only company the whir of the heater and the incessant sweep of the wipers across the screen. It was as well it was dark, for that way I couldn't even try to assess where Dominique had had her fatal accident, nor the extent of it. We reached the Chalet about seven thirty, and the first thing I did, while Lakey took a long-overdue shower, was to make a phone call, a call I hadn't been able to place from the airport, but one I had wanted to make all afternoon. To Helsinki.

Chapter Nine

February, 1988

There are things in life we'd all like to live again, hoping for a different outcome, but it can never happen. There are no "if onlys". But those faded photographs, plus a few recent ones, have taken on a new significance alongside all the complicated computer equipment, fax machines and modems we've had installed these past few months.

It was a long drive back from Ben's place in Müstair. I'd have been better taking his advice and staying on at the farmhouse with him and Sigrid, or at least coming back by train. But there wasn't time, so much to do to get things off the ground, and so I made the journey mid-week in appalling weather, blizzards and driving snow most of the way, worse, if anything, than last year.

Now, here at the chalet again, with the outstanding matters in hand, I'm rediscovering splendid, snowy isolation and setting out this thing, this something that matters. Like I told Ben that night, a year ago, there comes a time when crying has to stop, and it's an unbalanced mind that finds merit in crying the longest, whatever we may feel like inside. What happens after the crying is something else.

Frédérique will make the return journey to "The Refuge" in Ben's farm at Müstair next week, with the first two "refugees". In America there have been some nasty court cases where organisations similar to ours have tried to snatch back converts and rehabilitate them, but with some knowledge of Swiss law and heavyweights like Simona on our side, we may be able to avoid that happening here. And all the time, at the back of my mind, there's the irrational hope that one of them might one day be Charlotte… But I'm jumping ahead.

Frédérique Dantin, Dominique's younger sister, has joined us with a passion and fanatical determination to which I had thought only myself susceptible. It wasn't until we were going through Dominique's things that I realised just how wealthy she had been. Her father had left them a legacy of quite staggering proportions, which explained whey her mother had always been able to live in comparative comfort. After Dominique's death last year, the majority of her fortune came to Frédérique. Until she turned up on my doorstep I had as good as forgotten that there was a younger sister, the Dantins had divorced when the children were young, and unusually the parents had been given divided custody of the children, even more unusually the younger going to her father. Hence during all those years that Dominique and her mother had visited Geneviève and Charlotte at our place, they had understandably been reticent to talk of the husband or the younger daughter, a typically Swiss reserve.

Yet Frédérique's contribution, philanthropic and personal, would never have happened if she hadn't met Lakey that weekend.

After Lakey's disappearance she hadn't admitted at first that she had lent him money, and even hired a car in her name for him. I could see she was hiding something and we argued badly. What strange social conscience prompted her to such extremes I couldn't at the time understand, we went through a very bitter patch when I accused her of aiding and abetting a criminal. She had turned on me then, and said if that was what she'd done, hadn't I done the same by putting him up at the chalet for several days? It was only after that that we had sat down and thrashed out the whole affair. But if Sigrid Sorensen hadn't turned up out of the blue when she did, I'm still far from certain whether Frédérique would have agreed to join us in this strange venture. Let alone Simona...

There are those who maintain, pretty blindly I always think, that "these things are meant to happen". Try telling that to a policeman. But that first night at the chalet when I telephoned Helsinki, I still thought things could be made to happen.

John Trethewey

Friday the 13ᵗʰ 1987 - Black Friday

Almost the only thing I did that was actually successful or worthwhile that Friday 13ᵗʰ, last year, was the telephone call to Helsinki. One of the bonuses of having senior police rank was that you could do things that civilians would find impossible. Mrs. de Almeida – all the housekeepers here are Spanish or Portuguese – had put out cold meats and a salad for me, which she didn't always do, and I was able sufficiently to augment these from the fridge to make Lakey's first evening back in Switzerland tolerably homely. But the food without the good news would hardly have made him feel at ease. No, it was the surprising rapidity with which Helsinki Immigration called back, a welcome interruption just as we were sitting down to eat, that put the smile back on my face and some animation in his.

'Helsinki Immigration.' I didn't waste any words. 'I called them while you were washing. They checked on Suri and just called back.'

'And?' He paused in lifting a fork full of cold meat to his mouth. 'What's happening? Suri... Sigrid? Are they still there? For God's sake, Paul. What did they say?'

'I'm trying to tell you.' I couldn't resist playing the ham actor, poured more wine into his glass in celebratory fashion. 'They left this morning.'

'Left?' He stared at the wine glass as if it was poison. 'Shit. Left for where, dammit? All of them? I mean, did she go with ...?'

'Easy, Ben.' He was het up again, his hand shaking badly as he tried to lift the wine glass. The fork was still poised in mid-air in the other hand. 'They all left, yes. Finnish Immigration tells me they took the early afternoon flight to London. They're sending printed confirmation and passenger list to Cointrin, it'll be there by morning.' I was relieved to have got the news so quickly, for I wanted to convince Lakey that I could help him if he would help me. And there was a hell of a lot we had to talk about before either of us could help the other.

'London?' His face was blank. 'What in God's name does Suri have to do in England? You'd know, you said you had dossiers on loads of these people, does he have a base in England? If so, whereabouts? Because if he does, Paul, I'm going there, tomorrow, and stuff the Swiss law, the Swiss police and any stupid enquiry.' The truculent tone was in evidence again, and I didn't like it. But I couldn't blame him. It was uncanny, he was living out in front of me the identical reaction I had had to Charlotte's disappearance, and the same reactions were documented hundreds of times over in the dossiers lining the walls of my office.

'You don't have any money.' I was short on charity again, and instantly regretted my words. He tossed his fork down on the plate with a clatter and slumped back in his seat, suddenly deflated.

'I thought you...' He swallowed hard, his fingertips again straying to play with the table cloth. He was like a little boy whose favourite toy has been crushed beyond repair by a careless parent backing the car over it. My parental instincts again. 'Did they say anything else?' He was near breaking point.

'Yes.' I replenished the glass he had drained at one gulp. 'The tickets were all singles, and there was no indication of onward reservations.'

'Singles.' He repeated the word in a strangely flat tone, thinking through the various possibilities this opened up. 'Has he a base in the UK, Paul? Do you think…?'

'We should know that by…' I glanced at the stupid cuckoo clock on the wall as its little door opened and the daft bird mechanism stuck its painted head out and warbled nine times. '… within the next hour. I'm waiting for a call from Heathrow now.'

'I see. I'm sorry. I flew off the handle a bit, I think.' I hadn't heard anyone use that expression since I'd been at school in the forties.

'Yes, you did, but with every reason.' It was hot with the log fire crackling alongside and I took off my jacket. He studied the coloured epaulettes on my shirt.

'What rank do you hold, actually?' His glance implied that he had just realised that by rank I wasn't a plain constable. I told him the story then, starting way back in Carouge in the seventies and finishing with an honest appraisal of my immediate prospects with the police. Nil. I had been wondering how to gain his confidence without it looking artificial and his question had opened the door for me to talk about Geneviève and Charlotte. And so, Suri. After half an hour it was evident that he wouldn't be leaving for London next morning and it was pretty basic psychology for a listener to a story of such personal hurt to reciprocate with an equally personal account of his own miseries, if he had any. Lakey had enough to fill a book.

It was very late by the time we turned in. All through those hours I had the dichotomous double-edged sword of duty and inclination needling me. What I wanted to talk about – and Lakey no less – was what had happened on the Trans-Siberian Railway to make him such a threat to Suri that he had sent out Scholl on a Kamikaze mission, and what I very imminently had to report on in writing to the Commissioner was Scholl and Delta-Echo-Mike's suicidal approach to the airport. It was the old story; for me the two were inseparably connected, and for either line of enquiry to proceed I had to suppress the link. Suri. In every way to suppress it. Him.

The call from London came in much later, around midnight. A chap I had been at school with in the fifties was returning a favour. Suri and his group had arrived in London in the early evening and had been whisked away in a convoy of limousines. The address for the non-UK holders' entry cards, including for Miss Sorensen, was "Medina, Buckinghamshire". Lakey didn't know what "Medina" was, but I did. If I'd told him the truth about "Medina" there and then, he'd have left and tried to get to London, penniless or not, so I didn't.

A few hours later we were back in the airport again. It was the coldest day of the year, the temperature well below freezing, but the sun was shining in a sky of deep blue and a preternatural clarity about the snow-covered mountains surrounding the airfield seemed to bring them closer on either side. Neither of us, though, was in a mood to notice the weather.

I hadn't got past signing off the night duty Sergeant when the phone rang. The Sergeant was about to leave, took the call, then handed me the receiver.

'Another call from England, so I suppose it's for you. Sir.' he added as an afterthought.

'de Savigny.'

'Oh, good morning. This is American Express Card Services in Brighton. Uh... am I speaking to Geneva Airport, Police Department?' It sounded like a typical cold-caller voice, a person who spent half their working hours on the 'phone, and probably never met a customer as a human being from one day to the next. I said it was, and gave my name.

'Ah, that's very good. I'm trying to reach a Mister Lakey. Zürich police at Kloten tells us that his flight was diverted to Geneva yesterday, and we urgently need to contact him.' There was a diffident pause, then: 'Would it be possible for you to confirm whether or not you are au fait with the Lakey affair?"

'Until I know what your interest is, I'm afraid not.' I was chilly. I dislike these telephone voices and their impersonal manner. And something was bothering me at the back of my mind, but I couldn't pin it down. He tried again.

'I see. Yes, I understand. I think. Let me try putting it another way. Does the mandate for Mr. Lakey's arrest under Zürich police issue...' There was a strangled noise as he attempted the German. '... *Strafanzeigezettel* 3 stroke 8 have any significance to your department?'

This was more like it. With that kind of ID I felt I could say something more helpful than my last response. I said:

'Yes.'

'And Mr. Lakey is in Geneva?'

'Yes.'

'At the airport? In police custody?'

I thought I'd better say Yes to that as well, until I had formal written declaration from Amex to annul the charges.

'Yes.'

'I see.'

Whatever he saw, I didn't. I wondered why he was asking. All I knew for certain at this point was that Lakey maintained the Amex charge had been a put-up job to get him away from Moscow before Suri pressed real, more sinister charges.

'Can I ask what your interest is?' I queried, but the line was already cut, the triple dialling tone all that I could hear.

'Can I go now, sir?' The Night Sergeant was waiting patiently in the doorway. I nodded, my mind on the Amex business. I turned to Lakey when the phone rang again.

'de Savigny.' But it wasn't for me, it was for Lakey. I passed him the receiver, mystified. I was tempted to ask who was calling, and on what business, but with the man right there beside me I could scarcely quiz the caller before putting him on. Besides, I half-guessed it had to be Amex in Brighton. I expected at least to be able to listen to his responses, though, but there weren't any.

After listening for perhaps twenty seconds he grunted like an animal in pain and then slammed the phone down. I stared at him, waiting for him to explain. He sat down very abruptly and rubbed his eyes so hard with his fists that I thought he was going to do himself an injury. Thoroughly alarmed, I grabbed him by the shoulders, lifting him bodily from the chair to face me.

'For God's sake, man!' I slammed the door to my office with a well-placed kick. 'What's going on? Who was it?' Then, instinctively, I guessed who it was, and that one solitary guess was the crunch factor that finally set my mind irrevocably on the notion that Scholl was Suri's man, Suri's killer. I wondered with a sudden chill whether the previous call really had been Amex at all, or if it had been... It took a full minute for Lakey to recover, he looked as if he'd been pole-axed.

'The bastard, the shitty little...' He was shaking and had to sit down again. I went out into the corridor and brought him a coffee from a wall dispenser, and when I gave it to him he just sat there, staring into the plastic cup like a waxwork figure. Then he gulped down the hot liquid and squashed the plastic cup into a mangled heap and dropped it on the floor.

'That was one of Suri's people? Did they say how they knew you were here?' I pressed him. 'Ben, this matters... if they're watching you...' God knows what made me think that.

'Watching me? Of course they're fucking well watching me, you fool.' He sneered unforgivingly. Like so many of his countrymen, he had a facility with foul language unparalleled in the rest of Europe. 'What do you think Suri is? Some kind of fucking mind reader? That was one of his creatures, yes, but not in Switzerland, I think. No, I'd say that call came from England. They mentioned the American Express thing as well, and... and Sigrid. They mentioned her as well.' His voice had fallen to a murmur, flat and unemotional now. 'No, of course they're not watching me,' He stood up and crossed to the window, stared out into the blinding whiteness of the frozen snow covering the airfield. I saw his eyes follow the lift of a DC10 just taking off, a strange longing in his look. I was more uneasy than ever at my previous responses to the alleged American Express caller. And now I was almost certain it hadn't been kosher. It was only half past six in England. No-one starts work in that kind of place before nine in the morning in Britain. That had been the something in the back of my mind. Too late now.

'But that's ridiculous.' I was out of my depth, somehow too old to adjust and too inexperienced to analyse. If the first call really had come from Brighton, then this second call was either pure coincidence, which I didn't believe, or else Suri had unlimited contacts, and I didn't believe that either. 'One minute you're saying Suri has someone here watching you – God knows nothing's impossible where Suri's concerned, he has the means to do it – then in the next breath you're telling me the call must have come from England. If it's the former, we need to get you protection, and if it's the other, then we need proof. It's an internationally recognised offence to use a telephone with the intention to intimidate or to blackmail... Ben!' I had to turn him physically to face me. Incredibly, he was smiling.

'That was a good idea of yours, letting me stay at your place last night. If I hadn't, I shouldn't have been here now.' I didn't get it. Seeing this, he went on more gently, like a patient teacher to a retarded child. 'That's why they called, Paul. Not because they're watching me, but because they aren't, and they think they ought to be. I think they're running scared.' He grinned, a bleak and chilling smile without warmth. He was a better detective than I was, dammit the whole bloody world was getting to be a better detective than I was.

'How do you work that out?' I was mystified.

'The Sergeant. He said "Another call from England..." That means it wasn't the first. Nor maybe the second. Does the Police Office keep a log of incoming calls?'

You can see what I mean about the whole world. Not only had this not occurred to me, I hadn't even taken in what the Night Sergeant had said. I could excuse myself on the grounds that I'd only had four hours' sleep, but Lakey had had no more, and no less on his mind. I went through to Reception and had a look.

'You're right. There've been five calls, roughly every hour from midnight onwards, all logged from Amex Card Services in Brighton. But that call...'

'... was most certainly not the way credit card companies talk to their card holders.' Lakey smiled thinly. 'No. I think that was someone in... what's the place called? In Buckinghamshire?'

'"Medina"?'

'Yes. "Medina". Stupid bloody name. It's certain that was one of Suri's animals, and if I'm right, far from having someone watching me, he'll suddenly be feeling very secure and very safe in his little Sanyasins' parlour there.' I didn't follow and said so. Also, time wasn't on our side, the daytime replacement for Vinet would be arriving any minute and we had a full day's investigation ahead of us. Unconsciously, I had already dragooned Lakey into the force to help me.

'Get it together, Paul!' He begged a cigarette from me. I was tired of people talking to me like that, but this wasn't the moment. 'I know there hasn't been time to tell you all about the Trans-Siberian, God knows it's a long enough story, but everything to my way of thinking points to Suri running scared. Why was I going to Delhi? Because the Soviets thought - and I thought – that was the one place, the one country in the whole world we could put the squeeze on his bloody ALBATROSS for what is actually abduction, kidnapping if you like. Suri didn't want me to reach Delhi...' Too right, I thought, he sent out Scholl to make sure. I still had no intention of mentioning this to Lakey. '... but he wasn't taking any chances on me not getting there, which I guess is why he switched flights to London. And why he's now sitting tight in his bloody "Medina", or whatever it's called.'

'You mean...?' I bit back the words. I had been about to say that if Scholl messed it up – as indeed I thought he had – Suri would still not have been in Delhi even if Lakey made it there. 'How come scared?' I changed the question.

'Can I have another coffee?' He was pacing up and down the small office, his left fingers constantly near his face, the teasing of the nails recurrent. 'I think Suri knows I have – or had – enough on him when I was in Moscow, to make the case stick. I think he thought I would have had enough on him in Delhi, as well. And I think that phone call...' he gestured at the phone, '... means he wants to be good and sure I'm still in custody for the American Express thing, here, and can't just quit the country and pursue him to England. I think.' He concluded uncertainly. 'But it's all theoretical...'

'Not all.' I murmured. 'The call before yours was from... or purported to be from Amex in Brighton.' I told him what had been said. 'It's plausible, I suppose. It's certainly plausible.' I was hard put to hide my excitement, a strange, legal, abstract excitement I mean, at the probability that even the all-powerful Suri was sufficiently rattled by what Lakey knew, that he was desperate to ensure that Lakey really was in custody, and so not an immediate threat. It also bolstered my crazy theory about Scholl. And from a police point of view, if that first call had been fraudulent, it was the first time I had first hand proof of illegality on the part of Suri.

'The bastard certainly has wide contacts.' Lakey was still pacing, talking to himself. 'Only Sovenskaya, Fonjallaz and a few people in Brighton knew about the mandate for my arrest yesterday. I knew he was powerful...' He winced at some personal and recent memory. '... but that really is quite something, the cold calculated cheek of it, to telephone the Police Offices at the airport like that. I suppose if I hadn't been here, they'd have persisted in pretending it really was an Amex call, in Brighton, and tried to find out where... The bugger's not stupid, is he?'

There was no admiration in his voice. I had to agree that someone in this "Medina" place, Suri or one of his "Saints", was most certainly not stupid. But I was, now that Lakey had spelt out the evidence and the theory. It was irrefutable, and I hadn't seen any of it until his perfect exposition.

'One of two possibilities, then.' My mind was at last half-way functioning. 'The first call really was from Brighton, which means Suri has contacts inside American Express he has no right to have... though we might never be able to prove that. Or else the first call wasn't Brighton at all, but Suri's people playing games to find out... Like you said.' I stopped. I was going to ask him again what had been said to shake him so severely, but I had had a better idea. All incoming calls are automatically recorded for later checking, in case of anonymous or what are stupidly called "intelligence" calls. I decided to lift the cassette and take it home, where I could make a copy of it. Also, I didn't want the Commissioner hearing my gaffes of the last call before the one to Lakey. It was the first time in my career I had even come close to suppressing evidence. I was to do much worse in the days to come.

Now, of course, we know more about the whys and wherefores of those calls, and what prompted Suri's people to take such a risk. Not one that Suri would have authorised, had he known about it. No, it was a few of his insecure psychopaths, it turned out, who had on the one hand wanted to ensure – as I had guessed – that Lakey was out of the way, and worse, on the other, and much more in character, given vent to the sadistic streak in them that Lakey had so easily identified on the Trans-Siberian journey.

At that moment, however, the Day Sergeant reported for duty and I had to take refuge in my office to plan out the day's investigations. I hadn't a clue where to start. Before the Duty Sergeant settled in in Reception, though, I managed to lift the tape and insert a clean one. It felt like a burning coal in my pocket, the fires of conscience.

Chapter Ten

'Do you know where I can find a piano?' Lakey swung round from where he had been staring out over the apron, watching the aircraft movements. I wondered if I'd heard him aright.

'A what?' I was making up a list of "Action this Day" items for urgent attention and paused, my pencil in the air.

'D'you know where I can find a piano?' he repeated, studying his hands held out before him.

'You want to play the piano?' I was surprised.

'What the bloody hell else would I want a piano for?' He was short, that arrogant touch evident again. He lowered his hands, and made an effort to relax. 'Sorry. Yes, I want to play the piano.'

'Ah.' I was caught off guard. 'Well, there's one at the Chalet, but it hasn't been played for years, and it's probably very out of...'

'I mean here. Now. No?'

I suppose it was reasonable enough to expect a police officer who has spent twelve years in a place the size of Geneva airport to know most of what it has to offer. But it didn't feel like it. I dropped the pencil and tried to think. Then it came to me, I had seen a piano and quite recently. The new Air Traffic Control tower, a harsh black modern monstrosity, had a subterranean nuclear shelter, as most government buildings do in Switzerland. Given that no-one really expected ever to use it for its sinister purpose, I recalled that a couple of the rooms had been decorated as a club-room area for Air Traffic Controllers' occasional use. I was pretty sure I'd seen a piano in there on a recent visit.

'Seems a rather odd thing to want to do.' I said. I was still smarting from the way he sometimes spoke to me.

'So maybe I'm a rather odd kind of bloke.' He shrugged. 'Sorry. I didn't mean to... Look.' He appealed to me. 'If anyone knows this Suri you do, and no one detests him more than I do. But the way I see it, you've got more than you can cope with on the airport side of things. How do you think that makes me feel, Paul? I want, and I think you want, to get that bastard and his Sanyasins and his bloody "Saints", and we can't, for the simple reason you've got too much else on, and I can't because without your help I can't even buy a bloody sandwich.'

'Then there's Sigrid, she's on my mind every minute of the day and night, which may not mean much to the world outside, but right now she and I are the only world I care about. And what chance do I have, do you have, or any of us have, of nailing Suri with anything? I'll tell you what chance, the way things are. Bloody damn all, and that's why I'm so bottled up, screwed up, call it what you like.' He stopped and stared at me. 'Shit, Paul, if I didn't think there was at least some chance of us getting something done about Suri, I'd never have stayed. Surely you're not thinking I'll disappear on you?' I didn't know whether he was planning to, or whether this was the real man talking.

'I know.' I pushed the note pad across the table to him. 'Look at it. Just look.' I tapped the growing list for "Action this day". 'I have to clear this lot by two o' clock. Then I have to go over the files and ATC videotapes back at my place, produce a preliminary report for the Commissioner, get an update on Suri from the UK - or try, if I can call in a few old favours outstanding - and then trace the previous movements, criminal record if any and antecedents of this maniac Scholl.'

'That's what I mean.' He nodded. 'I was thinking you'd find it easier to get ahead without having to keep an eye on me all the time?' He gave that strange little laugh again that had nothing to do with humour. 'Because I'm not so stupid as not to see that you can't leave me at liberty until... Well, just until.' he ended, lamely. That was the crunch. Until what? I didn't deny it.

'There is a piano.' I said eventually. 'I'll show you, it's in the ATC building, and as I have to go there anyway, it's on my way. You a good player?' I asked.

'Rather.' This was an unusual streak in an Englishman, most of his countrymen tend to answer that kind of question with euphemistic junk. 'You know, how I spent my youth before I learned how to misspend it.'

'I don't know what kind of music you'll find there.' I said apologetically, confused by the enigmatic shifts in his character.

'I shan't want music.' he said sharply. 'I want a...' Again that laugh. I think he thought I wouldn't understand. 'I want a work-out, and for that I have all the music I need up here.' He tapped his forehead.

I left him in the basement of the ATC tower, locked in. He said he didn't mind, the way I was feeling right then he didn't have any choice anyway. Up on the top floor I found Le Comte once again at the Tower Controller's station.

'Paul.' He hurried over to me. 'How's it coming along? Did you get the tapes and things I sent over?'

'Things? What things?' I looked at him blankly. Those damned Sergeants had treated me like dirt for long enough, but they'd never actually held back on me before. As far as I knew. Oron was already on the phone.

'Sorry.' He hung up. 'My fault, they're still here. I thought they'd already... I'll have them brought up right away.' Another brief phone call. Then: 'I got some news through about this Scholl character, from Friedrichshafen. And I've had the ATC video tapes of Approach and Departure radar copied for you, I thought you might need them. Has Simona been back to you?' I tried to read some hidden significance into his inevitable twitch, but he was the usual inscrutable Comte. No hidden significance. I crossed to the windows and looked down at the airfield. It seemed a lot more than 24 hours ago that we had watched Scholl descending in the path of Fonjallaz's DC-9.

'No. Was she going to?' I turned sharply as he laughed briefly, a quite different Oron this from the tense and twitching Controller of the previous day.

'Christ, yes. She was up here first thing this morning asking about... Don't tell me you don't know?' He was laughing now, a warm and friendly laugh. What it cost him, when he was inwardly mourning the absence of Dominique Dantin, I'll never know. Perhaps a lot, perhaps nothing, I never asked him.

'Know what?' I was mystified.

He looked round with a furtive glance, and spoke in a lowered voice.

'You must have been the only one at yesterday's preliminary enquiry not to have noticed, then, Paul. Fonjallaz did, and so did Caroline Zbinden, and you can't count Mueller anyway, all he thinks of is wind shear and *vent-arrière* and his Visual landings total.' He broke off. 'You're serious, aren't you?'

'Perfectly.' I hadn't a clue to what he was talking about.

'Simona's divorce came through last month, you know.' he said obliquely.

I still didn't get it.

'I didn't know she was getting a divorce.' I said stupidly. My mind was too much on the matters of the moment to follow. Oron looked at me strangely.

'You mind if I say something personal, Paul?' he asked. I shook my head. 'If - when - Simona calls you, and she will, have an open mind, hey?' Now it dawned.

'You mean... she...?'

'Yes.' He laughed again. '*She*. There must be more to you than meets the eye, Paul.'

'Good God.' I was nonplussed. 'You're sure of this? I mean, you said Fonjallaz, and this girl Zbinden...?'

'Paul, you have been living alone much too long.' He clapped me on the shoulder. 'I have an idea... Suppose I invite you round for drinks, I mean you and her? I could get a Number Four for myself, make it look right... what d'you think?'

I thought it was an appalling idea, and was about to say so. But I didn't. I had suddenly remembered the previous afternoon, the way she had held me, the melting effect of her green eyes. Suddenly I wasn't appalled at all, I thought it was perhaps rather a good idea.

I'm not an adolescent any more, and romantic follies were never my forte all those years ago when I was. I knew well enough the difference between motivation driven by common sense and inclination driven by common hormones. If that sounds unduly clinical, you have to remember that I had at one time, even if not too successfully, been trained as a police officer.

'Good God.' I repeated. It had suddenly struck me that, whether I liked the prospect of knowing Simona Sentori better again or not, the suggestion could hardly have come at a worse time. I hadn't had so much to do and so little time to do it in years.

'Time enough to arrange that when this is all over.' Oron glanced over his shoulder, his extraordinary responsibility for all aircraft movements in evidence again. Seemingly reassured he turned back to me. 'Ah. Here they are.' A miniature lift in the wall warbled twice, automatic doors opened, and he lifted out a sizeable bundle of documents and a couple of boxed video cassettes. 'About Scholl...' he said. We sat down, and he told me what he'd discovered about Delta-Echo-Mike and the pilot Scholl.

Later in the morning, still in the ATC tower, I had that catastrophic interview with Mueller. Oron and Fonjallaz were entirely right, the man was devoid of all imagination, obsessed almost with his flying hours, and Visual Landings total. To a young airline pilot, landing on the Instrument Landing System, the ILS, is far too easy. His - or her - promotional prospects are considerably influenced by the number of Visual Landings accomplished. In the outlying Greek islands, for example, a visual approach is the only possibility, for such airfields have no ILS installations, but on the more sophisticated airfields in Europe, given their capricious weather conditions, ILS landings are the norm. Not infrequently I had heard pilots almost begging the Tower Controller to allow a visual approach, often using the short cut approach over Pétal, rather than passing St. Prex as was standard. More often than not pressure of traffic and not weather conditions obliged the Controller to refuse.

Mueller was an almost impossible witness, I had to drag every word from him, and as I still knew almost nothing at this point from Fonjallaz, I found myself in a cul-de-sac. What Mueller said wasn't worth hearing, and I had insufficient information to start with to make my questions sufficiently trenchant or probing to force a useful answer. After half an hour, he left, half an hour which had dented my professional pride even further.

Around midday I went back to the basement, and paused outside the door to the Controllers' club rooms. I don't know how much of the past three hours Lakey had actually spent playing that piano, but he was certainly playing it when I got there. Chopin, or Rachmaninov, I know, they're not the same thing, but I'm no expert. He wasn't bad at all. I'd heard worse on France Musique radio. I unlocked the door and went inside. For no obvious reason, my mind kept going back to Simona Sentori. "Paul, you look dreadful." she had said.

After a brief lunch break, it was back to my "Action this Day" list. Fonjallaz was on a round trip to Lisbon, and wouldn't be available until Monday at the earliest. I decided to hold on to the documents and video recordings Oron had provided until I could go over them at leisure at home. There was tension now, something I had only vaguely sensed the previous day. Stress, too, the need urgently to produce results for the first time in so many years that I had forgotten what was involved in a really complex police case. I had to have a preliminary report ready for the Commissioner by the time he returned from holiday on Monday. And I wanted to crack the Suri business without delay. Once again, Lakey had spelt out the problem as neatly as anyone could. I had two conflicting interests. What I wanted to do had to wait, and what I had to do really involved doing what I wanted to do first. And I couldn't. Stress? It was intolerable. With the Police telephone cassette still burning a hole in my pocket, we left shortly after two in the afternoon, and returned to the Chalet.

One of the differences between the Swiss and the British is that the Swiss in general consider it unthinkable just to "drop round" on someone in the way a British couple might on their friends. For all her cosmopolitan manners, Simona Sentori was totally Swiss. We hadn't been at the Chalet more than half an hour when the phone went. Lakey was hammering away at the piano - it was dreadfully out of tune as I'd expected, but his playing seemed to be dragging it back to a sort of acceptable pitch - and I had to close the door to take the call. Oron had been right. When he had advised me to "keep an open mind", I hadn't really understood. I couldn't imagine what a success story person like Simona Sentori would see in a deadleg like me. I had never known her well enough all those years before to have discovered that she needed to be the stronger partner in a relationship. Or her feminine streak that took pleasure in repairing broken wings. People like me. At the time the quandary I found myself in was quite acute. She wanted to come to supper, was offering to cook the meal herself - I remembered again her words "You look dreadful", this smacked of feminine protectionism against the widower's culinary incompetence - and I was not entirely averse to the suggestion.

But there was Lakey. I was again starkly aware of the dichotomous double-edged sword of inclination and of my driving obsessions: Simona Sentori for the evening versus my preoccupation with Suri, with Lakey and his girl, with my last-ditch stand against ALBATROSS. It was painful, not knowing what to say, and sounding so indecisive to her on the phone there. Simona is first and foremost a pragmatist - she couldn't understand my hesitation. Or rather, she must have misunderstood it as a peculiar but somehow fitting reticence by an ex-lover, for in truth that is what I was. I took a deep breath and said Yes, come round about 7.30, I'd like that very much, the usual noises. When I put the phone down I realised what I'd done, with Lakey's very accomplished piano playing reverberating through the house, I couldn't fail to. The question dinned in time with his Beethoven Bagatelles - what to do with Lakey for the night?

The sound of a car on the drive way was sufficiently unusual for me to go to the door to see who was calling - I had very few visitors. The driver was a svelte young woman in her early twenties, with short light auburn hair, two very blue eyes set wide apart below a jaunty fringe, and a skier's sun tan. Despite the bitter cold, she was dressed only in a blouse and slacks. And after I was through with my policeman's appraisal came the faint idea that her face was familiar. But I knew I had never seen her in my life before.

'Deputy Commissioner de Savigny?' She held out her hand, a beautifully manicured hand at that. The sunlight danced on her reddish-brown curls, and I caught a whiff of some expensive perfume. She was extraordinarily good-looking. Through the open window came the furious sound of Lakey hammering away at something tempestuous on the ill-tuned piano.

'Yes.' I was trying to remember who she reminded me of. As soon as she introduced herself it was evident.

'Frédérique Dantin. You were a friend of my sister, mother tells me. I do hope you don't mind me calling unannounced...'

'Not in the least.' I turned to let her into the house. The piano had ceased, and I caught sight of Lakey's pale face and fair hair pressed close to the window. On more grounds than one his interest was forgiveable. 'How can I help you?' I asked, motioning her to a chair. The log fire crackled comfortably. She remained standing, staring round in inquisitive interest at the vaguely shambolic old wooden-walled room, with its junk and papers everywhere. Mrs. de Almeida was all right when it came to ironing and wardrobes, but she couldn't handle the living area.

'Thank you.' She finally took the hint, blushing slightly. 'It's about my mother, Deputy Commissioner...'

'Paul.' I corrected her. Lakey had returned to the piano, was thrashing Schubert in a way I hadn't heard it done before. She winced.

'You have children, er... Paul?' Of course, just as I hadn't known her, she had never heard of Charlotte. I shook my head, uncertain whether I felt amused or upset.

'No. A kind of house-guest.' This reminded me I had no idea what the hell I was going to do with Lakey for the evening. His "work-out" on the old piano was getting past a joke, the timber walls were shivering with the resonance of the left-hand keys. I could hardly hear myself think. 'Shall I ask him to stop?'

She smiled to herself.

'If you don't think it would be rude, yes, perhaps.'

I went into the next room, and the only way I could actually get him to stop was to invite him to join us. What was it Le Comte had said? "...lived too long on your own..." I introduced Lakey to Frédérique Dantin rather vaguely, and he tactfully left us, muttering something about coffee.

'Do you mind if Mr. Lakey joins us?' I wasn't sure why she had called, but if it was to do with Dominique I could understand her not wanting other people around.

'Not in the least. In fact, he might be able to help, as he speaks English. He is English, isn't he?' She giggled faintly. 'He looks English.' The smile faded, and her face took on a strange far-away expression. 'I'm sorry. I'll come to the point. You see, I'm living at Dominique's. Well, as much as possible at my mother's place, but sleeping at Dominique's. That's rather the problem. Sleeping at Dominique's I mean.'

'I don't see the problem.'

'Well, my mother's got this thing into her head about the gardener.' She stared into the fire. I didn't know anything about a gardener. I thought at the time that she was confused with the grief of Dominique's death, but it wasn't the Dominique affair that was hurting her. It was her mother. 'Mummy's gone a bit strange, Paul. I'm sorry to have to come and involve you, because she told me not to, if she knew I was here now she'd be furious.' I didn't think it was the mother's strangeness that her mother had forbidden her to discuss. Patiently I waited for her to explain.

'Oh, I'm making a real mess of this.' She teased a lock of hair into view, inspecting it for split ends. 'I don't know where to begin...'

'Your mother?' I prompted gently.

'Well, no, it's the CB radio, you see.' She stared at me hopefully with those wide-set blue eyes.

'The CB radio? What's a Citizen's Band radio got to do with the gardener?'

'That's just it, we don't know. It's all in English, you see, and neither of us can read it. But Mummy's certain it's all sinister, because he was more or less living there, you see, and if it wasn't him, then it was someone else, and until we can translate what it says Mummy doesn't think it's safe for me to... Well, the fact is, I think Mummy's on the edge of a breakdown, and I thought, as you're half-English, I was wondering, I know you said you'd call tomorrow anyway but is there any chance of you coming round now?' she ended up.

She stretched her legs out towards the fire, suddenly relaxing, as if this explanation settled everything. I hadn't the foggiest idea what she was talking about.

Lakey came in then with the coffee, and there was a round of banalities before we got back to the gardener, the CB and whatever it was that was probably sinister and in English.

'Do you speak French?' Frédérique asked him. I hadn't heard Lakey in French before. He spoke it very passably. I shovelled a few papers off a spare chair and he sat down.

Considering the man's preoccupation with his girl in "Medina U.K.", and all he had gone through in the past ten days, I found his courtesy and warmth towards Frédérique Dantin surprising at first. It could have been that the piano playing had helped, but it dawned on me soon after that he was actually reacting to the girl's own suffering, identifying any support he could give her as what he would expect from others. It was a peculiarly Christian moment, full of silence and a strange warmth. When Frédérique started again to explain, it was evident that she was addressing Lakey as much as myself, and I wasn't unduly sorry. I hadn't understood a word of her first attempt.

'I'll start from the beginning.' she said. 'I'm staying at Dominique's, I arrived last night from Willisau. Daddy bought a house there after the divorce.' she explained. 'But I went to my mother's first. And she'd already been up to Dominique's place. That was what upset her so much. There was this weird peasant chap, some kind of gardener, there. When she arrived, he was actually in the kitchen, or so she said, and talking on some kind of CB radio Dominique must have had installed. That was a shock in itself, but she was too confused to ask him - or to understand clearly - what he was doing there. When I went up later in the evening, he'd gone. The house was locked, so he must have a key. But what really upset my mother was that he's been living there, she thinks for a long time, because she found a man's clothes in some of the wardrobes, and, well, you know the kind of things, razors, ties, some shirts and...'

'She thinks this man was Dominique's boyfriend?' Lakey was gently probing.

'She doesn't know what to think.' Frédérique shifted on the chair uneasily. 'Nor do I. Oh, I was never very close to Dominique, nor to Mummy since the divorce, Daddy and she went different ways, and we separated so young that... well, I don't really know much about Dominique.' she ended up. 'But Mummy is convinced that if I'm staying at the house on my own, and this gardener person has his own key, well, she's a bit over-wrought and I say, I think she's on the verge of a breakdown, and she thinks I oughtn't to stay there alone. And then there's these log books, all in English, by the radio.' She stared at us, as if that explained everything.

'Log books?' I looked from Frédérique to Lakey and back again blankly. 'What kind of log books?'

'That's just it.' She wriggled on the chair in frustration. 'We don't know. There are loads of dates and times and all kinds of notes, but neither of us has enough English to understand them. And that's what's getting Mummy all worried, she thinks Dominique's been having some weird kind of relationship with this gardener man, and she was so upset when she found him there...'

'So what would you like us to do? How can we help?' This was a quite new Ben Lakey to me, and altogether a much nicer person than the man I had been seeing the last twenty-four hours. Frédérique Dantin turned to him, studying his face intently. She seemed to take some satisfaction from what she saw there, her left hand involuntarily reached out to touch his arm in a gesture of warmth, or gratitude.

'I don't think there's anything... sinister, as Mummy calls it. But if I can't convince her of that, and I can't, she'll go round the bend. I'm sorry.' She turned to me, suddenly more formal. 'I know, you're a friend of hers, I shouldn't talk like that. But she really is beside herself, quite hysterical I should say.' She turned back to Ben Lakey. 'What I was hoping was that the Deputy Commissioner...'

'Paul.' I interrupted.

'Yes, that Paul could come up to Dominique's place and have a look at these log-book things, and maybe put my mother's mind at rest. Or better, that Paul could trace this gardener, through the police perhaps, and find out what's been going on...' Her voice tailed away. 'But it's an awful cheek, I know. At a weekend, as well. I wouldn't have asked, but I thought, the way my mother is, you might come round for supper afterwards, and that way put her mind at rest about whoever it is Dominique was... well, living with.'

She stopped and looked from one to the other of us. Her eyes suddenly clouded, and I sensed she was near to tears. In a touching gentleness, Lakey covered her hand with his, the other hand on her shoulder. If he hadn't been so obsessed with Sigrid Sorensen and Suri, I'd have wondered about this sudden physical warmth.

'Can I be of any help, perhaps? I haven't Paul's contacts to help find the gardener, but I know he has a hell of a lot on at the moment. Paul?' he looked at me defiantly, as if challenging me to deny that I needed the peace and quiet and the time to pursue the enquiries that so far I hadn't even started.

I was in a quandary again with that question. I didn't think he'd attempt to run for it, and I certainly couldn't refuse in front of Frédérique Dantin. And yet... I was unhappy at losing sight of Lakey, not so much for any stupid police reason as because I was worried that if he did make off, I'd have lost my grip on Suri. Whatever grip that might turn out to be.

'It's rather up to Miss Dantin.' I replied eventually. 'I have no objection, of course not.' He relaxed then, visibly pleased that I had made the only response possible under the circumstances. Fool that I was, I only had quietly to pocket his passport. But I didn't.

'You want to go now, I expect?' Lakey stood up abruptly. She looked from me to him in some confusion. She didn't know either of us, and she was very young, around twenty-two at a guess. It must have been something of a surprise for her suddenly to find an unknown Englishman at her disposal, and I suspect she shrewdly questioned his motives. I'd already worked that one out for myself: given the choice of doing nothing and bottling up his frustration against Suri, or helping someone else and at least doing something, he'd opted for the second. With my usual slowness, I suddenly realised this was the one way to get rid of Lakey for the evening. True to form, I nearly botched it.

'I have an idea.' I said. 'Mr. Lakey is quite right, I do have an inordinate amount to do and I am a bit pressed for time. It doesn't make me a very good host.'

I took care not to meet Lakey's eye.

'How does this sound? You go and take a look at these books or whatever they are. If you can find the gardener's name or anything about him, ring me here, and I'll get on to Rolle police and see what they can tell us.' I didn't say that a name or car number plate would be ample, the computer would do the rest. 'Then, if Mrs. Dantin is really as upset as you say, I don't think you should leave her alone for the whole night, whether there's any danger in staying at Dominique's or not.'

It was hard to talk about the place and not call it "Dominique's", even though she was dead.

'If you can find out what these log-books or whatever are all about, I don't see it makes much difference whether it's me or Mister Lakey who gets to the bottom of them. And let's face it,' I was trying far too hard, they were both looking at me with the same peculiar expression. They couldn't know what I later admitted to myself, it was the common hormones at work, and not common sense. 'Supper with Mrs. Dantin will certainly be a lot more appetising than here, and that way you could reassure Mrs. Dantin at the same time. Ben.' I added cordially.

'You can spare me for the evening then, Paul?' Lakey was very dry, he was looking at me in a speculative manner. He was wondering what I was up to, any moment now it would be he rather than I that would insist on his early return to the Chalet, to satisfy his curiosity at why I so obviously wanted him out of the way. This was an irony I couldn't handle. I decided a hint was necessary.

'I'm expecting someone.' I murmured. Frédérique's face had been looking more and more troubled as I had gone along. Now it cleared and she burst out laughing, her blue eyes sparkling in a mixture of relief and amusement.

'Gosh, I'm glad you said that. I thought you were some gooky old match-maker.' She glanced up at Lakey - he was a good deal taller than she was. 'No offence. I'm most grateful for any help you can give me, Mister Lakey. Only the way Paul was talking...' She giggled, the eyes impish again. 'I thought you must be the hungry werewolf of Rolle and anything would do.'

Lakey's face suddenly showed the strain he was living under. His eyes were hooded as he glanced to me and then back to Frédérique.

'Shall we go?' She stiffened at his tone, and bright patches of red stained her cheeks.

'I said something wrong?' She was very close to him. This was a generation I had never been able to fathom. They jumped from well-bred copy book manners to the personal level with frightening speed. Her eyes were reading his face again, her gaze fixed on him. He looked down, then away.

'No. You remind me of someone. That's all.' He shrugged. 'Sorry. I'll tell you about it some day.'

'Yes.' She jangled her car keys meaningfully. 'Do you have a first name, Mister Lakey?'

'Benjamin.' He grinned crookedly. 'But I prefer Ben.' He turned to me, the speculative look in his eye again. 'See you later?' His tone of voice said "see you tomorrow". We all shook hands.

It sounds stupid, but we all three agree, looking back, that was the moment that somehow cemented our mutual interest, and was the start of a bond none of us had dreamed of until that moment, and which, to be honest, none of us recognised for some time to come.

Chapter Eleven

I didn't hear Lakey return, but I heard the crunch of Frédérique's car turning in the drive, and Simona heard it too. The bedside lamp was still burning, and she half sat up to check the time. I knew what time it was, the stupid clock downstairs had just announced a cheeky four 'cuck-oos'.

'He's up late.' she murmured, She wrapped both arms around me and held me close for a long moment. Soon afterwards she fell asleep. But sleep eluded me.

I'd used the intervening hours until Simona's arrival working on the preliminary report for the Commissioner. After making a copy of the tape cassette I'd lifted from Reception, I'd played it several times. There was no doubt in my mind after that, that the calls purporting to be from Amex in Brighton were all made from "Medina". There was no earthly reason why Amex should have called so frequently at that hour of the night merely to trace Lakey, and then have done nothing to follow it up. And the call to Lakey was unmistakably from some creature in "Medina"...

I had stupidly thought for a short while that I at last had proof positive of an illegal fraudulent action by Suri's people, misrepresentation of identity to induce the police to reveal information to which they had no right. Then with an awful bitterness I had realised I couldn't use the evidence, for I was the idiot who had given all the information away in my stupid answers. If the Commissioner ever got to hear that tape... In a moment of despair at the whole sordid business, I had thrown the cassette on the fire, and watched the plastic casing melt round the coiled tape. When I realised what I had done, destroyed police property holding material evidence, I had put away the cassette copy I had made in a locked drawer, so that I shouldn't be tempted to do anything so stupid again.

After that I'd played the video tapes Oron had provided for me. They revealed no clue as to Scholl's motives, but at least their clock readings made it possible to detail the exact timings of his first appearance West of the airport, and the subsequent movements of both aircraft. I didn't know then of course the way Simona's mind was working - I should have paid more attention to Le Comte, perhaps - and I didn't want her to know I had those tapes, so I locked them away as well.

Finally I turned to the notes Oron had compiled on Scholl's movements.

These looked more promising, and I pored over them, checking every movement of his aircraft, every arrival, every departure. I was looking for the least clue that would link Scholl with Suri. There was nothing. Oron had done well to collect all this data in so little time, but it was really only a record compiled from the larger European airports and ATC centres where Scholl's aircraft had appeared in the last three months. What really would have been useful would have been the flight plans he had logged, but that was too much to hope for so soon after the crash. I found nothing to link him with Suri. I was so discouraged by now that I hadn't even bothered with the dossier Simona had had sent to me at Police Offices, there would be nothing there either, I was sure.

All I had to go on, then, were the Telexes of that Friday morning, and what I had actually seen and done. My preliminary report for the Commissioner was turning out to be a pretty thin affair, a collection of facts and times, devoid of motives or theories. The only theory I had I couldn't prove, and until I could prove it I couldn't include it. It was frustrating beyond belief.

By then it was time to make the place and myself presentable for Simona Sentori. Of all the moods I could have been in to renew our friendship, none could have been less promising. Only half an hour before she arrived, I was wishing she wasn't coming round at all. Had I only known... But then Simona Sentori is a very accomplished female and changing a man's mood is child's play to her. Also, and although she still denies it, I know now, she had come with set intent.

With just a hint of some expensive perfume, she breezed in like a human whirlwind, as if we had never separated and the last twelve years hadn't happened. And she didn't look a day over thirty-five, although she was actually over forty. Oron had been right, I had been too many years on my own. I found it hard to reconcile this animation and flamboyance with the meticulously formal manner she adopted in the Enquiry Rooms. And I didn't recall her being like this all those years ago, it was like meeting a young ghost who has grown up and come back. In the flesh.

She hadn't been in the house half an hour and I had all but forgotten about the mess I was getting into, and as neither Lakey nor Frédérique had rung to remind me of it, my mind was by now undividedly on Simona Sentori. I was thoroughly uncertain but unduly optimistic at the direction of this sudden interest. She was a superb cook, and had brought the materials for a whole series of exotic dishes which she knocked together in minutes. That was my fault, inviting her for half past seven didn't allow her to prepare the food in situ. I decided I had lived much too long alone.

We had drunk an ice-cold aperitif in front of the blazing log fire, allowing the warmth and the alcohol gradually to melt away our inhibitions, the result of too many years of alienation, too many battles.

She was wearing a stunning flaming-rainbow piece of clinging silk, which, set against her fair hair and golden complexion, produced an effect you won't find in any of the fashion magazines, they'd be banned as indecently provocative.

To start with I was at a loss. If Oron was right, she had a weird notion we had some place together, and I knew Le Comte far too well to suspect him of any malice. But I didn't know Simona, or women, well enough to read her intentions, and she is far too sophisticated for any man to be able to read the signs with any certainty.

Over a candle light supper she warmed to several themes, none that sounded like the normal dinner table games. I hadn't played those games for years, truth be told I'd forgotten how, and that, I think, was why she had come. She was through with them as well.

She talked a lot at first about her former husband, and then her general weariness at what she called the Game of Human Rites. And young First Officer Mueller.

'God knows what he's like on the flight deck, but there and then he was quite incapable of looking at anything but my...' she grinned quietly. 'You know. Tell me, Paul, is it because a man desperately wants to stare at a woman's bosom, or is it because he's biologically unable to prevent himself?'

Rather than answer the question, it occurred to me she might have asked because I was perhaps guilty of just that. She had not pressed the point.

There was an implicit sexuality about her topics that any other man would have picked up, but it was frankly lost on me. She had married late in life, it appeared, around thirty-eight, after too many years learning how to play the games she now thoroughly despised. After only five years or so of married life, and still without children, something had gone badly wrong. What actually prompted the divorce she was only prepared to hint at.

'You and I, we grew up in the world before AIDS, Paul. We chose to ignore the Old Testament, and we didn't want to be reminded, twelve years ago, that we were playing with the fruits of innocence. Now we know better...'

She had seemed to change tack.

'People like David are finding it hard to come to terms with the new rules. God's sake, how can a man still think of playing those sexual games nowadays? The grass on the playing field may look green enough, but the goal posts are rotten. Where does it leave a woman?'

Luckily it was a rhetorical question. And it told me all I needed to know about what had gone wrong with their marriage.

Soon afterwards she had got up to serve the main course, and over the candle flame her eyes met mine.

'What I always liked about you, Paul, is that you're entirely ingenuous.'

I wasn't sure I altogether liked that and seeing this, she had shaken her golden curls with a cheerful laugh, and pressed my hand to the wine glass.

'Come on, that was meant as a compliment. Drink to old times?'

She had raised her glass, and I had said something banal about drinking rather to a new future. Her eyes gleamed then, and with a clink of glasses she had rejoined:

'That was exactly what I meant. I don't think there is an ounce of guile in you, Paul de Savigny, and that is suddenly extraordinarily attractive.'

She had kissed me briefly then, and things were rather hazy for a little while after that. But it wasn't until we were well into the dessert that she left me speechless. She leaned across the table, we were comfortably close by then, and said:

'What on earth made you decide to become a policeman, Paul? You must know by now you're no earthly good at it.'

It was not a romantic comment, nor was it intended as such. I have said that Simona Sentori is first and foremost a pragmatist. I could have wished then that she was not. I didn't know what to say.

'Second Deputy Commissioner isn't that bad.' I ventured eventually, playing with the stem of the wine glass.

'Second Deputy Commissioner is extremely bad, Paul, for you.' Her green eyes sparkled in the candle light, and there was a cool appraisal in her look.

'You've been speaking to Le Comte.' I said flatly.

'With Michel Oron?' A warily speculative look crossed her face. 'He told you that?'

'No.' I lied. 'But yesterday in the Tower, after the 493 business...'

'Oh, that.' She looked relieved, and I knew why.

'What's so bad about Second Deputy...?' It was at this moment that Frédérique Dantin rang to tell me that they hadn't managed to sort the log books mystery, perhaps I could have a look next day. She added that Lakey would be staying until late at her mother's, she would drive him home and I needn't worry if he didn't appear until early morning. The way our conversation was turning, the last person I was worried about was Ben Lakey.

I lifted a bottle of cognac from the drinks cabinet on the way back to table. Simona had swung her legs out sideways and pulled my chair across beside hers.

'On second thoughts,' she murmured, 'the sofa looks more comfortable.'

I poured the drinks, the neck of the bottle clinking unfriendlily against the glass.

'Why did you become a Federal Air Commissioner, for that matter?' I was bitter. I couldn't add the second part of her question to mine, she was an excellent Investigator.

'I didn't mean it that way, Paul.' She had pressed against me, her head on my shoulder. I was confused, different emotions pulling at me.

'What way, then?'

'You could have done so many different things.'

'Like?' She kissed me again, it was not the answer I was expecting.

'Oh, I don't know. Did you never think of something more sociable? By the way, was there ever any news about Charlotte?' I put the glass down carefully.

'No to both questions.' She had taken my face between her hands then. Her touch was very gentle and her eyes tender in the firelight.

'Now I've hurt you twice, and I didn't mean to either time. Sorry, Paul. Maybe this is better: I don't think I could fall in love with a real policeman.' Seeing it wasn't any better at all, but a damn sight worse, she released my face and stood up. 'I think I've had a little too much to drink. Can I use the...?'

'Upstairs. Second left.' She hadn't come down again, it was I who had followed her a little while after.

Now, hours later, she was asleep, and I was not.

It was little consolation that, on a personal level, magic still happened. On a professional level I was probing the extent of the damage, and I didn't like what I was discovering about myself, still less what she found there. Not only no magic, but actually nothing at all.

There was a peculiar déjà-vu feeling about the morning. Twelve years previously... It was disturbing, she looked exactly the same to me that morning as she had all those years ago, but I couldn't kid myself that applied to myself as well. Lakey wasn't up when I went to make coffee in the kitchen.

'I think I made some mistakes last night.' she said, sipping her coffee. She had her head propped up against the bed-head, and the sheets tucked modestly around under the armpits. I didn't want to talk about that.

'Such as?'

'Not that, you idiot.' She put down the cup and held me close. 'Good God, I'd forgotten how sensitive you are.' She paused. 'I wish I hadn't, forgotten I mean.'

'Some people are like that.'

'Not enough people. Only you.' She sipped her coffee. 'Do you have to go to work today?'

'Do you mean do I have to, or am I on duty today?'

'Bloody policeman's mentality.' She sniffed. 'Both, I suppose.'

'Yes. Two o'clock till nine.'

'Only?' Her eyes widened and a smile crossed her face.

'Yes.'

'That's as good an answer as no.' She put down the cup again.

Later she asked briefly about my "house guest".

'You want me look after him while you're at work?'

'You're thinking of seducing him as well?' I was trying to be funny. It was only the crack of the back of her hand across my cheek that made me realise how far off the mark I had been. Before I could think what I might say to repair the damage, she had my face in both hands, and was doing a better repair job than I should have.

'I'm sorry, Paul. Dammit, forgive me for that. You...' There were tears in her eyes, I had never thought I should see this, not in the cool calculating Simona Sentori who had tried to make mincemeat of me in the Robin enquiry. 'My husband...' the words came with difficulty. '... used to speak just like that. Forgive me.' she repeated.

'I think the proper answer is "Yes", then.' I said. 'Please.'

Chapter Twelve

'How long can you stay?' I hadn't had breakfast in bed for so many years - truth be told I hadn't had anything in bed for so many years - that everything tasted doubly good.

'Why?' Simona swallowed a piece of croissant, flakes of pastry falling on the duvet. 'You thinking of having me tested for HIV pos...?' She seemed to choke and screwed up her eyes, her hand suddenly reaching for me. 'Hell, that was awful of me.' She shook her head in disgust, then opened her eyes to stare at me from a distance of a few inches. She was blushing. 'I don't know why I said that. Yes, I do. You see what I meant about David? After a few years living with a mentality like his, that's the kind of thing you get used to coming out with. Sorry, Paul. Especially after the way I lashed out earlier... After all,' her eyes crinkled, 'it was I that came to you, not the other way round.'

It seemed to me her former husband had a lot to answer for.'

'So how long can you stay?' I tried again.

'You talking about hours, days or weeks?' Her voice was very soft. But we both knew that the strangely animated tenderness in her face and in her hands was something not always easily sustained beyond a few weeks.

'Yes.' I shoved the breakfast things away significantly.

'Then so am I.' It was the meaningless trivia of lovemaking that we all try to believe in. We might have gone on like that for some time, but the bedside extension rang at that moment, and I wasn't so bad a policeman as not to answer my telephone.

'Paul? Frédérique... I'm calling from Mummy's place. She was wondering, were you thinking of going over to Dominique's this morning?'

I looked at the clock, I'd forgotten all about Dominique's affairs, and my meeting with her mother. It was already eleven o' clock.

'Is your mother going over, then?' I asked, playing for time. I was hoping to be able to get out of this.

'No, didn't Ben tell you... or isn't he up yet?' I didn't answer that, and she went on. 'Until we know what these stupid books are all about, she refuses to go near the house, something about "Dominique's sins" and the place being cursed. I told you, she really is acting very oddly. Listen, if it's all right with you, I really don't want to leave her here alone, and yet it's an awful cheek to ask you to go and look at those things without one of us...'

'No, it's not at all. I'd be glad to.' I meant it, any other time I'd be glad to. Just not that morning. 'So you're staying at your mother's for now?' She said she was, and I had to get up then to check my duty roster. I resumed the call on the downstairs phone. 'Tomorrow afternoon, about three o'clock?' She agreed to that, and it is ironic that I rang off thinking I had organised things rather well. I couldn't have known that what I would find at Dominique's would prove once and for all that Scholl had never even heard of Suri, and this delay was in large part of my own making. Simona had joined me in the living room by then, and was staring round much as Frédérique had the previous afternoon. I'd stashed most of the junk and papers in out of the way corners just before she arrived.

Now, in the light of day, all that candles and firelight had made look romantic suddenly sprang to the eye as the disordered accoutrements of a bachelor too long alone. I had never really thought of myself as a widower.

'I thought you said you'd tidied up.' She said it accusingly, but the way her eye dawdled over the dusty plants and the shoddily arranged books I sensed she was looking forward to imposing her own sense of order on things. Again I wondered what quirk of Fate had so suddenly, so forcefully set the magnetism flowing between us. It seemed unreal. 'When do I get to meet this Mr. Lakey? And you haven't told me yet why you're keeping him here?'

Fate wasn't that kind after all. This was the crunch I had known had to come. I could see no way of preventing Lakey and Simona talking, and it wouldn't be long then before...

'I'm not keeping him anywhere.' I said lamely. 'It happens he was involved in some financial misunderstanding in Moscow, we thought at first he was under arrest, then it turned out he wasn't. Moscow impounded all his luggage, and he has no money either. It seemed the least I could do, after they sent him like a parcel from Moscow to Geneva, more or less handcuffed to his seat.'

'Paul, nobody can be more or less handcuffed, they either are or they aren't.' She giggled. 'There's more to this than meets the eye. Still, if that's your story, I expect you'll stick to it.'

She flopped down on the sofa, looking mischievous, her lower lip again tucked under her very white upper teeth. A thoughtful look crossed her face. She shook her head, flicking a strand of blond hair out of the way.

'I think I'll wait and see what Mister Lakey says, when I get to see him. Wasn't he on the 493 flight?' She bounced up again, her green eyes accusing. 'He was, wasn't he? This was the man Fonjallaz was going to talk to you about? By the way...' With an impish look that I was starting to find very endearing she watched my face for some reaction, 'Shall I press your shirt for you before tomorrow's meeting?'

'Meeting?' I sat down beside her. Now that I was resigned to her finding out about Suri, I couldn't see it made any difference any more. I tried to kid myself that Lakey's involvement with Suri might provide a good reason for keeping him around the place, and yet not compromise my enquiries into Scholl. More than ever I was glad I hadn't mentioned my ideas about Scholl to anyone. 'What meeting?'

'As Vice-President of OFAC, *l'Office Fédéral de l'Aviation Civile*, I hereby convoke you to attend the Session of the *Comission Fédérale d'Enquete* tomorrow at ten o'clock, Deputy Commissioner.' She ran her hands affectionately through my hair, an uncomfortable reminder that it was quite markedly thinning. 'Oh God, wouldn't it be awful if I started to laugh or something. How embarrassing. I shall have to watch my step.' She blew me a minute kiss, then wriggled off the sofa and disappeared into the kitchen. 'Do you have a housekeeper,' she called, 'because, if I feel like this about you for long, I think she might come to disapprove of me.' She came back from the kitchen with a glass of orange. 'I shan't be able to do this tomorrow.' She lifted the glass to my lips. Suddenly she was pressing hard against me, her voice a passionate murmur. 'God, if I want you this badly tomorrow in the Enquiry room,' her voice turned into a giggle, 'I think I'll have to adjourn the meeting.' The orange juice spilt all down my front as Lakey gave a polite cough behind me.

'Sorry.' he said, 'did I interrupt something?' I spluttered some kind of greeting as I went to change my shirt, and when I came downstairs again Simona and he were deep in conversation. I could feel the tension building in me now, any moment he would start to tell her all about Suri, and it would be out. I muttered something about fetching wood and left them there at the breakfast table.

There was an unfriendly chill about the mottled white sky, with the sun just breaking through the overcast. Despite the dark circle of tall pines that surrounded the estate, the snow-glare was intense in the broad clearing behind the house. I fetched an axe from the shed and vented a lot of pent-up emotion and other things working up a sweat on the logs for the fire. I'd chopped enough to last over a week when I heard her come out of the house behind me. I didn't turn round, I just reached for the next log. But before I could lift the axe again, her arm circled my waist from behind and she laid her head on my shoulder, her other arm reaching for the axe and gently lowering it to the ground.

'Oh, Paul.' was all she said.

Lakey was back on the piano when we went in again, not on a "work out" this time, I think, but tactfully distancing himself, playing pianissimo. Simona immediately disappeared into the kitchen and I buried myself in the office. I took out the video tapes and the other stuff I'd locked away, realising now how immature it had been even to dream of not discussing them with Simona. Immature and unrealistic. But I hadn't known then...

'Can I run through that stuff this afternoon?' She was standing in the doorway to the office, looking oddly school-girlish in a little pinafore over the borrowed dressing-gown, and with her eyes streaming from cutting onions. I stood up and went across to her.

'You think Suri...?' My voice was very soft. Clearly, whatever Lakey had said, it seemed she had drawn the same conclusion, that there was some link between Suri and the ill-fated approach of 493. I didn't know then that she knew me well enough to understand that this might be my interpretation, but nobody else's.

'You're the police offic...' She stopped, and brushed her eyes with her sleeve, we were both remembering what she had said the previous evening, "You're no earthly good at it." she had said. I don't think either of us questioned it any more.

'What did you mean, you "don't think you could fall in love with a real policeman"?' She just stared up at me then, her green eyes studying my face intently, looking for something that I couldn't identify.

'A real man, though.' Her voice was a mere murmur. She took my hand. 'I told you, I'd had a little too much to...'

'Yes.' I didn't really want to pursue it. 'You said that.'

'I said too I'd forgotten how sensitive you are.' She nestled her head against my shoulder.

'Something more "sociable", you said.'

'Yes.'

'Like taking in Lakey? Or taking on Suri?' She thrust me away from her then, at arm's length, and threw her head back defiantly.

'Maybe.' She sounded very doubtful. 'But only if, Paul, only if you know what you're doing. Do you, Paul, do you know? Darling...' Her sudden switch of approach had me wrong-footed, and I blinked a bit at this. '...this could be what you've been waiting for to happen since... since Charlotte went. Or it could go disastrously wrong. So disastrously, I don't want to contemplate what might happen if...' She stopped, and pushed past me to the desk with the video cassettes and the documents. 'Can I run through this stuff this afternoon?' she repeated, 'while you're at work?'

'You want to?' My voice was lifeless, I was being torn every which way and didn't know where to turn. I think in my heart I was scared she would destroy any possible link between Scholl and Suri, despite my suspicions. Or was it that she too would prove to be a better detective than I was?

'I want to do anything that might stop you hurting yourself, Paul. And if you don't mind, then, yes please, because I want to help.' She stopped, and we stood in silence. For some time.

'Something's burning.' said Lakey from the doorway behind her, then, seeing what we were doing, 'Oh Christ, sorry, that's the second time I've done that.' But he was grinning, and suddenly so was I.

'The onions!' Simona pulled her dressing gown around her where it had fallen open, and skipped past him towards the kitchen. 'Hell, I've burned the onions. Why couldn't you have turned them off?' she called accusingly to Lakey. The Chalet hadn't seen so much animation, so much life, for years, and nor had I. In a dispassionate moment of self-examination I saw my professional life falling apart at the seams, and my personal life suddenly promising things I hadn't believed in for years. More irony.

Leaving the things piled up on the desk for Simona, I followed the other two into the kitchen.

There was a strange loneliness about being back in my office that afternoon, for the roster only scheduled one officer on a Sunday. Immediate emergencies were covered by the Gendarmerie, over on the French side. I sat and stared sightlessly out over the apron, oblivious to the aircraft movements. My thoughts were tangled, confused, I no longer even felt the hurt of Simona's flat statement: "you're no earthly good at it."

She was right, I wasn't. "I don't think I could fall in love with a real policeman." she had said, too. That was supposed to have made me feel better?

I wondered how I had ever got into this state, where in my career things had started to go the wrong way. But I knew the answer to that and it was no help. I pulled out the files and started to write up the report on the Scholl affair.

I'd got as far as the point when Oron had taken over in the Tower, sending out the fire crews and the VIP coach, when the appalling thought first shot through my mind. I had nothing on Scholl whatsoever, other than that he had tried to fly head on into a commercial airliner. It didn't matter that I had no proof that he had ever heard of Suri, still less been ordered to do it by Suri, what mattered was that no-one knew anything about Scholl. I was the only person authorised to enquire into his activities. And the way my mind was working, I was determined to find proof, at any cost. Even if it meant...

The appalling thought was so awful that rather than identify it as inexcusable, I sought every means I could to justify it. But there was no way round it. I was actually contemplating falsifying the evidence, worse still creating it if need be, to indicate an involvement between Suri and Scholl. I was physically shaking with the enormity of what I was tempted to do. I got up and, oblivious to the bitter cold and the fine sleet that was falling, I walked all the way across to the ATC tower in the hope of finding Le Comte and some sanity. But he wasn't on duty that afternoon, and when I got back to my office and wearily opened the file again my mind had half-accepted that such actions would be justified, with Scholl dead, and Suri every time beyond the law. But could I bring myself to do it?

Time after time I stood up and paced the office, stopping again and again at the window, as if staring at just one more landing or departing aircraft would give me the inspiration I needed. Scholl was the key to everything. How had he known where to find Swissair 493, how had he timed it so perfectly? What had been the signal that got him on the eastbound ILS at the precise moment that 493 was passing through 5,000 feet to Runway 23? Where had he flown from? From Oron's detailed notes, I saw that he hadn't been to Friedrichshafen for over a week, and there was no evidence of his take-off from any major European airfield on the 13th at all. So he'd flown from some minor strip. I jotted this down on a blotter, and began to draw up a theory.

I couldn't see any way Scholl could have known that the Lakey flight was approaching Cointrin, its timing, its SQUAWK ident for Heaven's sake... That was a clincher too, only a very sick mind would have wanted to show the identical SQUAWK ident approaching from opposite quarters simultaneously. People as sadistically sick as Suri's lot, perhaps? I made more jottings.

So how had Scholl known when to time his approach from the South and the West, it was the split-second timing that was puzzling. The near-miss conflict between the Iberia and the Speedbird over St. Prex was of no interest, it was merely a fortuitous distraction for Scholl. Slowly my mind came to the only conclusion open to it. Scholl must have been in collusion with someone at Air Traffic Control. Only that way could he have known when to stop flying around in French airspace, as he indubitably had, and make for Geneva via the hidden approach behind the Salève. Quite excited now, I started to add some flesh to my skeletal sketch.

I could safely exclude the Tower Controllers from any suspicion, as also the Geneva Approach and Departure frequency operators. But they were only the tip of the iceberg. The high-altitude flights were all controlled by Swisscontrol from another centre well away from the airport. It seemed abundantly plain that someone there, perhaps a Suri sympathiser, had contacted Scholl as soon as 493 had started descent and been passed to the Approach frequency. There was quite simply no other way he could have known when to start his suicidal approach. More jottings.

But where he had flown from? And how to prove the so tenuous link from Swisscontrol radar? There was no way I could see myself getting hold of every single tape recording from Swisscontrol for the morning of the 13th, not now, they'd have wiped the tapes and used them again. And how to locate his airfield of departure? The dossier from Oron had a transcript of Chamonix control's conversation with Scholl, and his untruthful story about diverting from Nyon to Fribourg, but Nyon lies well within the zone where flight plans and SQUAWK idents are required, so he hadn't come from there. That alone made Scholl an outright liar, quite apart from seemingly homicidal. Sufficient to tie him in with Suri, though? Not yet, nagged my inner voice, not yet.

I dragged out a large scale map of the lake and environs which showed every airfield. There were eight of them, but only three outside the flight plan and SQUAWK ident requirement zone. But he could have come from further afield. Like Sion, or Fribourg or from France even. I wondered then belatedly, whether he had had a flight recorder. Although it was Sunday, I tried telephoning the Technical department.

Miraculously, there was someone there, and better still, there had been a flight recorder and voice recorder. Did I want to drive over and collect the reports and recordings? When I asked why they hadn't been sent over automatically, it was the old story. Some Sergeant had made unkindly noises about an old man's foibles, and said it could wait. I didn't pursue the matter, and was about to drive over to the oddly placed subterranean Technical department that is built into a bunker underneath the main runway when the phone went again. Cursing, I answered. At the back of my mind, or sensing some telepathy, I thought it might be Simona, but no telepathy, no Simona. It was the *Pharmacie Principale* on the Departures level, they had a shoplifter and would I come up immediately? In no mood for loutish shoplifters, I locked the dossier away in my desk and went up to Departures. I was furious.

By the time I was through with the shoplifting affair it was past six o' clock, and whoever had been at the Technical department had gone home. No flight recorder tapes, no voice recordings. It was maddening, whichever way I turned I came up against delays, dead ends or blank walls. I toyed for a moment with the idea of breaking into the Technical offices, then dismissed the idea as crackpot, I didn't like to think what the consequences might be when the Commissioner heard about it. But you can see the extent to which I was obsessed, even to have thought about it.

I reviewed the notes I had made. Friedrichshafen, that was where Scholl had based his aircraft. He certainly hadn't flown over from there on the Friday, but it was the only address I had for the man. I consulted a few handbooks, and then, wondering what kind of police arrangements there were at Friedrichshafen field, sent them a tentative Telex, on the off chance. The reply came back within minutes, which suggested either a much superior police arrangement than Cointrin had, or a very bored Duty Sergeant who was glad of something to do. Half a hangar, the Telex said Scholl had owned. I reached for the airline schedules. There was a morning flight to Friedrichshafen with Delta Air Regionalflug. I picked up the phone and immediately made the reservation. Dammit, I was supposed to be investigating Scholl on the authority of a Federal Commissioner. The fact she had suddenly become my lover was neither here nor there. Or was it?

"We shall need your full report into the antecedents and movements of the late Monsieur Scholl..." Simona had said. She had also said: "Paul, you look dreadful." I stared at my reflection in a wall mirror. She certainly had a way with unflattering comments.

'Single or return?' yawned the clerk at the Inter-line ticket office. The usual bad manners.

'Wait.' I checked the return schedules, the afternoon flight would allow me five hours at Friedrichshafen field. That should be enough. It would mean missing Simona's *Enquête Fédérale*, but that was probably all to the good. I grinned at a recent memory, something she had said. "If I want you this badly, I'll have to adjourn the meeting..."

'You still there?' The clerk yawned again. I confirmed the return flight for the afternoon, and she said she'd send the tickets down within the hour. I returned to the Telex then and sent off a whole series of questions to the West German police office at Friedrichshafen airfield, with copies to the *Polizeizentrale Friedrichshafen Stadt* for good measure. I wanted to learn as much as possible in the shortest possible time the next day, and although the German police are as efficient as any, they tend to be short on imagination. Armed with my exhaustive list of questions, they wouldn't need any imagination, I thought. I took the liberty of signing the Telex with the title of Commissioner of Police, Cointrin Airport, Geneva. There would be time enough to sort out the difference when I got to Friedrichshafen. There was also hell to pay when I got back.

Chapter Thirteen

'Good God.' I stopped in the doorway and stared at the unrecognisable orderliness of my living room. Simona was lying on the sofa with a brandy in her hand, the picture of contentment. The whole place had been utterly transformed.

'You don't mind do you, Paul?' She had jumped up as I came in.

'Mind? No, but... this must have taken you *hours*,' I protested.

'Yes.' She grinned, that impish look again. 'Hours and hours.'

'Good God.' I repeated. It took several seconds to locate the drinks. I splashed a large brandy into a glass. 'On your own?'

'Don't start that again.' She was mischievous. 'Your Mr. Lakey has gone out. Some girl who called round... how *did* he meet someone as gorgeous as that as quickly as that?'

'Long story.' I sat down beside her. She glanced at her watch.

'I can't stay, you know that, don't you?'

'I don't even know where you live,' I said. I was wondering whether her intention to depart had anything to do with the papers she had wanted to read through. Not that I could see she would have had time to go over any dossiers after re-constructing the entire living room to her own design.

'That's the problem.' She nodded as if in agreement. 'I've no clothes here, and I can hardly preside over tomorrow's Enquiry in your dressing gown.' She giggled, her arm round me. 'So, I think, darling...'

'That reminds me. I'll have to give the Enquiry a miss.' I explained about Friedrichshafen, and the early flight. Her eyes misted at that.

'Oh, Paul. That's excellent, exactly what I would have done.' She kissed me with sudden vehemence.

'So will it matter that I'm not there?' She shook her head.

'Not now. I've read the dossiers anyway. Will there be someone to present the Preliminary Report?' She was momentarily official again, the raw pragmatist in her coming to the fore.

'If they bother to turn up.' I said bitterly. 'The Sergeants at Cointrin are a law unto themselves, it seems to me. And I don't think the Commissioner himself will want to read it...'

'He's back, is he? Ummm.' She chewed her lip pensively. 'That's a pity.' But when I asked her why, she gave a secretive smile, and changed the subject. It turned out she was right. 'About this man Lakey,' she went on. 'Did you know he knew Jim Jones?'

I was staggered. Apart from entirely re-designing my house, and going over my police files for me, she'd found time to learn all about Lakey and his past.

'You mean... *the* Jim Jones. Of the People's Temple? But he couldn't have... I mean...' I stopped then. It was possible, I recalled that Lakey's print-out showed he had spent three years in the States in the early seventies.

'Mr. Lakey has had a very uncomfortable career.' she murmured, sipping her drink. 'He didn't just lose this latest girl-friend, Sigrid something...'

'Sorensen.'

'Yes, something, to Suri. Another friend of his joined Jim Jones's People's Temple as well, years and years ago...' She curled up comfortably on the sofa, and pointed meaningfully to the log fire that was burning low. I obliged with more logs, then ran my hand along the fender. It had been freshly polished, the burnished copper gleaming. I didn't know what to say. Mrs. de Almeida wasn't a patch on Simona, not in the same league. Then again, I'd never had breakfast in bed with Mrs. de Almeida. 'What are you laughing at?' she wanted to know, so I told her, and we didn't get back to Lakey and Jim Jones for some time after that.

'You know, Paul,' she said, 'I never thought a man could have better reason for loathing those Sects than you do, after Charlotte, and... what was your wife's name?'

'Geneviève.'

'Yes, Geneviève. But Ben Lakey... He didn't just lose this girl to Jones and the People's Temple back in the seventies, he implied she went out to Guyana with the Temple and died in that terrible mass suicide...'

'It wasn't mass suicide.' I corrected her. 'It was mass murder. They made children and adults alike drink cyanide, and those that wouldn't drink, they injected instead. In the tongue, in the arm, any place. I don't call that suicide.'

'How horrible. I'd forgotten, you're something of an expert.' She paused. 'Like I said yesterday, something more sociable? Maybe this is the right kind of ground for you, Paul. But anyway, Lakey. For him history has had a nasty way of repeating itself. Now he's lost Sigrid thingummy too, to Suri. You think he has any love for these Sects?' She paused. 'There was some legal affair in Switzerland, too, wasn't there?'

I was casting my mind back to the computer report from *Polizeizentrale* in Berne, but she went on.

'Something about a slander or defamation, he was sued by Meridian Medicaments in the early eighties.'

'He mentioned all that as well?' I wondered how on earth Simona had had time to discover all this. In the same few hours my own achievements had been pretty pathetic.

'Yes.' She glanced at the clock again, and I thought she was going to say she had to go. But it wasn't that. 'I hope Mister Lakey is having more luck with the girl who called this afternoon than his other girlfriends...'

'I don't think she is a...' I interrupted.

'No, I know, but the problem with Meridian was all to do with some girl-friend. He hasn't been very lucky in his relationships. To put it mildly.' The clock again. 'I expect he'll be back soon.' she said meaningfully.

'How soon is soon?'

'Oh, not very.'

'Don't you have a home to go to?' I said. She curled up on the sofa again then, very relaxed, her eyes glowing strangely in the firelight. It was hard to remember now the way she had breezed in the previous evening, confident that she would work a miracle. I still hardly knew her.

'If that's an invitation, I might just accept it.' Her voice was very soft, like her hands and her lips. Then, later : 'David cancelled the lease on our villa from the end of the month. He's been there this weekend, clearing out his stuff. That's why I didn't want to be there when he... Don't misunderstand me.' She was suddenly insistent, remembering I think how easily I jumped to the wrong conclusions. "Sensitive", as she called it. 'That wasn't why I came here, or stayed. Although...' she shuddered as if suddenly chill, 'I can't stand being near the man any more.' I didn't know what to say to that so I sensibly said nothing.

Monday, February 16th 1987

The flight back from Friedrichshafen was awful, the aircraft like something out of Disneyland, a propeller driven box-like and rattling thirty-seater that couldn't fly high enough to avoid the cumulo-nimbus that was lying heavy over the bridge of the alps all the way from Lake Constance to Lake Geneva. I was physically shaking as I walked unsteadily from the plane to the Terminal, a heavy attaché case of papers in one hand.

Turbulence in the air was nothing compared with the jolt I got on the ground. The first thing I saw in my office was a mound of papers and other affairs piled high on my desk. Before I could put my bag down, the Commissioner appeared at the open door to Reception. He caught sight of me as I came in from air-side. A volatile character at the best of times, there was an unusually aggressive air about him, and I felt suddenly very apprehensive. He nodded towards his office wordlessly, and, humiliating though it was, I knew I had no option but to follow him.

'Sit down, Paul.' He was curt. I could see that from his point of view his situation was not easy. He was six or seven years younger than I, but carried full responsibility for airport police investigations. He sat down behind his desk and reached for the dossier, the Preliminary Report. 'I wonder if you can visualise, Paul, just what it was like for me today.' His mild tone was at odds with the mottled red that was suffusing his cheeks, I had to grit my teeth and wonder a while longer just what it was that was riling him so badly. There were so many possibilities that I couldn't begin to guess.

It turned out that, for no good reason, he had decided to represent the airport police in my place at the OFAC Enquiry chaired by Simona. He had not had time to study the Preliminary Report in detail before appearing at the Tribunal rooms to read the damned thing in public. I winced inwardly as he reached across and flicked the pages to the item in question that had so discomfited him.

'".. and so,"' he read, '"with a view to seeking ATC clearance on the delayed Delhi flight, I went to..."' He choked at this point, his fingers actually prising at his collar, as he seemingly struggled for air. '"...I went to breakfast."' he concluded. His protuberant pale eyes peered balefully at me across the desk. There was a mixture in his look of embarrassment for his own situation and contempt for mine. 'You went to **BREAKFAST!?**' he bellowed. 'The first case of any importance that has the misfortune to come your way in how long, ten years is it, and what do I have to read out to the Enquiry? The Second Deputy Commissioner went to breakfast. Jesus wept, Paul, I knew you were a clown, but I never thought you...'

'Was there anything else you wanted to say?' I was on my feet. I didn't have to take this. It was just dawning on me, God knows it must have been evident enough for any poor fool to have seen in the past, but somehow I'd always managed to miss it, no wonder the Sergeants treated me with total contempt. They were simply copying the top man, the Commissioner. No one had ever spoken to me like that though, nor called me a clown.

'Yes. Sit down.' He was bitingly abrupt. Unwillingly, and feeling very small, I did as he said. 'What's this?' He held up a copy of the Telex I'd sent the previous evening, the list of questions to Friedrichshafen, signed with his name and title. 'Who authorised you to do this?' he demanded. 'How many other footling little bits of paper have you sent around the continent with my name at the bottom?' he wanted to know.

'Just the one.' I muttered. I hadn't the guts to do what I wanted to do above all, to walk out and quit. Nothing to do with any determination to get Suri, now, and so putting up with this appalling behaviour. I just didn't have the guts to do it.

'Just the one.' he echoed hollowly, and let the flimsy fall spectacularly on his desk, where it lay for what seemed an age, a time during which I said nothing and he just sat and stared at me. Eventually, he picked the Telex copy up and placed it neatly in the folder. The sound of a helicopter landing almost outside the window seemed to shift his concentration. 'Would you step to the window, please, Paul?' He was under control again now, I thought. I unwillingly followed him to the window. 'Take a look.' he said, pointing to the nearby fire-fighting practice range. I followed his line of sight.

They must have spent most of the day bringing back Delta-Echo-Charlie and rebuilding the broken fragments in a semblance of its original shape, I thought. They'd been lifting the bits out of the Jura crash site by helicopter. Nothing could make the aircraft look real or whole again, but the accident investigation team were doing as good a job as anyone could. I knew it was standard procedure to reconstruct a crashed aircraft with a view to discovering the precise cause of its malfunction. The only malfunction in Delta-Echo-Mike, I thought wearily, had been the intentions of its pilot.

'That's the aircraft.' The Commissioner stated the obvious. 'Or part of it. And a coffin in the city morgue holds the remains of its pilot. Name of Scholl, I understand. Who was he?' He stopped then and stared at me aggressively, as if I had brought the plane down single-handed. So I told him who Scholl had been, summarising for him what I had learnt in Friedrichshafen, the contents of my heavy attaché case.

'All right, next question. Why did he do it?' Again the aggressive face to face accusing look.

'On that score, I have no firm opinion as yet, sir.' I was icy. Whatever supposed errors I had committed, and whatever imagined embarrassment the man had suffered in my absence, he had just lost any semblance of respect I might have had for him. I had never believed anyone could speak to me in such a fashion. 'With your permission, I would like to visit Bex aerodrome tomorrow morning, first thing. I gather that is where his aircraft has been housed for much of the winter.'

'Granted.' He grunted the word as if against his will. 'Now, who is this Lakey man? Is he under arrest or not?'

'Unless American Express have rescinded their warrant... but I'd need to review the materials on my desk to answer that.' I was treating him with the same contempt now in which he plainly held me. 'As to who he is...'

'I know who he is, you poor foo...' he broke off, and wiped his fleshy face with his hand. 'Oh, Paul, Paul, Paul... when did you last actually have anything larger to handle than a lost suitcase or credit card?' he asked, suddenly mellowing and pushing me to the desk again, and the chair. I honestly couldn't remember, and said so. 'Just so.' he murmured. 'I think I owe you an apology perhaps.' "Perhaps" was putting it mildly. I thought so too. But I didn't think I was going to get one. I said nothing, resumed my seat. 'I know who Lakey is.' he went on wearily. 'He's an aberration that Moscow put in our direction, these things turn up once in a while. You've read Fonjallaz's report?' he shot a quick up-from-under shaft across the table.

'If it's more recent than Saturday, no sir. I understood he was in Lisbon?'

'That's right, of course, you won't have seen it.' Yet, I felt like adding. Yet.

'Is it significant?' I asked dryly. He stared at me then and burst out laughing. He had a high-pitched voice at the best of times. It was not a humorous sound.

'Significant? Depends on how you interpret significance, I suppose. Not to the case we're working on, no, not remotely.' So he discounted any link between Suri and Scholl. This didn't surprise me. 'But I think you'd need to be thicker than a blue-arsed baboon, Paul, not to agree with me that a man who's been bested by the Maharaj Suri has no small significance for you. Hey?' he persisted. 'Well?'

'I can see what you mean.' I agreed coolly.

'You can see what I mean, can you? Wonderful, bloody marvellous!' He stood up, the cheeks glowing with that mottled purple again. With a visible effort, he brought himself under control. 'How many years is it, now, Paul, since Charlotte? No, let's say since Geneviève died?'

'You bastard.' I spoke through my teeth. Now he had really succeeded in getting under my skin. I knew well enough that it had been Geneviève's death that had effectively also signed my death warrant as far as any career prospects with the Geneva police were concerned, I wasn't so damnably stupid that I hadn't been able to work that out for myself at some point in the intervening years. But I didn't need this farmer-faced beefy Chief Constable with his cackling laugh rubbing salt in the wounds either. If no one had ever spoken to me the way he just had, I'm certain no one had ever called him a bastard before and remained in the police force to tell the tale.

'Uh-huh.' He sat down, looking suddenly smug, strangely comfortable. 'I was beginning to think...' He stopped then, and there was a bizarre silence that neither of us seemed to want to break. He was letting the message sink in, God knows he had spelt it out clearly enough. First with the questions designed to reveal my incompetence as an investigating officer, then the reference to Lakey and Suri hinting at my lack of objectivity, and finally the direct mention of Geneviève's death as a turning point. He could hardly have spelt out more cruelly my situation, my prospects.

'Do you want me to give the Scholl case to Vinet?' He asked a direct question, and he got a direct answer.

'No, sir.' I bit the words off crisply.

'Very well.' He swivelled in his chair and stared down at the re-constructed pieces of aircraft in the wintry gloom outside. 'Today is Monday. Tomorrow, you say, you want to visit Bex? Tuesday. Wednesday you have...' he consulted a wall chart roster, '... a nine hour duty. Oddly you seem to have earned some leave... God knows how,' he muttered under his breath, 'from Thursday through Monday.' He rather enjoyed the Americanisms he'd picked up from some cheap TV series. 'All right. Here's the bottom line. I want your full report on Scholl, on my desk, fully documented, by the end of shift Wednesday. Then you can take your four days' leave, and...' I thought he was going to add a gratuitous "Good riddance", but his voice tailed away.

'That doesn't give me very much time, sir.' I didn't care any more what I said, but some element in my distant training broke through, I was recording a protest.

'Jesus wept.' he roared again! 'How much time do you need, for crying out loud? You've just had three days in which as far as I can see you've achieved sweet nothing. "Not much time..."' he mimicked.

The remainder of that interview is, I think, unworthy of recording, neither of us would come out of it very well. When I was finally able to leave him, pass through my outer office and collect the unwieldy collection of evidence and documents on my desk, and make it to the car park, I was so angry I could scarcely hold anything without dropping it.

Vinet must have heard all or most of our altercation in the Commissioner's office, and with some lingering remnant of decency he volunteered to help me carry the impossible pile of things. I wasn't too proud to refuse his offer, which probably sums up everything that was wrong with me and my position in Geneva Cointrin Police Department.

Chapter Fourteen

I wasn't sure I wanted to meet Simona in the state I was in after that. All through the snowy hills up above the motorway the words chased round and round in my head, like a litany: "I knew you were a clown...".

It was almost a relief to find the neatly written note on the sideboard:

"Had to go Saanen, Cherokee collided with hang glider. Call you. L & k. SS."

I knew there weren't many Federal Investigators in OFAC, but I didn't see why it always seemed to be Simona they called out. Saanen was a hell of a way away. But at least I didn't have to meet her yet. I wondered what her face had looked like when the Commissioner got to the bit about "so I went to breakfast...".

Still smarting bitterly from the altercation with the Commissioner, I started to sift through the sundry mixture of Scholl's belongings and assorted documents I'd found on my desk. If the Commissioner wanted results within forty-eight hours, he'd bloody well have them. I think it was then that the terrible notion recurred, that I could justifiably invent evidence. I'm not saying it was a crystallised clear idea, but in the darker recesses of my mind, there yes.

An hour or so later, Lakey returned. Again I heard Frédérique's car on the drive as it crunched away on the packed snow. He came straight over to me, unconcerned that he might be interrupting something important.

'Time's running out.' He looked terrible, his eyes red and his jaw working nervily. His fingers were dancing a tune against his thumb, and I wondered what had happened to cause this. He looked meaningfully at the drinks sideboard, I nodded.

'Not for me. Help yourself.' He poured a stiff whisky, a drink I abhor, then came and stood over me, staring down at the untidy pile of evidence on the carpet.

'So that's how it's done.' He gulped at his drink. 'Doesn't look very orthodox to me.' Perhaps if I hadn't had that run-in with the Commissioner I wouldn't have reacted so sharply. He made some apology, I pushed away the heap of stuff I was tagging and asked him what he wanted. He'd slumped down in the armchair opposite and was staring moodily over my shoulder to the photographs on the far wall.

'That's your family?' he asked obliquely. 'I understand you never found your daughter, Charlotte she was called?' He was speaking very rapidly, the words tumbling from his lips. 'I don't think I'm very surprised, really, I think you're an academician, a theorist, a Casaubon, you just collect people's stories, their miseries, and house them in dusty folders in that stuffy little office of yours. You never investigate them and you certainly don't do anything about them. I think you just go on collecting more and more such cases, so you can go on reminding yourself how badly hurt you've been. It's a therapeutic bum-ride for you, you kid yourself you're doing something just so that you can ensure that you never have to actually do anything about them... And I think I know why you don't, Paul, it's because you can't. Nobody can, least of all you... Oh, God.' He stood up stiffly, and turned to hide his face from me, the tears were moist on his cheeks. 'I'm sorry.' When he spoke again his voice was uneven. 'I shouldn't have said all that. It's not your fault you don't have the...' He stopped then, and wiping his face turned to stare at the mound of belongings at my feet again. "Not very orthodox." he had called it. I suppose he was right.

'Was that all?' I was more glad than ever that Simona had had to go to Saanen. 'Or is there more?'

'Scholl's stuff?' He toed the heaped plastic bags. 'Strange man, this Scholl, he flies head-first into a Swissair jet, crashes and dies, and no one knows the first thing about him. Or do you, now?' He squatted down on all fours in front of me, and stared into my eyes. 'Four days ago, I thought you were going to help me get Sigrid back, charge Suri with something he really couldn't squirm out of, whatever the technical legal words are for kidnapping or abducting someone, and holding them, probably against their will in "Medina" or whatever that place is called. I must have been mad.' He made a snorting noise, and stood up violently. 'If I had any money, I'd...'

'The problem is that Sigrid may not be being held against her conscious will.' My voice was toneless, distant. I couldn't cope with his hysterical outbursts, and I could only grasp at the single concrete point he'd raised.

'You what?' He sneered. 'You're not suggesting that she's sitting inside "Medina" holding Suri's cock, and all of her own free will, are you? Don't you know anything about this ALBATROSS? God's sake, you've got enough files gathering dust...'

'I'm beginning to wonder whether you really know anything about it.' I said angrily. 'You accused me just now of being unwilling or powerless to act against him. Sure I am. Like you are. Perhaps my dusty files, as you call them, are proof not of my uselessness but the fact that in more cases than not, the ALBATROSS brain-washing is so damnably successful that the missing youngsters don't consider themselves as "missing persons" at all, they think Suri's some kind of Godhead and all the world outside are aggressive mental deficients. Have you read any of those case histories,' I cried, 'because you wouldn't have to read many to see that a lot of those families actually traced their relatives to places like "Medina", and may even have got to see the missing person, only to find that, technically, legally, there was nothing they could do. Nothing. If a person over the age of majority says "I am staying here of my own free will", even if anyone half way normal could sense this was not the uninfluenced mind speaking, there is nothing whatever that the family can do. So they write to me.' I finished lamely.

'That's what I bloody well mean.' Lakey was shouting now, his fists clenched as he faced me across my living room. 'You're their last bloody chance, so why don't you get off your cowardly arse and fucking well do something?' He screamed the final words, quite out of control, then threw his glass in a frenzy against the staircase, where it shattered into a thousand slivers. He turned on his heel and without another word went outside.

I had just put the phone down when he reappeared, shivering like a man with fever. Stepping unseeingly past me, he made for the arm chair and slumped down in it. I thought he had cracked-up badly this time, which is why I had immediately tried to get hold of Frédérique, the only other person who knew him. Now I handed him a fresh drink, he looked up in surprise.

'I promise not to break this glass as well.' he muttered.

'Well, that's something.' I left him there and went into the kitchen, and was in the middle of cutting some sandwiches when I heard the crunch of the car on the drive again. Frédérique came in without knocking, and I heard them talking in low tones through the open door. I suddenly remembered I hadn't kept my rendezvous at Dominique's to look at those damned log-books or whatever they were. She appeared beside me.

'Is there nothing you can do?' Her voice was a murmur. 'I think he's breaking up.'

'I think he already has.' My own voice was very soft. 'Has he told you anything about the Trans-Siberian journey?'

She shrugged helplessly.

'This and that. Nothing concrete.' Always the same Suri story, nothing concrete. 'But if he did... would it help, could you start proceedings against this ALBATROSS, or the Suri man?'

'That would depend on a number of things.' I piled the sandwiches on a plate. 'You want to stay a while?' Again the shrug.

'I could...' she sounded doubtful, 'but there's my mother. She was upset not to see you at Dominique's this afternoon.' She avoided meeting my eye.

'I was in West Germany this afternoon.' I said. It felt as if I'd been most places between Hell and back that afternoon.

'I told her you were probably very busy. The funeral's on Wednesday morning, at the village church. Can you make it?'

Wednesday. And the Commissioner wanted my final report - signed, sealed and delivered - by Wednesday night. I nodded.

'I'll be there. Listen, can we go over Dominique's things after the funeral?' I didn't think Madame Dantin would want to hold a wake after such a ceremony. She said that would be fine, and we went back into the living room. Lakey was hunched on the edge of the armchair, shivering.

'I'll make up the fire.' Frédérique went out quickly to collect firelighters and wood.

'Ben.' I handed him a plate. Wordlessly he took it and started to chew the sandwich with a monotonous motion of the jaw, as if eating was a duty he had to get over. 'About this Trans-Siberian journey.' I started.

'The journey was all right.' he interrupted, his mouth full. 'It was Sigrid that... besides it all started long before we got to the train.' His eyes were strangely glazed, he was eight thousand miles away, and she was beside him. I wasn't sure how good an idea this was, he'd quietened down for now, but I thought he was probably a very sick man. And I don't mean he was ill. He stopped chewing and there was a long silence, only broken by Frédérique getting the fire going with tongs and bellows.

Well, the outcome was that Suri might have faced criminal charges, had they been pressed in Moscow. But Sovenskaya had scotched that, which is why the Delhi business had developed. Whether the Indian authorities would really have cared less about some Swedish passenger on an Aeroflot flight grounded for the night, I very much doubt. However, the Soviets and some back-room boffins in Berne had thought it worth a try, but even they had been very far from sure. That explained why they'd gone to such lengths to get Lakey to Delhi without any police involvement. The very fact that Swiss authorities and some obscure Soviet department had worked so closely against Suri gave me some hope, though. I hadn't appreciated until I heard Fonjallaz's version of events in Moscow how widespread the international dislike of ALBATROSS was, at all levels and in many countries. Now, in the early hours, Lakey had gone to bed, Frédérique home to her mother, and I was chewing over what significance if any there was for my theory in the international deprecation of ALBATROSS and Suri. Did this make it more likely, or less, that Suri had somehow organised Scholl's suicidal mission against 493?

It was late, and I was making no headway - or rather all the headway I was making was pushing me in the opposite direction, that Scholl had nothing to do with Suri, which was unacceptable - when Simona called. I remember now, over a year later, her exact words. She said, with the impish giggle she knew I couldn't resist:

"Had a good day at the office, dear?"

Resisting the temptation to give her a blow by blow account of one of the worst days of my life, I must have made some less than memorable reply. Unaware of the turmoil surrounding me at the Chalet and at work, she was bubbling over with everything that made things tick in her life.

She had an insatiable appetite for anything to do with flying, which was how she came to be an Accident Investigator for OFAC, and such a good one that she had become Vice-President. Most especially she was intrigued by incidents that seemed to make no sense. I don't mean she was morbid, far from it, but she took immense pleasure in unravelling the unfathomable, especially if it had anything to do with flying or aircraft. The Scholl case would have been made for her, if I hadn't been working on it already. She would never have made the mess of it that I was doing.

'Did you see the news?' she burbled. 'About the accident, I mean, out beyond Saanen? Quite unbelievable, Paul. Can you imagine, CAVU and bright sunshine...' CAVU was airline jargon for ceiling and visibility unlimited, cloudless skies. '...and this woman just flew smack into a rainbow coloured hang-glider at 2,000 feet.'

I said I hadn't seen the news, how dreadful. She must have sensed then that something was wrong, for she stopped burbling and made more comforting noises. I asked her when she might be back in Geneva - I meant Rolle - and she said Wednesday evening. Everything was happening on Wednesday, I thought. There was a tight silence then, as if she had a question she was afraid to put. When she finally plucked up courage I found it so moving it brought a lump to my throat.

'Can I bring a suitcase?' she asked with a nervous laugh. 'I've a sitting on Thursday in Lausanne.'

'Just one, then.' I said with a laugh no less nervous.

'We'll have to talk about that.' she promised, I could visualise her tossing her head in the way she did. 'Any progress with the Scholl thing?'

I was tempted then to tell her to stay away from Rolle and the Chalet for good, I didn't want her status compromised by a relationship with "a clown" of a policeman. If I'd been ten years younger I might have said as much, but she had enough on her hands, and was old enough anyway to decide for herself what she chose to do with her life.

'Not a lot.' I said I would tell her when she got back, and a little while later she rang off. Leaving me with a confusion of thoughts, a lot of bruised feelings, and a pile of evidence that all pointed to only one thing: my total and utter incompetence as a police officer. I hadn't lived through as impossible a day since Geneviève died. Leaving the mess in the living room, I went to bed. The stupid cuckoo clock chirped twice as I stepped over the broken glass at the foot of the stairs.

Four hours later I was up again. Of the forty-eight hours given me by the Commissioner there were only thirty-six left. I wanted to be on the road early.

'What the hell?' I stopped on my way downstairs. Lakey was stooping over the broken glass with a brush. He glanced up and looked at me sheepishly.

'Just clearing up.' he said. 'Will I come with you to Bex?'

'If you like.' I hadn't wanted to suggest this, for fear of arousing his paranoia at being watched, but I certainly didn't want him running round loose in the state he was in.

'About last night...'

'Any coffee on the go?' I waved him to silence. 'Forget last night.' He looked at me as if I were mad. 'You knew Jim Jones, I think Simona said?'

'Yes.' He straightened from where he had been picking up the glass. 'Yes. I met Jim Jones.' He dropped the pieces of glass into the bin.

'That's a good enough reason for anyone lashing out.'

'Thanks, Paul.' was all he said.

Before setting out for Bex we sat down together and logged all the tatty bits and pieces from the aircraft - anything mechanical and the interior were still being reconstructed - and sorted the charts, documents and a hundred and one odds and ends that had made up Scholl's life. It is remarkable how much you can learn about a man in an hour with a methodical survey of the accoutrements that surround him daily. It was Lakey who pinpointed the crucial absence of a log book or books. There was no reason then why it should have occurred to us that these were lying on the late Dominique Dantin's kitchen table, where she had intended wrapping them up and posting them off to Scholl the day she died. Lakey had in fact already seen them there, but knowing nothing about flying, and with them being mixed up with radio logs as well, he had not understood their significance.

And so, with the crucial evidence missing, and the flight-recorder and voice recorder tapes still to play through when we got back, we went to Bex. I had done few more tedious and useless pieces of investigative work in all my years in Cointrin.

Chapter Fifteen

Tuesday, February 17ᵗʰ

It was a foul morning to drive anywhere. It was well past dawn but the February sky was like night. Huge snowflakes were blizzarding across the motorway, driven by a gusting crosswind that shook the car and made steering difficult. The headlamps and fog lights reflected back off the driving curtain of white, and the hiss of the tyres in the slush was unsettling. If these conditions persisted, we might not make it to Bex at all.

'I'd have thought they'd have given you a police car.' remarked Lakey as we turned right on to the motorway above Rolle, and I increased speed.

'Would that make you feel safer?' I handed him a cigarette. He shook his head.

'I'm allergic to police cars.' he said enigmatically.

'What have you got against the police? Apart from me?' I tried to put him at his ease. He didn't answer for a moment, drawing on the cigarette. Then:

'You ever been inside a Swiss prison, Paul?' I couldn't remember, I didn't think I ever had.

'Surprisingly, no. Why?'

'They put me away for nearly six months after the Meridian affair.' he said bitterly. 'You think I love the Swiss police?' I hadn't known he'd been in prison as a result of the slander charge brought by Meridian Medicaments.

'But that was a civil action.' I recalled. 'Nothing to do with the police...'

'When you can't pay damages, they still put you in prison.' he said drily. 'It was four years ago, and the only capital I had was the house I'd just bought. I wasn't a millionaire, I hadn't bought a bloody villa, I'd bought a broken-down farm house out in the wilds that I'd hoped to do up with a woman called Sylvie Gueudet.' He sniffed, reminding me of Le Comte. 'Bloody Sylvie. If anyone should have gone to prison, it was her.'

'What happened?' I vaguely recalled something about a documentary. The car skidded badly as I braked to allow a lorry to pull out in front of us, and for some seconds he let me drive in silence.

'With Sylvie, or Meridian?'

'Both.'

'Where do you start?' He extinguished the cigarette, opened the window a fraction and flung out the stub. A burst of snowflakes invaded the car, and he wound up the window with a curse. 'That was silly of me. You know I make television advertisements? I mean, my living is directing them?'

'Yes.'

'It's not a bad way of making money, but when you're self-employed as I am, what the Swiss politely call "independent", but it's the same thing, you look to better things.'

'Like a mini-series you mean?' I interrupted. 'Drama, or a soap like the Schwarzwaldklinik?'

'Do me a favour.' He sounded injured. 'I wouldn't be seen dead with my name on the credits to that kind of... No. We were trying to break into the Documentary market.'

'We?'

'Me and Sylvie. She was a very good lighting and sound technician.' He paused. 'Among other things.'

'Go on.' This was all news to me.

'Our first contract was for the Swiss Co-op, it was a big thing, very lucrative. That's where I got the money for the house.' He paused as we swung off the main motorway on a link road around Lausanne. 'This is Lausanne?'

'Yes. Why?'

'Drive a bit faster, it was here I was in court.' But I didn't drive faster, not in those conditions. Visibility was down to twenty yards and the road thick with freshly fallen snow. 'We had a lot of friends from all over the place, people in the film world. There was a man called Richard Benson, he'd been a teacher and gone into scripting documentaries as a living. He told us he'd got the contract for a documentary to try and improve the image of Meridian Medicaments. There'd been several spills of chemicals in the Rhine at Basel, and there were noises too about vivisection, malreatment of animals, that kind of thing.' He grunted. 'It was a whitewash job they wanted, not a true documentary. Just one problem, I didn't know then that Benson was an animal rights nutcase, and I couldn't have guessed that Sylvie would pick up that garbage hook, line and sinker.'

'But you knew her well enough otherwise, didn't you?' I was working on what Simona had told me. The slush was flying high around the car now, the snow falling if anything still more heavily at this end of the lake than nearer Geneva.

'We were living together, doesn't mean you know a person.' He was terse.

'Benson... what did he do?'

'Hah.' He made an unfriendly noise. 'Well may you ask. He stood in the witness box and told the world I'd cheated him of forty thousand francs clear profit. The bastard. It's as well for him he left Switzerland before I got out of prison...'

'Yes, but what did he actually do?' He had shown the same bottled-up violence the evening before, and it wasn't attractive.

'To cut the long one short, we were doing a job on rats. The film was actually called "The Rat". Meridian was at pains to reassure the world that the animals they used for testing new medicaments were humanely treated, stupid word to apply to animals, I thought, but anyway... So we spent six months working on that, we really had a good tight team. Sylvie was ace on the tricky lighting in confined spaces, and we had some very good film. The difficult bit was the sound track.'

'Why difficult?'

'You sound too enthusiastic, you're doing a hard-sell, the viewer turns off. You make it too dry, too factual, they still turn off. Well, in the end I thought we had it just about right. Took the master video tape along to the SSR people in Geneva. That was the French version, you see, we planned a German sound track later in the year.'

'So what went wrong?' I began to see what Simona had meant about him having a "difficult career". Six months in prison for a film about a rat?

'Bloody Sylvie is what went wrong. And the old hormones. Hey, watch it...' His last comment had caused me inadvertently to swerve badly out of lane. Luckily traffic was light, no one in their right minds was driving that morning unless they had to. Conditions were as bad as ever.

'I may be a bit slow on the...'

'I'll tell you. SSR accepted the film as seen in the studio that day. They liked it very much. Great! Money was in the bag, I thought... The transmission date was scheduled for a month or so later. That was in case we had to cut anything, give us some leeway. Well, we didn't cut anything... *I* didn't cut anything.' He fell silent for several minutes then and there was only the swish of the wipers and the hiss of slush under the snow tyres. I waited.

'One night, quite late, I had to go to the cutting rooms, we had our own small studio in the nuclear shelter... is that an offence?' He grinned faintly. I didn't answer. 'I couldn't understand why the door was locked. Until I found Sylvie inside.' He swallowed, and begged another cigarette from me. He was so broke, he couldn't even buy a packet of cigarettes. 'I didn't understand what she was doing at first. Then I did. She had the master video on the editor. And a script on the desk. Well,' he exhaled smoke acridly. 'She was recording a new sound track over the old one. Not at all the text we'd shown SSR. If I'd had an ounce of sense I'd have called the police there and then, and dobbed her in. But she promised, there on the cutting room floor, she promised she was just doing it for an experiment, to show some friends. Friends.' he snorted. 'Some friends she had. She meant Benson.'

'On the floor?' I queried. I was a little short on imagination, perhaps. He looked sheepish.

'I was younger then, and she was very... well, you know.' I understood the hormones comment better now.

'I know. Yes. I think I do.' I had the picture now. 'She sent off the doctored master-video in place of the real thing?'

'Half past eight on a Tuesday night I turn on the television. Christ, Paul, it was only my second documentary after the Co-op, the only thing I'd ever made apart from 30 second adverts for dog food, toilet paper and the like. You don't get a break like that every day. And never again. Two minutes later my phone's ringing, Meridian chairman promising to bust me for all I had. The text was very bad.' he added softly.

'What did it say?'

'You should read the transcript. Let's just say that every time an animal appeared, the voice-over screamed vengeance on the unpitying cruelty of the butchers at Meridian, testing completely unnecessarily on defenceless... you know the kind of thing.' He stopped then, and I wondered what had happened to Sylvie, or the Benson man. 'Sylvie disappeared to France, and the arch-hypocrite Benson took the witness stand against me. Christ, can you stomach it? It was his text Sylvie had recorded, and having got his foul lies across on the media, he had the gall to stand up in court and say it was all my doing. He actually demanded damages too. Didn't get any though, which is why they put me in prison. No, Paul, I have no love for Swiss law, Swiss police or Swiss prisons. Perhaps you understand better how I felt flying handcuffed in a Swissair jet. Is it far now?'

It wasn't, but Bex airfield is out in the wilds, and the weather was so bad I took a wrong turning. We ended up on a track on the banks of the Rhône, the current swirling huge quantities of silt-grey water down to the Lake. It took me half an hour to extricate myself from the backwoods of the Rhône valley, and it was past ten when we drew up outside Bex club house.

Some forty yards away from the buildings I was forced to stop behind the red and blue flashing lights of a police patrol car that was blocking the narrow track. In front of it was a yellow PTT Telephone company van, and beyond that a brown Peugeot saloon so badly bogged down in freshly fallen snow that they'd had to fetch a petrol-engined snow plough from the air club buildings to dig it out. I could see the distinctive orange Police issue hi-viz clothing on the man wielding the plough, everybody else had more sense than to stand about outside their vehicles in the blizzarding winds. A curtain of powdered snow was lifting from the white expanse that was the airstrip, and already ice was obstructing the view through the car windows like a gauze mesh.

I left the car and approached the police patrol car in front. The driver opened the back door to offer me some protection from the wind whipping around my ankles.

'You the forensic blokes?' he asked, then, catching sight of my uniform through the open greatcoat, apologised. 'Sorry sir, you must be Deputy de Savigny? Thought you were from Martigny forensic, we were told they had a car coming out. What's going on, sir?'

'I was going to ask you that. You got the message from Cointrin then?' I noticed he was alone. 'That's your co-driver?' I gestured to the figure steering the snow-plough, man and machine dwarfed by the intensity of the snow storm swirling around them. He grinned.

'Drew lots, didn't we? One of us had to lose. Cointrin police, hm? I didn't know there was a police station at Cointrin, tell the truth. Can I ask what we're looking for?'

'Information.' I wasn't sure that he wasn't another of the Vinet brigade, that last comment of his had made me wonder.

'About?'

'Man called Scholl. You never heard of him, I suppose?'

'I do watch the news sir. That'll be the maniac that tried to ram a Swissair DC 9 inbound from Moscow, no?' He wasn't Sherlock Holmes, I decided, the clicks as he connected thoughts were painfully audible. 'And if Cointrin Police want "Information" about a man called Scholl, and if they're looking for it at Bex airfield, I guess it's a safe bet he landed or took off here some time.'

'That's about it.' I agreed. 'What's with the Telephone van? And whose is the Peugeot up front?'

'The PTT van was my idea.' he said, trying unsuccessfully to sound modest. 'There's a large club membership, though you won't see many of them in this weather.' he interjected. 'Because of that, they have a taxometer that shows when every telephone call is made, the day and the hour, and how much it cost. I didn't know what we were going to be looking for, but I thought it might be useful to know when the telephone was last used, and who by. A penny-pinching sort of mentality, though, wouldn't you say, sir?' I didn't say.

'And the Peugeot.'

'Not my idea, sir.' His face clouded with disapproval. 'We couldn't just bust the door down, so the Inspector tried to locate one of the Club Committee to let us in. As it's a working day, he didn't have much luck. The Peugeot belongs to Mr. Aeschbach. Mr. Aeschbach is a bank manager.'

His tone of voice spoke volumes about what he thought of Aeschbach.

'And what's he doing here?'

'Rather you judged that for yourself, sir, begging your pardon.' I wondered what he'd got against the Peugeot driver. Perhaps Aeschbach had refused the constable an overdraft. At that moment, the orange-coated officer with the snow-plough gave a signal and I retreated to my own car as the convoy got under way and we drove on to the buildings.

I quickly understood his reservations about Urs Aeschbach. The man was a toady little creature, with an immaculately trimmed little beard and moustache to match. On the Clubhouse Committee he was a nobody, he had part ownership of a Robin based at Bex, and the combination of these two factors made him nauseatingly self-important.

Bex airfield Clubhouse is really a rambling collection of ill-designed and shoddily constructed wooden buildings. Even the heavy covering of snow still left them unromantic in the extreme. But as long as Aeschbach had the key in his hand, this was the Ice Palace to end all Palaces. He wiped the snow from his boots with ostentatious care and unlocked the battered door with the reverence of a minor banker opening a safe deposit box, which is what his normal work consisted of. He started tut-tutting within seconds of crossing the threshold, we had to send him back to his car in the end, he hadn't a clue about not messing up finger prints or forensic investigations.

The place was bitterly cold, the temperature way below freezing in the unheated building, and it stank. We found the cause of the stench in the main club-room, a pile of rotting food, cheese mainly, on a table beside the sofa where Scholl, presumably it was he, had spent the Thursday night. I didn't think there could be that many vagrants who elected to spend their nights in Bex club-house. There were clothes too, and one of the first things I came across in the pockets was a crumpled Friedrichshafen Car Park ticket. Scholl, without a doubt.

'What has been going on here?' Aeschbach was still fussing around uselessly, getting under our feet.

'That is what we have come to find out, sir.' I was politely patient.

'It is most irregular. Most.' I had known he would say something pointless like that, sooner or later. I agreed it was most irregular, and would he please stop touching everything, as the forensic team had not yet arrived and I didn't want them accusing him of crimes he hadn't committed. He stared at me blankly.

'Crimes? I? I have committed no... Oh.' Understanding finally dawned. 'You mean fingerprints?' I assured him I meant fingerprints, and he gave a little effeminate laugh then and sat down in a corner like a scolded school boy. It wasn't until later that he had come over all bossy and we had to send him outside.

We spent four hours at Bex altogether, we got to interview the farmer who had hired out his hangar to Scholl, a bandy-legged little man with bright blue eyes almost hidden in wizened folds of skin, and we had the whole place finger-printed. I'd brought with me copies of the deceased man's prints from Geneva, and left them for comparison at Martigny forensic department. Then we had checked out the telephone, and it was here that I had to call on the insupportable Aeschbach for help.

'Who uses the airfield in February?' I had asked him, 'Anybody?'

'In weather like this,' he assured me, 'nobody.'

'But someone has been.' I pointed out. 'And recently. Living here.' He began burbling again then about it being unacceptably irregular for people to live in the Clubhouse, and I had to cut him short. 'What I'm getting at,' I said, 'is this: who would have been likely to use the telephone here, in the last two weeks, say?' He had consulted a wall-calendar then, eventually coming up after much humming and hawing with the answer:

'Nobody, I think.' I thanked him and it was soon after that that we had to discourage his meddling by getting rid of him. The telephone was the only lead I had, but it was a clincher for me and my theories. Scholl had made call after call - the prints we found on the handset were indubitably his, and there were no others, implying that some cleaner had done a thorough job before Scholl had moved in. In that respect, Aeschbach was right, nobody had used the phone. Except Scholl. The taxometer showed he had made upwards of seven hundred francs worth of calls in five days. It was this that had caused bank manager Aeschbach to have an almost apoplectic fit.

Of course, there was no way of knowing who Scholl had called, or where. But the real break was the call he had made at just after six in the morning of Friday, February 13th. Who had he been calling, and had he been confirming some message from an incoming call? Such as from Moscow, or even from Swisscontrol in Geneva? A twenty centime call probably made it local. It was that call alone that made the visit to Bex worthwhile for me, everything else that day could have been done by any half-competent constable. In fact, it was.

Furthermore, with the range Scholl's aircraft had, he could have made it to Zürich, I thought, with time and to spare. Had he received a call, telling him to fly to Zürich to down 493, and only been contacted en route to head for Geneva instead? I recalled that my Telex from Zürich had come in soon after five, the runway had been closed for an hour already by six o'clock... It wasn't until the next day that I discovered the Curtiss wouldn't have had the range or the speed to make it to Zürich and then the lengthy flight over the Matterhorn and France, and thus the whole theory was flawed.

The two constables had gone by now, and I left a very competent looking forensic team in control, asking them to have Scholl's things from the Club-house stored at Martigny until we had more news of his funeral and any family.

Family? God, this was something else I hadn't even started to follow up. I remembered in Friedrichshafen having seen some correspondence - I groaned inwardly, not relishing the prospect of going there again, and very far from certain that the Commissioner would authorise the fare for a second visit. Perhaps the West German police... they had been very helpful the previous day. But it was one more distraction. I heard again the Commissioner's high-pitched anger : "I knew you were a clown..."

'Now what?' Lakey was back at the nail-biting. 'Back to the Chalet?'

'To Cointrin, first. I have to follow up some things.' I glanced at my watch. Half past two. 'Why?' He shrugged.

'I keep thinking of Sigrid, there in England. God knows, I saw enough of their techniques on the train. What kind of follow-up treatment they'll be putting her through in that "Medina" place, I...' He swallowed.

'This is confidential.' I said in a low voice. I had lived long enough alone with my theory, and also I was trying to give him hope. I didn't know I was putting a rope round my neck and tying the knot on my career. 'But you have a right to know.'

I told him briefly of my conviction that Suri had called up Scholl and made him fool around on the approach circuit as 493 was coming in to land. He stood rock-still for what seemed an age when I'd finished outlining the theory.

'Well?' I demanded, 'what do you think? Is it possible? Were you important enough to Suri for him...' He interrupted me then.

'What do I think? I think three things. First of all, I think the idea's stark staring mad, as mad as Scholl would have to have been to even dream of doing it. Except, he did do it, didn't he, which is why maybe it's just conceivable...

'Secondly, I think that if by some miracle you're right, we need a good lawyer drafting the charges today, this afternoon. And thirdly, I think that if you're wrong, which God forbid is equally conceivable, then I shan't see Sigrid again. Ever.' He examined his hands again, like he had before asking for a piano.

'Thanks a lot.' I was morose. I hadn't wanted to tell him of my idea, he'd forced me into it as a way of encouraging him. The effect was, if anything, the reverse. He had discouraged me.

He didn't speak a word all the way back to Cointrin, an hour's drive. I parked right beside the ATC Tower, and left him once again in the basement recreation room. As I waited for the lift to the top floor where I hoped to find Oron he was slamming away at the Funeral march like the Day of Judgment was just around the corner.

Chapter Sixteen

Oron had been on early shift, and had gone by the time I reached the Tower Controllers' floor, but he'd put out the things I'd asked for. There were airways maps and ATC charts I would need to work out where Scholl had been geographically speaking, and not only in the unreal three-dimensional world of latitude, longitude and altitude. There was a note, too. Apparently Fonjallaz had been asking to see me again, and had made a tentative rendezvous for five o' clock at Police Offices. I didn't want to see anyone in my office, but I calculated that the Commissioner would probably have gone home by then. I tried telephoning the Swissair co-ordinator's office. No joy there, Fonjallaz was piloting the afternoon flight back from Munich.

Two hours to wait. I stashed the charts and documents Oron had left for me in the car, and collected Lakey from the basement. The vision of another run-in with the Commissioner was almost enough to put me off going over to my office, and I wasn't sure how he would react to seeing me still with Lakey. But in the end I went anyway. Basically, I wasn't prepared to be intimidated from my own office by some butcher-faced bully boy. But I very nearly was.

My desk was again littered with an assortment of documents and more of Scholl's bits and pieces from the crashed Curtiss. Vinet was doing his two-fingered typing act at Reception.

'You're back, are you?' he grunted, studying my face with a sly kind of look I didn't enjoy. 'Find anything at Bex?'

'Yes. The Commissioner in, is he?'

'Gone to a conference at Eaux Vives. You wanted him?' he sounded surprised, and when I said no, I didn't, he smiled meaningfully and went on with his typing.

We spent the intervening hours continuing with the identifying, logging and tagging of the newly retrieved belongings, Lakey seemed happier having something to do. He was writing a label when he stopped suddenly and looked up.

'I was thinking about what you said. About Suri and Scholl.' I got up and closed the door through to Reception.

'What about it?'

'What kind of proof do you have? I said we ought to get a lawyer on to it, drawing up the charge. What charge, Paul?'

I tied the knot firmly on the label I was attaching to a torn and empty wallet before answering.

'That's what I've got to find out.' I glanced at the wall clock. I had twenty-four hours left in which to do the impossible. Unless...

'But the charge... Would it be an Interpol case? Would it mean us flying to Britain, to face it out with Suri?'

He was way ahead of me, I hadn't thought it through to that kind of stage yet. Yet? What was it he had said, "so that you ensure you never have to do anything...". Was he right? Did I really prevaricate with inaction to avoid facing the fact that in reality there was no possible action?

'How do you bring a charge against a man in another country?' he wanted to know. 'Won't you need some kind of irrefutable proof that... that I was such a threat to Suri after Sigrid's kidnapping as to have forced him to... Hell, Paul, we'd need the Soviet authorities in on that as well. You can't really believe, I can't believe that even Suri has the nerve to... Or maybe he has at that.' He was talking to himself, and now he stood up, his left hand darting to his mouth as he sought out a piece of raw nail. 'Maybe he has. Maybe he damned well has... Not the way you put it, not mass murder, that's...' He looked at me deprecatingly, 'that is a bit far-fetched. But you remember that filthy phone call the other morning? If they can do that sort of thing, who's to say they aren't up to intimidating people in bigger ways as well?' He paused. 'Those phone calls from Bex? Is there no way you can trace them?'

He hadn't got as far as working out that Scholl would have had to have a contact at Swisscontrol. God the irony of that thought now, the bitter, stomach-churning irony of it. Of course Scholl had had a contact at ATC, he had been Dominique Dantin's lover, dammit, but I only found that out twenty-four hours later, and by then I had turned in the report to Police H.Q. at Cointrin, and the damage was irrevocably done. But the hideous irony of it, that he had indeed known someone at Air Traffic Control. But someone who could not have passed him any information, for she had died just hours before he had.

'You can see why I've had this thing on my mind.' I said. Compared to Lakey, I must have sounded comparatively dispassionate.

'And I accused you of not doing...' There was contrition in his voice. 'I think I owe you an apology.'

'You raised the question of what charge? A lawyer?' I was musing on this, because I didn't have an answer. 'Extradition is one way, but that might take months. You have a British passport?' I confirmed. He nodded. 'Because that might just work... What's Miss Sorensen's? Swedish?' Another nod. 'Hm. Pity. It's many years since I was in London. Sweden House would be the place to start, I fancy. Or the Embassy... same thing, really.' I was still musing aloud. Vinet opened the door with what sounded like his foot.

'Telephone for you.' As he spoke, the extension buzzed on my desk.

113

'de Savigny.' It was Fonjallaz; the flight was diverting to Berne with a passenger suffering a suspected heart attack. He would have to postpone the planned meeting. I was staggered he'd found the time to call and tell me, it isn't every day a pilot has to make for the nearest airfield for similar reasons. But then I hadn't got to know the kind of man Fonjallaz was at that time. I only really got to know him after I'd resigned. And that was three days away.

'We might as well go.' I stood up, and wondered whether to take Scholl's additional bits and pieces home with me. The way my mind was running, and with Dominique's funeral scheduled for next morning, and then the agreement to go over her affairs after that, I was planning to study the flight recorder and voice tapes that evening, and work through the night on my Report, if need be. That way I could turn it in to the Commissioner well ahead of his deadline. And now, it was something that Lakey had said, I knew what I was going to do with that report. I was going to give Suri a hiding by putting out a warrant for his arrest, sending the British police, Swedish diplomats too I hoped, to his doorstep. I was going to fabricate the evidence against him. It never occurred to me that my own Commissioner of Police might block the action. It had occurred to Oron the morning I had showed him the Moscow Telex, but Simona had been right when she had said I was ingenuous. God knows, I was learning a lot about myself those days, but I had still an awful lot to learn. The operative word, I think, is indeed "awful".

I jumped with what could only be called a guilty start, Vinet thrust the door open again, it was as if he had read my thoughts. Lakey stared at me strangely, but Vinet appeared not to notice anything untoward.

'This just came through. I've put a photocopy on file.' I glanced at the flimsy. It was from the Zürich offices of Amex, rescinding Lakey's arrest warrant for default on debt. He glanced at Lakey - to my knowledge it was only the second time Vinet had spoken to him. 'Congratulations, Mister Lakey.' He didn't sound as if he meant it, he sounded vicious. 'You're a free man again. Make the most of it.' With a sour look at me, he closed the door again.

'Come on.' I said. 'These damned Sergeants make me...'

'Does he always talk to you like that?' Lakey looked surprised. I didn't answer that, and we left for the Chalet then, carrying the bulky belongings between us. We had reached the car before he spoke again. 'So it's Interpol, and an arrest warrant, is it? For Suri?'

'It's Interpol.' I agreed. 'And then we'll see.' He turned to face me then, his back to the car.

'We'd better.' He spoke very quietly, and I knew then that if we didn't get results from Interpol and British CID very quickly, he would take the law into his own hands. All it would have required from me was the foresight to have impounded his passport when he first arrived. But I hadn't. And by now my mind was wholly on the impossible, the creation of evidence that would bring down Suri. I had never done such a thing in my life, and I had never known anyone do it. God knows, I wasn't much of a policeman at the best of times: "... you're no earthly good at it." as Simona had put it. What, then, I wondered bitterly, would I be like as a crooked policeman?

Lakey punished the piano cruelly that evening, I recall thinking that his attack on Chopin was as brutal as mine on the truth.

I had played the voice recorder tape to start with, noting Scholl's repeated and meaningless strings of expletives. I wondered at first whether these weren't the result of intolerable stress in a Kami-kaze pilot flying to his death on orders from some... what was the word I had used... God-head. We know now, of course, it was simply the ramblings of an unhinged mind.

But there was nothing on the hour-long tape to reveal any motive, and I think it was that that unnerved me. I had been banking on hearing the name Suri somewhere on there. Nothing. Just rambling repeated chords of foul language, interspersed with radio communications.

I turned then to the flight recorder analysis, this was the kind of thing Simona was very used to reading. I wondered where she was, what she was doing this evening, and for a little while I sat and allowed the distractions of the previous weekend, my newly arranged living quarters, and her scent hanging in the woollen pullover I was wearing to work their charm. It was with an effort that I dragged myself back to the job in hand. Suri, Interpol, the British Home Office and an imminent charge. I would have to be damnably clever.

Using the charts and ATC airways maps I plotted and followed Scholl's course that day. I even imagined for a moment that perhaps he hadn't been contacted by telephone before leaving Bex, but had been passed a visual signal while overflying Montreux at 1,000 feet. The idea was ludicrous, of course, and when I thought of what the Commissioner would say to that...

What was depressing me most of all was that there was nothing from the supposed accomplice at Swisscontrol to tell him when to turn in towards Cointrin. Everything in my latest theory had hinged upon such collusion, but the voice recorder was devoid of any such incriminating evidence. This was damnable. But I didn't give up.

After the flight recorder and map-work I took a break. Lakey and I discussed briefly where this left matters. He was lugubrious, he thought I was going to have to relinquish the theory, and let the Interpol warrant drop. He didn't appreciate what Interpol is, or how it functions. It is not a police force with rights to bring charges at whim. It is first and foremost an information gathering and dissemination service. But if we had had the dossiers of Interpol on our side, then a charge through the Strasbourg Court...

But he didn't appreciate how these things can drag on and on, sometimes for years, nor the expense involved. The discussion we had then did, however, affect the outcome of events in two profound ways. Although I didn't know it then, that was the moment he gave up all hope of my achieving anything by way of redeeming Sigrid Sorensen from "Medina", and so decided to abscond. And the second result was that I decided to start to write the report immediately. I knew it would take several hours, perhaps most of the night, and I was through with pussyfooting around on fruitless enquiries. Frédérique called round soon after, ostensibly to renew the invitation to the funeral next morning, but in reality to see how Lakey was. He was visibly in a dreadful state again by then, and she invited him out for a drink at some country restaurant, despite the appalling weather. It seemed tactless to advise her to drive carefully, and so it was I was able to get down to the report in peace and quiet. And to my wholly inexcusable inventions.

Chapter Seventeen

There was a violent storm blowing, the wind was howling ferociously around the old wooden building, and now and then gale-force gusts caused the whole structure to tremble. I had left the shutters open, and the falling snow was so dense that the blackness of the night was transformed into a shimmering curtain reflecting the artificial light falling through the panes.

My mind was made up now, and I had to fight the temptation to break open the despised bottle of Scotch to help inspiration along. How to go about it was the problem. I wasn't stupid enough to insert a blatant and outright forgery into the file, something that could be proved as a fake within a few minutes. No, I had in mind "seeding" the report with just sufficient pointers to support my theory, sufficiently to get action stirring against Suri. And then Lakey, and Sigrid Sorensen would have to take their chances, and let Natural Justice take its course. I had lost all faith in the Christian version of justice. Which I suppose was why I was taking the law into my own hands, an appalling admission for any police officer. But how to do it?

I recalled tagging some bank statements that had been found in the wreckage of the Curtiss, and there were some cheque book stubs as well. I had wondered where Scholl got all his money from, there was no sign of him having worked anywhere. Flying yes. Work, no.

Something here didn't add up. Flying is not a cheap pastime, and Scholl wasn't an occasional flyer, he flew regularly and extensively. So where had the money come from?

The South American entries on the bank statements were frequent, and sizeable. There were other transfers to and from West Germany as well. Some looked small enough to be payments of interest on investments, others were definitely large capital transfers. But on whose account, and where was the money coming from?

I did some quick arithmetic and was staggered at the total I came up with. Over two years, Scholl's accounts showed receipts of over four hundred thousand francs annually. Five times my salary. The purchase of the aircraft, which was documented separately, had been paid for in cash, not bank transfer, so with separate funds. And Scholl hadn't done a day's work all that time. So how had he earned the money? It was at this point that a germ of an idea began to worm its way through from the back of my mind to consciousness.

I had never heard of anyone spending lavishly every year without earning a centime of it who wasn't involved in something pretty shady. The idea gave a little wriggle and inched forward. The South American connection gave me to think there could be a drugs involvement, and the mobility of a man with his own aircraft supported this. But were there other possibilities? I was looking, after all, for a connection between Scholl and Suri, and I was ready by now to give any such connection a helping hand.

But what link could there conceivably have been? What incredible hold could Suri have had on Scholl that would pressure the man into flying head-on into a landing airliner? I was more inclined by now to Lakey's way of thinking, that it had been a stunt to scare Lakey witless and demonstrate Suri's omnipotence, I had more or less given up the crazy notion that Scholl would have been prepared to die for Suri. I had never heard of anyone carrying their devotion that far. But the question remained, what would have made Scholl do it? Other than... more and more money.

The creepy crawly notion that had been wriggling around in the darker corners of my mind came worming out into the open. A sudden deluge of snow against the window panes coincided with the fiercest gust of wind I had ever known, the whole building seemed to shake from the foundations upwards, and I had to go upstairs and check the sky light for damage. When I came back, I didn't return to the desk at once but started pulling folders from the shelves of the office. Dossiers sent to me by all those who Suri and others had robbed. Robbed of their own.

It took me a while to find what I was looking for. The paper was yellowed with age and from being stored in a smoker's office, but I thought that might actually lend some veracity to the criminal notion I had come up with. I was going to try to forge some correspondence between the Suri Sect and Scholl, and seed it in the final report on Scholl's death as if it had been found in the wreckage.

I forget who it was had sent me the Suri notepaper, they'd purloined it from the Sect's West German base in Bavaria as some kind of proof that ALBATROSS was not the charitable organisation it claimed to be when demanding tax exemptions, something like that. It had been Scholl's West German passport that had nudged me in that direction. Now all I had to do was to fit together a good enough reason for Suri to have engaged Scholl on sufficiently nefarious or sufficiently frequent business to have paid him handsomely - the one thing that was not in doubt about Suri was that he was a multi-millionaire, and could afford to fund someone like Scholl with the kind of sums on the bank statements. But for doing what?

It was the photograph of Charlotte that spurred me on then, in more ways than one. It was seeing her faded enlargement on the wall, her little girl's face grinning amiably, but the voice I heard was the tone she had used on her mother after Suri's crowd had started working on her, the screams, the daily invective. Suri deserved whatever he got. And it was the total and untraceable disappearance of Charlotte that gave me the ammunition I was looking for. What else would Scholl have done for Suri with his flying skills other than move people illegitimately from country to country? It was so obvious that I half laughed aloud at the simplicity of the affair. But an inner sense of caution held me back, I tested the wording of the forged letters several times before I was happy with the content and signatories' names and status. Then I went to the old Geneva Police Department typewriter and, using the Suri notepaper, carefully dated and typed three documents that I thought would fit the bill. If typing falsified evidence on a police typewriter didn't churn me up, signing Suri's name did, copying the neat script of his own handwriting in one case from some correspondence in one of the dossiers.

It was well past midnight, and some sudden reaction, to the late hour, or to what was happening to me, revulsed me. I got up and paced the length of my house then, upstairs and down again, seeking some justification for what I was doing. There was a merciless quality about the night, and the storm, the wind and the snow, and my intentions, something Shakespeare would have understood very well.

I wondered what would happen if Simona were to come back unexpectedly at that moment, and I knew the shame of what I was doing would probably render all of me "no earthly good", and not just the policeman in me.

Feeling a peculiar unemotional emptiness inside, I sat down again and started to piece together how to "seed" the dossier with the three documents that I intended should provoke international legal action and present Suri with a real headache.

I correlated the dates of some of the larger movements of funds to Scholl's account, and made notes on the relationship I wanted to draw between Suri's alleged requirements of Scholl as outlined in the forged letters and the payments that appeared to have followed. There was no irrefutable proof of gross illegality in those letters, nor in the payments, but it wasn't direct proof I was aiming for. Anything too concrete could too readily be refuted. If, as it seemed, there was a growing international disapproval of Suri, this would be ample to get things moving in the courts, even at a low level of activity. I didn't think I dared hope to achieve more than that.

Leaving the prepared documents on the desktop, I went upstairs again, and while I was in the bathroom I heard the slam of the front door. Lakey was back. When I returned to the office, he was standing, staring curiously at the three letters on the ALBATROSS headed notepaper. Intrigued, his eye moved from the letters to the notes I had scribbled on the pad beside the typewriter.

'This is my office.' It was a daft thing to say, for he'd read the damned letters by this time and I was merely making things worse by standing on some non-existent dignity. He picked up the top letter, read it again, then turned to me, holding it out to me.

'You can't do this.' There was a horrified look on his face, such pure revulsion as I had never seen in any man. But I had felt it only minutes previously. He was staring at me intently. 'This... this is pure invention. For God's sake, Paul, you're a policeman...'

'No-one else seems to think so.' I pressed my fists to my temples as a strange kind of painless sensation shot through my head. 'Besides, you want to get to Suri, don't you? I mean, let me get this straight, I am doing this for you, aren't I?'

He gazed at me, appalled.

'For me? This? Are you out of your mind? For God's sake,' his voice was a whisper in the storm and the night, 'this Scholl man might be entirely innocent, has that occurred to you? Dammit, man, supposing he was trying to make a crash landing, you said something about heavy icing on the wings, didn't you? My God.' he was pacing up and down in the confined space now, waving the letter in the air.

'A crash landing? Sure he made a "crash landing", five thousand feet up on the Jura.' I was brutally trying to defend the indefensible. 'Don't be so stupid, Ben. You were flying in 493 when Fonjallaz had to take avoiding action, so you know better than anyone...'

'Yes, I know better than anyone.' There was an odd hollowness, a strange resignation in his voice but I was too angry to identify it. 'And I know something else, that this is obscene, Paul.' He was shouting now. 'Christ, you don't really know the first thing about Scholl, whether he maybe has a wife who doesn't even know he's dead yet, perhaps? Or a family in... in South America or Germany or somewhere?' He pointed to the belongings we had labelled and logged together. 'If you think this is going... you must be out of your mind.' he repeated softly. He turned then and went into the living room, poured two stiff drinks, and handed me one. 'I want nothing to do with it.' He was still holding the letter in his hand and still pacing he read it again, a third time, his voice incredulous. 'I can't believe that you're really doing this...'

'I've done it.' My voice was brittle. He had stopped beside the window, and was staring out into the falling snow. 'Dammit, Lakey, only yesterday, in this very room, you were screaming blue murder because I didn't do anything. Well, now I have, now I've done something. Something for you, and for Sigrid and for Charlotte and all the poor buggers documented in my dusty files, as you called them...' My voice tailed away as I saw the look in his face.

'Yes. You've done it. My God, you've done it. Well, I want nothing to do with it, Paul. You hear me? Nothing. If you go ahead with this thing, you can count me out of... God's sake, I've been there, remember?'

I didn't understand.

'Been where? What are you on about?' Angrily I tried to snatch the letter back from him, and as he wouldn't let go, it tore down the middle, leaving us holding a half each like two sword fighters practising with safety foils.

'I've been there. I've stood there, in the dock. Face to face with perjury and false witness.' he replied. There was an icy glint in his blue eyes, and an insuperable bitterness in his voice. With a flick of his wrist he tossed the torn letter on the log fire and watched it catch light, the licking flames orange and blue. 'Six months in prison because of it. I wouldn't wish that on anyone, not my worst enemy. Which Suri is.' he added with that strange dry laugh of his. 'But Scholl, he wasn't my enemy...'

'Scholl is dead.' My voice was cracked, it didn't sound like my voice at all.

'And the truth dies with him, is that it? Is that what you're saying? How very convenient.' He turned his back on me in disgust then. 'Well, dead or not, and whoever Scholl was, I want nothing to do with this hare-brained scheme of yours.' He glanced at the telephone, and licked his lips very briefly. I thought then he was going to call the police station and have them send out a car to take me in. But he thought better of it and returned to the sideboard and replenished his glass. He held out the bottle to me, a strangely sympathetic gesture, I shook my head. At the same instant the bloody cuckoo stuck its head out of the wooden clock casing and chirped once and the telephone started ringing.

I took the call upstairs in the bedroom. I guessed it could only be Simona at that time of the night, and I was in no mood to talk to her in front of Lakey. Even as I climbed the stairs though, I felt a peculiarly light-headed sensation of relief, of anxiety dismissed. In my heart I knew I was more than glad that Lakey had come back and caught me at the puerile forgery. For that was what it had been. Only hours previously I had wondered what I would be like as a crooked policeman. There was a stupendous irony that I was even worse at that kind of thing than at my normal work...

Simona's cheerful voice greeted me, entirely unaware of the mess I was making of the Scholl case, my career and my life.

'*Buona sera, carissimo!*' Her voice was tender, the Italian very romantic, and it sounded as if she were telephoning from a bathtub, there was a lot of splashing and a noise like a tap running. I didn't think the hotels in a small place like Saanen ran to telephones in the bathrooms, and said so.

'No, I'm back at my apartment, in Berne.' she explained. I hadn't known she had an apartment in Berne, but knowing me as well as she did, and fearing my "sensitivity" would jump to the wrong conclusion, she went on before I could get a word in. 'I was hoping to take the MOB down to Montreux and pick up a connection to Rolle tonight, but things are so bad out here in the Oberland, the MOB stopped running by six o'clock, and they don't think there'll be any trains tomorrow until the afternoon.'

The Montreux-Oberland-Bernois was a narrow-gauge railway linking the Oberland with the Riviera and Montreux. If they stopped running, then conditions had to be unbelievably bad in the mountains.

'You did the right thing.' I said, and meant it. I couldn't imagine what I would have done if she had made the discovery Lakey had just made.

'How's that Scholl report coming along?' she wanted to know.

'Tricky.' I kept the answer brief.

'The Commissioner, hm?' She obviously knew more about the set-up at Cointrin than I had until the previous day. 'Was he very bad?'

'Unfriendly would be an understatement.'

'He didn't look too pleased on Monday, at the Enquiry.' I could hear the splashing of soap suds again. She sighed, and I thought for a terrible moment that she had already had enough of the "clown" and wanted out. But it wasn't that. She giggled. 'You really did give him some awful lines to read.' There was a long pause. Then: 'I wish you were here,' she said, splashing water against the wall, by the sound of it. Her voice was very soft.

'Well I'm not.' I said. She told me afterwards, a long time after, that even before she had called she had somehow sensed something was wrong and had to hold back from quizzing me there and then about what, exactly. 'But I wish I was, as well.'

'Tomorrow...' She said it faintly, and I heard her giggle as she started to blow bubbles, that's what it sounded like, a guggling noise that I found startlingly erotic. Which was exactly what she intended.

My God, she had done it again. This woman could change a man's mood at a touch, from a hundred miles away, with just a few words on the telephone. We exchanged a few more noises, I forget what, and when I went downstairs it was as if I had not yet started on the Scholl report, the inventions I had toyed with were a distant dream and to make things even better, there was a full glass of Cognac waiting for me.

Lakey was in the armchair by the fire again, watching the tell-tale orange and blue forked flames as the ALBATROSS note-paper went up in smoke.

'What now?' He looked haggard and sounded weary. It wasn't until a long time afterwards that I learned he'd spent the evening making his plans for his disappearance next day, and that the only thing he had had on his mind that night until he had discovered my lunatic conspiracy had been how he was going to get across the country to Müstair in some of the worst weather of the decade.

'You burned all of them? The jottings too?' I wanted to be sure he hadn't kept some for future use, God knows I am ingenuous like Simona said, but not completely blind. A smile crossed his tired features and he stared at me with an artificially bland innocence.

'Burned what, Paul? Jottings, what jottings? I saw no jottings...'

I grinned. He was all right.

'Pretty poor guest I'd be,' he muttered, draining his glass, 'burning my host's jottings, wouldn't you say? Can I have another drink?'

'Pretty poor host, I'd be, to say no.' The grin flashed across his face.

'All action is sin, someone once said.' He looked meaningfully at the fire. 'Who's to say? What time's the funeral?'

Chapter Eighteen

The next morning the snow lay deep outside, but the wind had dropped. Occasional pale patches of blue sky opened and then closed over again, framed by the billowing clouds that hung low over the Jura, strange and unearthly relics of the storm.

Even rising at dawn, as we did, I had had to revise my plans for that damned report, and for its content. My latest schedule had me at the funeral by ten thirty, after that at Dominique's house for an hour, then home at the latest by two o'clock. There I intended to compose the Final Report, load the Mitsubishi with all the stuff I'd brought home from the airport, and deliver the whole lot just before end of shift at Cointrin. Then back up to the Chalet, and Simona... and four days' leave.

But the first thing we had to do was to dig out the car and clear the drive as far as the road, and that was an hour's work between the two of us. To give him his due, Lakey was no slouch and put his back into the wet and chilly work of clearing snow. I know now, of course, that he was looking forward to imminent liberty, money, a car, and his journey across the length of the country to his home in Müstair, which in large part explains why he set to with a will.

The actual funeral, in an unheated stone church off the village square, was a frigid and unmoving affair, very Calvinist, and short on anything meaningful by way of religious content or faith. Mrs. Dantin and Frédérique sat in isolation in the front pew, and a man I guessed to be the father remained at the very back of the church. Whether they had met or spoken before the service or not, I don't know, but by the time the funeral dragged to a chilly close, I saw he had gone. Oron sat behind Frédérique, and there were few enough other mourners to be counted on one hand. This could have been the result of the weather, the country roads were in a very bad state, the snow ploughs all fully occupied on the Route Nationale and the motorway, it would be hours before they were free to plough the back lanes. But Oron had made it. I still didn't know then that he had had a thing going for Dominique, which was perhaps why he had made the effort to be present despite the appalling weather conditions.

Outside the church, in a freezing wind and under a grey overcast sky, the Pastor had hastily shaken a few hands before making a rapid and I thought unseemly departure. I only learned later that his wife had been rushed to hospital by helicopter the previous night with pneumonia, and the last thing he had wanted to do was to officiate at the funeral of a person who, according to a tearful Mrs. Dantin, had not set foot in any church for years. But Mrs. Dantin had brought pressure to bear, she didn't hold with the modern vogue of cremation, and had managed to get her daughter into the village cemetery. The way she talked about it sounded more like getting her daughter a place in the local secondary college.

Oron had left immediately after the service, acknowledging us with a brief wave only before driving off. Nobody had had the least desire then to go over to Dominique's and anyway, it was far from certain we wouldn't have to plough the track from the road to her house, and it was with some relief that I heard Frédérique suggest we should all go back to her mother's for hot drinks and some lunch. I was able to excuse myself from that, God knew I needed the time to write that damned report, and get it to Cointrin by five. So once again we postponed the tedious and not unemotional task of going over Dominique's affairs. And thus once again we postponed discovering the only concrete facts within five hundred miles to be learned about Thierry Scholl.

It would be entirely in line with my limited powers of observation for me to have overlooked some sign by Lakey at this point, a glance or a nod in Frédérique's direction, but I didn't. He had himself under tight rein that morning, he was all set for a long journey and he wasn't going to compromise it now by giving any clue to his intentions. So when Frédérique made a three point turn and drove away with Lakey and her mother as passengers, I didn't know that that was the last I was to see of Lakey for quite some time.

There was a strangely deserted air about the village square, normally by that hour there were skiers in Winter, parking their cars and heading for the ski lifts, and a few locals gathering at the village inn. Conditions were so bad, though, that anybody with any sense was staying indoors.

As I crossed the square to my car, one hand already fumbling in my greatcoat pocket for the car keys, I noticed a Toyota Land Cruiser, its roof thickly covered with snow, illegally parked in front of the Co-op across the square, with its engine running. In some countries this would signal an immediate police interest, the occupant suspected of planning a smash and grab or whatever. Not in Switzerland, though. Such things happened, but so rarely as for such a vehicle and its position not to arouse suspicion. And yet…

I couldn't work out at first what it was about vehicle or occupant - there was a single figure hunched behind the wheel - that had caught my attention. Then I had it. There was a CB radio antenna on the roof, and the occupant was at that moment talking into a hand-held microphone. On a sudden instinct, I crossed over to the parked vehicle and tapped on the door panel. The driver stared at me through the misty window, and then he lowered the pane an inch and glared at me through the gap. He still had the microphone in his hand, and was speaking even as he turned to look at me.

'... call you back in a moment. Samurai over and out.' He clicked off the microphone. 'Well? What do you want?' He spoke with the stretched and nasal vowels of the local Vaudois. I couldn't see much of him through the gap between the opaquely misted window and the door frame, only a glimpse of a weather-beaten face and an untrimmed sandy beard and moustache below two crinkled and wary close-set brown eyes.

'I wonder if I could ask you a few questions.' I didn't like his tone.

'Fuck off.'

In the movies they flick those damn warrant cards with an ease I'd never mastered. It took almost half a minute to extricate my wallet and then the warrant card and open it. I held it to the window.

'de Savigny, Deputy Comissioner, Geneva Police.' I pressed the card to the glass, shivering in the bitter air.

'Yeah? You can still fuck off.' A bleeper sounded in the van, he pressed a switch. 'Samurai... Hi, Alias. Hey guess what? I gotta flick on the pavement all the way from Geneva, an' he wants to ask me "some questions".' He mimicked me in a voice that sounded nothing like mine. I had a notepad out now and was taking down the number plate and make of the vehicle. He saw me through the snow-covered windscreen and I heard him drawl something more urgent to whoever Alias was. Then he was out of the vehicle and looming over me, an immense man, the worn leather jacket he wore barely big enough to encompass the great barrel of a chest. He looked like an all-in wrestler.

'You got a problem?' There was an anti-authoritarian arrogance about him that I'd come across many times before, if not recently. As the Commissioner had so painfully spelt out, they hadn't given me much of a workload the last few years. In fact, I thought, sizing up the man briefly, he was in his own way the civilian side of the coin to the Commissioner. Both bully-boys playing heavy in the rough and tumble world, with the difference that the Commissioner happened to wear a uniform and was paid by the State, whereas this oaf despised uniforms and the State.

'Yes. You.' I turned my back on him and walked around the vehicle, giving it an ostentatious once over. But there was nothing wrong with his vehicle.

'Well?' He was truculent, hands on hips and arms akimbo.

'You want me to book you, it'll be a pleasure.' I couldn't stand creatures like this, never had been able to. And I wasn't good at handling them either.

'Yeah? What for?' He leaned towards me aggressively.

'It is an offence to park a vehicle at the roadside with the engine running.' It was too, Swiss anti-pollution laws were very strict. There had been a famous case where a tourist had stopped in a lay-by for a rest, but left the engine running to power the air-conditioning. He had driven off two hundred francs poorer, the most expensive parking lot he had ever had.

'You gonna book me for that?' He reached through the door and switched off the motor. 'Go ahead. I'll plead innocent.'

I sighed. This wasn't the way I had intended the conversation to go.

'Can I ask you why you're parked here?'

He tapped his nose.

'Curiosity killed the...'

'For God's sake.' I cut in harshly. 'I don't want to book you, I want to ask you a few questions, that's all.'

'Ah.' He drew the leather jacket closer around him as the first snowflakes began to fall from a leaden sky. 'O.k.'

'The church.' I said. 'Is that why you're here?'

'What about the church?' He was suddenly guarded, and I knew I had guessed right. I had found the gardener.

'Mademoiselle Dantin, the funeral. You knew her?'

'Yeah.' He scratched his face thoughtfully. 'I knew her. Didn't get an invite to the funeral though, did I? But yeah, that's why I'm here. Representing the clan, so to speak.'

There had been a vogue for CB radios the past few years, with adults reverting to school children's code names and a whole radio jargon that they took pitifully seriously. Names like Samurai and Alias were typical of the genre.

'Clan? Mademoiselle Dantin was a CB-ist?'

'One of the best.' He looked sombre, and I glimpsed for a moment another side to the man. 'What's the police interest? No law against having a CB radio.'

'No. But there is against using one.' I looked at the increasingly heavy snow that was falling and then across the square to the local inn. 'Can I buy you a drink?'

'Me drink and drive?' He was back on the sarcastic tone. 'Officer, whatever are you saying...'

'I'm saying can I buy you a drink?' I clapped my hands against the cold. A strange look crossed his face.

'Deputy Commissioner, huh?'

'So?'

'I guess you can afford it. Okay. Do I leave the van here?'

I nodded.

'That way I can book you if you don't co-operate.'

'Hey man.' He raised his eyebrows exaggeratedly. 'That was almost funny.'

I can imagine that to the generation to which Frédérique belongs and Dominique belonged, the generation I never could fathom, such a man had some sort of crude rustic charm. There was certainly a fund of goodwill and warmth behind the cynical individualist exterior. He was modest too, it took a lot of persuasion to get him to admit that his interest in Dominique had been entirely platonic. I believed him implicitly, there was no duplicity about this character, despite his bravado, he just couldn't stand uniforms, or anyone that wore one, and said so unequivocally.

He had known Dominique for about eight months, but when I suggested he might have lived there he stared at me through the bushy eyebrows, then tugged at his beard and roared with laughter.

'Me, live at her place? Beauty'd have had more chance with the Beast. Christ, it was once in a blue moon I even had as much as a sandwich there. Besides, she had a boyfriend, and oh man, was he a tight-arsed little funny-boy, he couldn't stand the sight of me, and nor me him come to that.'

But when I'd asked about the boyfriend, he clammed up and I had to buy a second beer to get him talking again. The boyfriend had been so possessive - that was the way he put it - that he'd stopped going round for a while when he thought the boyfriend would be there. When he said he couldn't remember the boyfriend's name, I thought he was having me on, perhaps trying for a third beer, but it was true. Samurai - he asked me not to reveal his real name - was a man who kept life simple with a monumental distaste for curiosity and unnecessary complications, which, he said apologetically, was why he had resented my initial questions.

His interest in Dominique had started as a CB radio contact, what the CB-ists call a faceless voice, and when he'd finally tracked her down, and go to know her, the limit of his involvement was cutting wood from dead trees in the garden for her fire, and having occasional barbecues there with a few of the CB clan. Of the boyfriend he knew almost nothing. It had been a real *coup-de-foudre* for her, he said, a lightning affair that she had suddenly terminated, with a lot of smudged make-up the next few days. He had a colourful way of putting things.

'You were there this weekend, though.' I said. 'Madame Dantin...'

'Screwball woman.' He drained his beer in a single gulp then ran his hand through the tufts of his beard, wiping away the foam that had caught on the moustache. 'Then again, I guess she was upset...'

'All of that.' I agreed. 'When did you last see Dominique?'

'Hey.' His eyes had narrowed then. 'That's a copper's question. I don't remember.' he added, but I knew from the suddenly flat tone of voice that he was lying.

'How did you hear about the accident?' I tried a different tack.

'Din' you read the police report?' He looked surprised. 'It was me that found her, Chris'sake.' That explained why he hadn't wanted to say when he'd last seen her. What was it Martin Verre had said? "Took them hours to cut her remains free."

'...more's the pity.' He was still talking, but more in reminiscence now. 'I saw how bad the snow was that morning, last Friday, and I got up specially to go over and offer her a lift to the train at Rolle. Can manage most weather in the Toyota,' he waved at the Land Cruiser across the street. 'But a Golf... When I got to the house, she must just have left. Then when the phone rang I thought it might be her mother, so I answered, which I'd not normally have done.'

'And was it?'

'No. Some guy who rang off without a word. So I went after her, the way the snow was coming down that morning I think she was crazy to try to get to... Anyway.' He stopped then and I saw yet another side to this uncomplicated man, he really wished he'd been at the funeral proper, not just an observer from a steamed-up estate wagon.

I left him then, saying I'd be in touch about Dominique's key, and promising to explain to Madame Dantin. I didn't think he was the type to lift anything from Dominique's, and in any case, she'd given him the key. It wasn't for me to try and take it away from him. I didn't care to think how he would react if I tried. It was only days afterwards that I made the connection between Scholl's twenty-centime phone call from Bex, and Samurai's voice at the other end at Dominique's. Whoever coined the phrase "ignorance is bliss" didn't know what they were talking about.

Chapter Nineteen

The only thing that was "final" about my Final Report on Scholl's suicidal approach to Cointrin that Friday morning was my imminent demise. To say it was the best I could do given the circumstances is no real answer; that it was the first inquiry of any scope to come my way for several years, perhaps that's a better excuse, but as a defence still inadequate. *"Tout comprendre, c'est tout pardonner"*, Oron tried to console me with that. If you know all the facts you can forgive all the assumptions, he thought. The Commissioner didn't see it that way.

But when I got to the airport early that afternoon to type out the report and deposit the evidence and testimony, if you could call the sketchy collection of papers that I had "testimony", the police offices were deserted. This was unusual, except on the occasions when only one officer was rostered and then called away suddenly, as I had been on the Sunday to the shop-lifting business. By rights there should have been both Vinet and the Commissioner there. Not that I was in a hurry to see either of them.

I left the sealed plastic bags of labelled belongings beside my desk and crossed to the window, expecting to see Vinet's patrol car somewhere out on the apron or the tarmac. In fact there were two cars, way away, by one of the three Pavilions that house the Boarding Gates. I could make out Vinet's Sierra and the Commissioner's Audi, and one of the blue Peugeot wagons favoured by the Gendarmerie, all parked in a line in front of Gate 34. A number of supporting vehicles formed a half-circle around a Royal Jordanian Tristar. A black Mercedes limousine appeared, driving at speed towards the aircraft, and some way behind it a baggage train towing half a dozen luggage trolleys was pulling out from the main Terminal buildings.

I unhooked the radio from my belt and pressed the SPEAK button.

'Police One to Mobile. Come in Mobile.' I switched to RECEIVE, and caught the middle of a sentence, the Commissioner's high-pitched and irate voice:

'... that that clown de Savigny? Get him off the air, Sergeant, and tell him to...'

'We are maintaining radio silence, sir.' Vinet's voice, he was making a valiant effort to sound courteous. Only I didn't find it valiant. 'I think you had better get off the air.'

I cut the connection, and lifted the telephone to call the Gendarmerie over on the French side. The harsh unprofessionalism of the Commissioner had opened the wounds again.

'Gendarmerie?' The soft-spoken Gendarme was a woman, the majority of the French Gendarmes at Cointrin were women, there was no sexist nonsense over their side, unlike at Geneva Police. I gave my name and the safety-code that prevented just anybody calling up and impersonating the police.

'What's happening?' I wanted to know. 'At Gate 34, I mean.'

'I'm afraid this is an open line, sir, and I am not at liberty to answer you... in case the Press...' she murmured as an afterthought by way of explanation.

I tried the Tower next, asking for Le Comte, I knew he would have the answers. But he didn't. He was apologetic, discomfited at having to say nothing, but far too professional to risk his career and whatever else was at stake by obliging me as a friend with classified information over an open line. All this did nothing to improve my morale.

The direct telephone link from Geneva Central buzzed harshly, this was not an open line, and I answered it promptly.

'Eaux Vives Special Branch, Haegler.' It was one of those abrupt business-like voices. 'Who am I speaking to?'

I gave my name and rank.

'Patch me through to the Commissioner.' No please and thank you in this voice.

'We're maintaining radio silence.' I informed him. 'I'm not sure I can...'

'Who said anything about the radio?' The voice at the other end was impatient. 'Just transfer the call to Swissair at Gate 34.'

I did as he asked and went back to the window then. The disembarking passengers were now moving crocodile-fashion towards Gate 34.

Given that there was nothing I could do, and I had no intention of driving over to join them, above all if there was a bomb scare or something, I called the janitors' number to have some empty cartons sent up for Scholl's belongings. Within minutes there was a tap at the door.

'Evening, Monsieur de Savigny. You want boxes, I got boxes.' Sandor Kosjac was a small wiry Hungarian, an emigré from the uprising in '56. He used to enjoy ribbing Vinet on the rare occasions he passed our way. "You ever need a real policeman, just call Kojac. Kosjac - Kojac, get it?" Vinet couldn't stand him.

'Surprised you aren't out there as well, waving a flag.' he said.

So much for open telephone lines and radio silence. The whole damn airport knew what was going on. Except for me. Some Arab dignitary just in from Amman had asked for and was being given the full VIP treatment, explained Sandor. A police presence was required. I hardly thought this merited radio silence and all the telephone restrictions, unless it was someone like a PLO man, and I would have known if... The thought crossed my mind that perhaps I wouldn't, no-one told me anything round the airport any more. I wasn't a has-been, I was a non-starter.

After Sandor had left I closed myself in my office and settled to the typing. The choice I had to make was stark, did I or didn't I suggest Suri as the prime mover against Swissair 493? If I didn't, I had no motive for Scholl's madness. If I did, I couldn't prove any of it. I put off the moment of decision a while longer by filling out the Appendix forms first, lists of belongings found in the crashed aircraft.

I completed a second Appendix, describing in detail the movements of the Curtiss, using the Flight recorder report sent over by the Technical Bureau. The third and final Appendix was the Voice Recorder Transcript.

Finally I could put off no longer the actual composition of the Report.

I crossed to the window again, unable to settle at the typewriter. Outside, alongside the fire-fighting practice area, was the scarcely recognisable air-frame, a rebuilt skeleton, all that remained of Delta-Echo-Mike. It was hard to forget how it had looked winging in through the mist and the sleet, face to face with the red and white DC9 on final approach.

Staring at the broken glass of the cockpit I wondered what on earth had possessed Scholl, how he had felt sitting in there, flying the iced-up old crate at 2,000 feet through the driving snow, with the aircraft bucketing in turbulence and an eleven knot tail wind.

What possible motivation, what driving compulsion could make a man fly head on in the face of conflicting traffic? How did it feel, seeing the blinding triangle of its landing lights directly in front? I tried to visualise Scholl's hands on the flight controls, how his eyes must have been everywhere, oil pressure, engine revolutions, fuel, minimum clean and stalling speed, flaps, height, indicated air speed, and all this with the landing gear intentionally still up.

One thing was certain, Thierry Scholl had been no mean pilot. A line from my first flying manual came to mind - years ago I had wanted to learn to fly, but Geneviève had persuaded me to use the money for better purposes. Every pilot has heard it, and most treat it with the reverence of the Eleventh Commandment:

"There are old pilots, and there are bold pilots, but there are no old bold pilots"

And there were no answers.

I sat down at my desk, and started to type. And then, when I'd finished, I went through to the Commissioner's office and placed the whole dossier squarely in the centre of his desk. I turned to leave. He was standing in the doorway.

'This is Wednesday?' His tone was acid with sarcasm. 'Didn't I see...?' He crossed to the roster on the wall. 'Yes.' He turned back to me. 'de Savigny, Second Deputy Commissioner, rostered from nine through to six.' He stared at the wall clock ostentatiously. 'You overslept, perhaps? Or have you been in the habit of coming in four hours late while I've been on vacation?'

'There was a funeral I wanted to attend.' I spoke through clenched teeth, biting back what I really wanted to say.

'Ah, yes. The ATC girl. I'd forgotten.' He looked down at his desk. 'This the Scholl business? All wrapped up? Those boxes in there... his things? Right, then.' He stared at me quizzically, there was something he wanted to get off his chest, and he was working out whether this was the moment. I didn't say anything, and he decided to let it go at that. He glanced at the clock again. It was almost six.

'Well, Paul, enjoy your leave.' He looked at the door meaningfully. I was hard put not to slam it.

I remembered too late that I had agreed to buy some food for dinner. The shops were all shut when I left the airport, we'd have to eat out. A celebration dinner with Simona? I wondered. The way I felt about life then there was precious little to celebrate, except the promise of life with Simona. If she'd still have me.

And then there was Lakey. What was I going to do with Lakey? I was in no mood to buy him dinner as well. It was time Simona and I worked out what the hell we were and where the hell we were going, and I didn't want Lakey alongside. Perhaps Frédérique... I had just passed the turning to her mother's place, and on impulse I reversed and back-tracked.

Frédérique's car was in the drive, so I turned in and parked behind. The odds were that Lakey was still there, they'd struck up a rapport that was almost a brother-sister relationship in the past days. I thought I should let them know I would be out for the evening.

It was Mrs. Dantin who answered the door. She looked terrible, very strained and pale, and there were moist smudges under her eyes.

'Hello Paul.' She stared at me across the threshold, the hallway light behind her framing her hair like a halo. 'I was thinking of you just now, isn't that funny?' Her lips were trembling, and her voice was unsteady. 'I was thinking... Your Charlotte, and my Dominique. I was just remembering how they used to play toge...' Her voice broke and she looked away as the tears started to roll down her cheeks.

Frédérique's face appeared in the doorway from the living room, but she didn't see me with her mother there, blocking the hallway.

'Who is that, Moth...?' She came forward and then stopped, a strangely apprehensive look crossed her face as she caught sight of me. But she recovered immediately, and hurried to her mother's side to comfort her. I was both embarrassed and moved, feeling like an intruder on their grief. God knew, I'd been through much the same trauma with Charlotte, and then Geneviève.

I explained why I'd called and Frédérique thanked me cordially enough, but she didn't invite me inside. I thought then that her coy expression, and her suggestion that "Ben might even stay the night" had something to do with me and Simona, and Lakey keeping out of our way. In actual fact, of course, he'd already gone, which was the real reason for her strange behaviour.

The lights were on in the Chalet when I parked the Mitsubishi in the drive and wearily walked across the frozen snow to the front door. Simona had beaten me to it, and I can remember now the turmoil of thoughts and feelings as I opened the door and stepped into the safety and comfort of a home that was suddenly more real and more welcoming than it had been for years.

I didn't understand the strangely tender look that she gave me as I walked in, nor her urgent passion.

'I don't want food,' she had said when I admitted I hadn't bought any. 'I want you.' And she had proved it with an urgency that left me at a loss to know what was so special about Second Deputy Commissioner de Savigny.

I know now of course that she knew something that I didn't, not about Lakey or about Suri, but about myself. She had been in Berne all day and was shocked at just how thorough a bastard the Commissioner was. Even I hadn't suspected how vile he could be either.

We were lying in bed, about an hour later, I remember it now, she was staring at me in that weird way she had, just staring and speaking volumes where words would have been wasted, when there was the ring of the doorbell.

'Hell'. We both said it together, a simultaneous and shared reaction.

'Not your friend Lakey?' she groaned. I shook my head, and thought for a minute I might ignore it, but then the ringing was renewed. Whoever it was could see the lights were on and the car in the drive. I pulled on my trousers and went downstairs.

It was a very briefly worded telegram. Only two lines long. I remember thinking as I read it what a total bastard the Commissioner had to be, wasting police funds and his time on such gratuitous offence:

'SCHOLL REPORT UNACCEPTABLE STOP VINET WILL TAKE OVER STOP MISSING VIDEO & AUDIO CASSETTES URGENTLY REQUIRED'

It was signed with the Commissioner's name and full title.

When I went back to bed, things weren't the same.

Simona had to be in Lausanne the next day.

'I want to go on to Berne from there,' she said, 'and fetch some more things from the apartment. I'll be back tomorrow night. See if we can't make a long weekend last...'

She was trying hard to shake my mood of depression, but even the Simona magic couldn't take my mind off the blue and white telegram propped accusingly on the mantelpiece over the empty grate. She looked at me across the table, her green eyes reading my face with a look of concern.

'Oh, Paul. It doesn't matter,' she tried to persuade me. 'Let Vinet have the stupid Scholl case, and welcome.' But there was something else in her look, I couldn't place it at the time because I didn't know whom she'd seen in Berne the day before. It wasn't until quite some time afterwards she told me whom she'd met and what she had, entirely by accident, learned about me and Geneva police force. If I hadn't resigned that weekend, my days at Cointrin would have been numbered anyway...

At the time I couldn't have known, of course, and she kept the information to herself. I'm still uncertain now, a year later, what on earth prompted her to move in with me, what she found attractive in a policeman whom she herself considered "no earthly good". But we're still together, I'm no longer a policeman, and "The Refuge" in Ben's farm is up and running, so perhaps it really doesn't matter any more.

But it mattered at the time, it mattered more than anything else.

Long after Simona's car had purred off up the drive, very conscious of her perfume and her presence in the house, and now of her absence, I was still sitting at the table, staring at the faded enlargements on the wall. "These things are meant to happen..." I didn't think so. Not the Tumbril in the Sky, not the hundreds of other "tumbrils", not Charlotte, and not Geneviève. Not Scholl, and not Dominique Dantin, or Sigrid Sorensen and Ben Lakey and Sylvie Gueudet and Richard Benson... Or Simona?

Lakey. My mind wandered to Frédérique Dantin, this was the first night since his arrival that Lakey had not spent at the Chalet. I went out then, and on the spur of the moment I drove, finally, to Dominique's villa. Tuesday's snow had been cleared from the roads by now, and I was there within twenty minutes. God knew I had been promising to look over her belongings for long enough, and I expected her mother would need some help with the financial papers. I wondered briefly what the father's rôle might be in clearing up Dominique's affairs. I didn't know until I started to go over her papers that he was dead, and that the man I had seen in church at the funeral had no connection with the family.

The first thing I saw in the driveway was the black Toyota Land Cruiser. Samurai was there again. I only realised then that I had no key to the house, for I had not called Frédérique to tell her of my visit. My mind was functioning even less successfully than usual.

'Well, Deputy Commissioner de Savigny.' Samurai climbed down from his Land Cruiser. He wasn't a man who went in for hand shaking. 'Now what?'

I told him I wanted to go over some of Dominique's affairs, specifically the strange books by the CB radio. He had the grace to look vaguely discomfited at this, and instead of moving to the back door and letting me into the house, he climbed in the back of the Toyota, and reappeared a minute later holding three or four leather bound volumes.

'I guess these might be what you want?' He handed them to me.

'You borrowed them?' I knew nothing about CB-ists, or their habits, I didn't even know if these were his books, or Dominique's, truth be told I was more impressed that he didn't mess me about, just gave them straight back.

'Something like that.' He had scratched at his beard then, the way he did when he was thinking. The thought crossed my mind, it hadn't occurred the previous day, that Samurai might be a bit simple.

'Thanks.' I flicked through them. They were actually aircraft log books, but converted for use as some sort of CB log, that was certain. There were contact names, dates, and even the gist of conversations in some cases. The majority of the entries were indeed in English. 'Do you know why Mademoiselle Dantin used to write these in English?' I asked Samurai. But he didn't know. I'm sure he didn't know, there was no trace of the man's distaste of the day before when I put this question. If he didn't know the answer, he didn't mind being asked. 'Can I look at the inside of the house?'

He unlocked the back door and let me in to the kitchen. The first thing I saw, centrally placed on a side table, was a large and powerful CB radio. And beside it, more log books, strikingly similar to the ones Samurai had retrieved from the back of his van.

'You didn't take these, then?' I looked at him. 'Why?'

'No interest.' he grunted. 'Different.' I revised my opinion for the second time that morning about Samurai. Now I thought he wasn't actually simple at all, just pretending. Whatever, he was a strange type.

I sat down, and opened the first of the books on the kitchen table. A second later I was on my feet again. It was entirely automatic, and what my mind was doing or what I was thinking at that moment I shall never know. I had just opened Thierry Scholl's log book for Delta-Echo-Mike.

Chapter Twenty

These things are meant to happen. Again that thought, as I sat ignominiously in a public waiting room in the Police Reception at the airport, while Vinet located the Commissioner. For all I knew he might already have done so, and the bastard was keeping me waiting for the sheer hell of it. I could visualise the cynical smile flitting across his fleshy face as he skimmed the contents of my letter. The grin that would follow the smile, and the way he would swing the pivot-chair to the left and stare out over the tarmac. At this moment Vinet appeared in the doorway. His face was a scowl and he looked murderous.

'The Commissioner would like to see you now.' He was gritting his teeth as if it was physically painful to speak to me at all. I wondered what the hell was wrong with him, I'd have put money on his being overjoyed to see the back of me. Perhaps the Scholl case was already giving him ulcers. I followed him into the Commissioner's office. 'Second Deputy de Savigny, sir.' Still the gritted teeth, the artificial manners. He closed the door with a whisper of wood on carpet that was even more violent than slamming it.

I'd been right about the swivel chair, but not the smile. The Commissioner was grave, and I thought for a terrible moment he was going to play cat and mouse games. He was indeed staring out over the apron, his back turned to me. My typed letter lay open on the desk. Beneath it I saw the corner of some kind of passport protruding. They'd found Lakey, that was my first thought, they'd found Lakey and I was in deep, Christ knows why I thought that, but that was my first reaction. Then the Commissioner turned to face me, and I learned that, after all, these things are meant to happen.

'Paul.' He stood up, and crossing to a side cabinet filled two glasses with mineral water from a litre bottle, placed a glass in front of me and sat down again. 'This can't have been an easy decision for you.' He waved at the letter face up on his desk. 'Hey?' He leaned forward across the table and peered at me, his porcine eyes trying to read my expression. I wasn't going to give him the satisfaction.

'No.' I could dispense with the 'Sir', I thought.

'Well, well, well.' He rubbed his eyes with the back of his knuckles in a mannered way. 'Well, well. Who'd have thought... and there I've been trying to reach you all morning.' Before I could wonder why, he suddenly sat up straight, businesslike. 'Let me ask you a question, Paul. What made you decide to become a policeman, all those years ago? You must have known way back that...'

'... that I was no earthly good at it?' I felt a mirthless smile cross my face. 'Yes, I knew. But I didn't know that when I joined, did I?'

'You think you're a failure, then? A no-hoper? No hiding place, no place to go, a quitter?'

'For Christ sake.' My voice was harsh. 'What is that you want me to say? That I'm a sucking no-hoper, ready for the Kami-kaze cross-cut? Jesus!' I burst out, 'I didn't want to see you today, I'd planned on getting in before seven, and clearing out...'

'Whoa, hey, steady on. Paul, Paul.' He glug-glugged some more bottled water into my glass. 'Steady. You've got me wrong.' His crackly voice broke pitch with injured hurt. It struck me as preposterously ironic that he should be the one to sound hurt. I sat down again and drained the full glass in a single gulp. 'How old are you, Paul?' He changed tack, catching me off guard with his gentler manner. 'Fifty-two, three?'

'Fifty-one.' I didn't see why I had to suffer this monstrous travesty of a polite conversation.

'Fifty-one. And you really mean this?' He pointed to my letter of resignation again. 'Is it the Scholl business, or Suri and Lakey, or is it Vinet and the Sergeants? What, exactly, Paul?' he demanded. 'I need to know this, it matters, believe me.'

I didn't answer at once. It was a good question, a reasonable question under the circumstances.

'It's none of those things.' I answered eventually, 'And it's all of them. Your question was entirely apt. I should never have become a police officer. Happy now?' I was hard put not to sneer.

'The Suri dossiers.' He veered yet again to another angle. 'Why is it that nothing ever came of that venture? You took it very seriously, if I remember. What happened? Not enough time? You hardly had too much to deal with here.' He held up his hand to rob the suggestion of its implicit insolence.

'No.' I answered truthfully, wondering where the hell all this was leading. 'No, it wasn't overwork, nor insufficient time. It was something much more basic.' I swallowed. 'As you've bothered to ask, I'll tell you. It was fear. Plain, old-fashioned fear, fear of failure...'

I paused, toying with the empty glass. A manic shriek filled my ears, a demented man called Blake.

"Give me the gun! I can't stand f a i l u r e!"

The Commissioner was staring at me strangely and cleared his throat meaningfully.

'… but I don't suppose you'd understand that, you're a success-story, a man who doesn't fall down on the job.' I stopped. I didn't really know why I was telling him all this, fundamentally he was a man I had despised, and here I was telling him what a great guy he was.

The pivot chair squeaked as he swung it left in the way I'd visualised. He wasn't smiling though, and I began to wonder again about that passport peeping out from under the letter.

'All right.' He seemed to come to a decision. 'Agreed. I formally accept your letter of resignation, and on account of the hitch you encountered with the Dantin matter in the Scholl investigation, I'll propose to Police HQ that this be recorded as resignation on compassionate grounds. As of Monday....' He paused and stared at me. 'There could be problems with severance pay, though. That bother you?'

'The pension will be safeguarded, surely?' I hadn't even thought about this side of resignation, that I would have no proper income for the next fourteen years. *Fourteen years*. Christ. It was only now sinking in that I had thrown in the towel on more than just a lousy job. It was suicide.

'Pension's no problem. I was thinking of a lump-sum, but I'd have to have some focus...'

He swung back to me.

'What will you do about Suri?' It was a direct question. 'Will you go on trying, to find Charlotte I mean, and to intervene against him? Or is that all over now?'

'It'll never be over.' My voice was soft. 'Never. Now that I'm a free agent... well, there's this Lakey business for one thing.' I assumed he was *au fait* with the Lakey story.

'Yes.' He slid the passport out from under my letter, flipped it open, irritatingly keeping the name out of sight. 'Yes,' he repeated, 'there's this Lakey business, as you say. I think that's the way for you to go, Paul. I think...' He stopped, then reached to the intercom on his desk, held down a button and spoke to Vinet. 'Call the Med-dep. I'm coming up now.' Vinet made some acknowledgement. The Commissioner stood up. 'I have a surprise for you.' He was smiling, but it wasn't the smirky, smug grin I'd envisaged, in fact I'd never seen the man in such a human light. I didn't realise then that my resignation was a God-send to him, it had spared him the trouble of ousting me by more unorthodox means.

The Med-dep was a miniature pharmacy and clinic on the top floor of the admin building, reserved for aircrews needing minor medical attention. I couldn't imagine what "surprise" the Commissioner could have for me that was in any way connected with anybody in Med-dep, and the notion that Lakey might have smashed his car and been flown back to Cointrin overnight seemed far-fetched in the extreme. Still clutching the passport and a flimsy yellow folder, the Commissioner led the way to the lift. We travelled to the top floor in silence. Then the lift doors slid open, we passed through a glazed door and were in the medical atmosphere of Med-dep, the pungent odour of disinfectant very strong.

'Wait here, will you, Paul.' The Commissioner waved me to a small waiting area and walked straight in to the dispensary. I heard his voice through the glass door, and then he was coming out again, followed by a tall very blonde woman wearing a faded track-suit and dusty trainers.

'Miss Sorensen, Paul de Savigny. Paul, Mademoiselle Sorensen.' I had stood up as they approached, but the room was suddenly spinning, my thoughts reeling. Sigrid Sorensen, here in Geneva. While Lakey could be almost anywhere in Europe.

Automatically I had extended my arm to shake her hand, but now I saw that both her hands were thickly swathed in fresh white lint bandages, and I suddenly felt sick. Suri.

When I managed to tear my eyes away from the bulky bandaged hands to look at her more closely, I got another shock. She was very slender, a tall girl, with an almost boyish figure, diminutive breasts and long legs, but it was her face that caught and held my attention. She was a blonde Eurasian, part Oriental, I couldn't begin to guess what mixture, and one of the most beautiful women I had ever seen.

It struck me then that Lakey had never actually said a word about his girl-friend except that she was Swedish. For no good reason I had assumed that with a name like Sorensen she would be white.

I stared, mesmerised almost, at this extraordinarily lovely face. Her hair was very long, brushed straight, falling over one cheek and shoulder. Her eyes were a deep cornflower-blue, slightly slanted above high slender cheekbones, and the Oriental-European skin was a unique peach-gold, at that moment though marked with the tell-tale dark patches of fatigue around the eyes.

I glanced again at the bulky white bundles that were her hands. She blushed and lowered her eyes. The Commissioner coughed gently.

'Exactly my reaction, Paul. Exactly how I felt. My apologies, Miss Sorensen.' He was speaking in heavily accented English. He waved her to the leather chair and she sat down gratefully. I was still examining her face. Now that I had taken in the startling beauty, and that universal serenity that Eurasians seem to emanate, I could identify too a deep-rooted hurt about her. It wasn't just fatigue, nor the anguish that Lakey had carried as an imprint. This was a person suffering actual physical pain. And a lot more besides. Her impassive features seemed to exaggerate all this rather than mask it.

'Where… I mean when...?' I stammered. The Commissioner gave me a meaningful look as if to say "I told you you were a lousy policeman."

'Miss Sorensen arrived this morning, train overnight from London via Paris. She contacted the *Bureau de Police* at Geneva station, they took one look at her, and sent her straight over with an escort. You saw the way Vinet looked at you...' He chuckled. 'He's lumbered with a dead maniac called Scholl, while you have much prettier...'

He was interrupted then by Sigrid Sorensen who suddenly seemed to come to life, like a clockwork doll.

'Monsieur de Savig-nee?' She had a strangely childlike voice. 'Is Ben still staying with you? They told me...' she waved a bandaged hand at the Commissioner, 'they said you were putting him up... and that you know something about...' She stared at her hands for what seemed an age, 'about Suri and ALBATROSS?'

'Your hands.' I said. 'I've never seen that. But I've heard about it.' I glanced at the Commissioner, his face was stony, and not this time because of anything I had done. 'Several times I had reports of that happening, but not for a couple of years now. For a dancer it's typically the legs or feet they go for. If it's the hands, or the fingers, you're probably an artist, or a musician, a pianist?' I stopped. The banal typescript reports of this most bestial of Suri's "fidelity tests" were nothing compared to the vision of those lumpy white bandages. I felt physically sick as I thought of what they must have done to her, to her hands, her fingers, to necessitate so much lint. A stapler, I remembered that more than once I had read of that, or a staple gun. It was an effort to tear my eyes away from that appalling testimony to the lunatic sadism of Suri's mob.

'I am a musician.' She was very soft. 'I play the flute. I mean, I did.' she added. Her eyes met mine. They were moist, the whites very accentuated. 'They threatened to... they said they would...' There was a catch in her voice, and she bowed her head so that the long gleaming blond hair fell fully across the side of her face, covering her eyes. Her voice was a faint murmur and neither the Commissioner nor I heard what it was that "they" had threatened.

The Commissioner waved briefly to someone in the dispensary, and a white-uniformed nurse came out quickly and sat down beside the Swedish girl. She must have been applying clean bandages before we arrived, for her face reflected the revulsion she felt at what had been done to Sigrid Sorensen in "Medina".

With an imperious jerk of his head the Commissioner nodded to a side room, and I was in no mood to resent it. I was appalled. I was way out of my depth and didn't understand what was going on.

'It's true, then?' He was brusque, I think he was as horrified as I was that anyone in their right minds could hold down someone's hands and fire staples into the living flesh with a staple-gun, and even more horrified that they could get away with it. I was almost certain that was what they had done. Or drawing pins. The fact that Sigrid Sorensen was in Geneva probably meant that no charges had been brought against Suri in the UK. I wondered if the Commissioner had seen her injuries, nothing less would account for this quite unwonted humanity in the man.

'I've come across reports, never seen it. Do we know why she's here?' It was a stupid question, one that reinforced totally the current belief that I was a lousy policeman.

'Lakey, of course.' He looked at me as if I were simple. 'The Suri people told her we had him in police custody here. Just one more way of tormenting her, I think.' He looked at me strangely. 'I always knew something pretty powerful was driving you,

Paul, something that kept you going against this ALBATROSS madness when there was nothing actually that you could *do*. I'm only now beginning to understand it. And you.' He looked at me with a strange humility. 'There was a lot we didn't bother to find out.' He glanced at his watch. 'I've told her - Miss Sorensen - that you are free to escort her, to re-unite her and this Lakey. I assume you are, willing I mean?' I nodded. I was wondering how she had got away from "Medina", where she had had her injuries treated initially. Without police intervention? It was scarcely credible that any doctor or hospital could have treated her and not notified the authorities. There was a lot I didn't know.

The Commissioner was still speaking.

'And you can have any facilities available, *any* facilities Paul, that we can offer, if it'll help you pursue this Suri creature and his sadistic maniacs.' His face was mottled red again, and the collar too tight around the fleshy neck. His voice was high-pitched. 'Christ, I have a daughter, not her age, no, she must be going on thirty, this Sorensen woman, but I have a...' His voice tailed away as he realised what he had said.

'I had a daughter, once.' I was dry. 'I know. I know what you mean.'

'Shit.' There was an uncharacteristic stillness about the man then, his voice bitter, his lips compressed. 'Yes. I'd forgotten. That was unforgivable of me.'

'No it wasn't.' I was mild. 'For once we see eye to eye.'

'You'll take her to Lakey, then? And...' Unusually the Commissioner seemed at a loss for words. I had never seen this before. '... if there's anything you need from us... Better still, I'll brief Martin Verre at Rolle. That way, you won't need to...'

He didn't finish. but I knew he meant I wouldn't have to tangle with the intolerable Vinet or the other Sergeants. I had never known the man to show such compassion. In hindsight, I know now it was only just dawning on him the kind of atrocity Suri's "Saints" were capable of, and it rankled badly that such activities should be beyond the law. Ten years too late he was just catching up with me.

'I'll look after her.' By Christ I meant it, I felt I had been given one last chance to pursue Suri, one last chance to get the monstrous little rat in the dock, photographs of this girl's hands as mute evidence to the man's sordid illegality. 'Has she made a statement?' I suddenly began to think like a policeman, thirty years too late.

'Of a kind.' The Commissioner sat down heavily behind the unoccupied desk and waved me to a seat opposite. He drew out two typed sheets from the yellow folder. 'Of a kind, she has.' He glanced down the two pages, his eyes narrowing as he read out the salient sections.

'"... late at night, in the early hours of Wednesday February 18th, I was invited to prove my allegiance to the Power of Healing and the Almighty... the Transactional Leader Sanyasin called Jana urged me to enter the Room of the Faithful in a state of grace and nakedness... I entered the Room, a darkened closet really, wearing only my 'mala', a medallion of the Maharaj Suri.'"

He looked at me across the desk with his porcine eyes almost bulging out of their sockets.

'She did all this of her own free will?' He was nearly apoplectic with astonishment. 'And then we get to the...' He wiped his face and tried to ease the collar of his shirt around his throat.

'"... At first I was very relaxed, the result of two hours of Sensory Meditation prior to the Fidelity Test. Now the Sanyasin Jana told me to lie face down in the shape of an X on a broad wooden plank, with my arms, hands and fingers outstretched. She massaged and caressed me into a State of Grace."'

The Commissioner reached out for the ubiquitous bottled water and poured a glass for himself absently. I knew what was coming next, this was exactly the kind of documentation that the "dusty folders" in my little office housed. He went on reading in a hoarse voice.

'"Jana explained that the Allegiance and Fidelity Test required of me a sacrifice that would be considered Holy in the eyes of the Maharaj, and that this differed in each person's case. She knew that, as a flautist, my hands and my lips are essential to my music. While continuing to massage me through the six levels of Graciousness... "'

The Commissioner lifted his eyes from the text.

'The what?' he demanded, as if I had personally devised the term.

'I've come across it in some of the reports.' I admitted. 'Some say it's hypnosis, others call it brainwashing. The crudest report was from a South African woman, who said it was a plain orgasmic manipulation. Take your pick.' I shrugged. I felt physically sick. The Commissioner grunted, as if he wished he hadn't asked, and resumed his text.

'"... the six levels of...", yes...: "She said that the Healing that would follow the Sacrificial Suffering..."'

'Do they always talk this kind of garbage?' he wanted to know. I nodded wordlessly. He skipped a section and flipped to the next sheet.

'"... that would follow the Sacrificial Suffering would give my musicianship the Blessing of the Maharaj and of the Deity. She then instructed the other two Sanyasins present to fire metal staples into each fingertip, then along the sides of each finger, this being a pre-requisite for Holiness."'

The Commissioner refilled his glass and emptied it in a single gulp, then tossed down the typescript.

'She goes on to say she thinks she fainted almost immediately, and when she came to, she was in her room, with her hands crudely bandaged in sack-cloth.' He peered at me again across the table. 'She says she got up, put on the only clothes she had, and immediately tried to leave the house, carrying only her passport, which she had resolutely refused to give to the "Medina" officials for "safe keeping".

'Realising that she didn't even know whereabouts "Medina" was in the UK, and knowing she could not leave the house by the main entrance, it seems it's watched day and night by some sort of Receptionist, she made her way to the kitchens. She had hoped to find some food there, but came across a cache of money, almost two hundred pounds. She took this and then left the house by way of a pantry window.

'She walked, she says, several kilometres to High Wycombe where she made her way to the Hospital and was treated in Outpatients.' He looked at me obliquely. 'Now we come to the really impossible part. "After treating my injuries and bandaging my hands the doctor tried to insist on calling a police officer to interview me."' He scratched his chin. 'Quite right too. But when she heard that she would be questioned and encouraged to press charges, she immediately discharged herself, using the stolen money to take a taxi to High Wycombe station, from where she travelled to London and bought a ticket via Dover/Calais to Geneva. She says she travelled by train because she thought Suri might report her to the Police, and charge her with theft, and the airports would be watched. Can you credit it? *She* was worried *Suri* might charge *her*? I've been in touch with the British police. They say they've never heard of her. I haven't had time to make enquiries of the Hospital people yet.' He put the two typescript sheets back in the folder. 'To think she travelled for almost twenty-four hours like that, no luggage, no medicines. She says she didn't eat either, to try to keep people from seeing her hands... I can scarcely imagine it.' His voice was soft. 'What must they have been thinking of at Dover Immigration? Or Calais, for God's sake? She can hardly have been able to hold her passport...'

'You've obviously never seen the pig-sty conditions the railways, Sealink and the Channel ports consider acceptable for international travellers.' I pointed out. 'It's a grossly uncivilised system. No one but the British would put up with it. And the Belgians.' I added, remembering what a dump Ostend harbour-station was and always had been.

'Even so...'

'She made that statement here? This morning?' I reached over and picked up the folder. 'But she won't press charges, right?'

'No. She won't do it.' There was bafflement in the Commissioner's eyes, incomprehension in his voice. 'I've asked, I've begged her to, under oath. I've told her not to worry about the money she took, in case that's what's bothering her. But she just gives that terrible reproachful little smile, and says she can't do it. I was hoping that you might be able to persuade...'

'They never will.' I was remembering the hundreds of files in my offices. 'I've seen worse injuries documented, and the victim typically never objects to talking about the event. But can you get them to press charges? It's bizarre. They all say the same thing. Every damn time. "I can't." And then they clam up. It's been a brick wall to me for several years.' I added. The Commissioner was looking at me strangely.

'Can I ask you a personal question?' He was oblique. 'Does Madame Sentori have any idea about your involvement in the Suri thing?'

'Is that a leading question?' I smiled in spite of myself. The Police Commissioner was well-informed.

'I was just thinking...' he was musing aloud. 'She trained in law. Didn't she?'

'Yes.'

'Well... you wouldn't want to compromise her situation, but I was thinking...'

'So was I.' Again a dry smile. 'So was I. Is there anything else I need to know about Sigrid Sorensen before we leave. We *can* leave, I presume?' I had taken good care not to let on that Lakey had disappeared, and I wasn't going to. I was going to make immediate tracks to Frédérique and introduce her to Sigrid Sorensen. And force her to tell us where Lakey had gone.

'Nothing she can't tell you herself.' The Commissioner glanced at his watch again, he wanted to be back in his office. 'I'll be in touch about the severance pay.' he murmured. 'And I think, Paul, you've made the right decision. You know what they say...' He made to shake hands, the same old sweaty palm. '... these things are meant to happen. Hey?' With that, and a brief wave to Sigrid Sorensen and the nurse who was helping her to repair her make-up, he was gone. Leaving me with the quite impossible task of explaining to Sigrid Sorensen that Ben Lakey had disappeared and could by now be in any one of a dozen countries, but was almost certainly not in Switzerland.

Chapter Twenty-One

The sky was heavily overcast and the gusting wind was hurling snowflakes in violent flurries that took my breath away as I escorted Sigrid Sorensen to my car. She was shivering - she had no coat, no luggage, and no clothes other than the faded purple tracksuit she was wearing. I opened the door for her, and she awkwardly manoeuvred herself into the car, trying not to let her bandaged hands touch the metalwork. The nurse had given me a borrowed Swissair Travel-bag containing her passport and some ointments, spare bandages and painkillers. I slung this on the back seat.

She had only spoken once since the Commissioner had left us, to ask me to turn up the deep collar on her tracksuit, and to close the zipper to the neck against the cold. Otherwise she had followed me silently, very erect and with great dignity, first to the lift, and now across the snow-covered carpark.

For her part, I think, she was coming to terms with the reality that she was finally free of Suri and his damned ALBATROSS, and about to meet Ben Lakey again. For my part, I was trying to work out how to tell her that she wasn't going to see Ben Lakey today, and perhaps not for quite a few days. Then there was the clearing of my office on my mind as well, raising the spectre of what I had done, thrown away any chance of a regular income for the next fourteen years. Simona could hardly be expected to think this was an auspicious start to a relationship.

And now this silent slender girl beside me, bracing herself against the movement of the car with her feet, her bandaged hands neatly in her lap, and her gaze fixed on the white expanse of road outside. Meant to happen?

'You sound as if you know a lot about the Maharaj Suri and ALBATROSS?' Her voice was distant, her eyes fixed on the slush-filled motorway ahead. 'And about me. Has Ben talked a lot about me?' She turned towards me, that strangely impassive look on her face still in place.

'No. Hardly at all.' I glanced at her. The wind was veering nastily in sudden gusts, and I had to keep my mind on the driving. 'Nor about the Trans-Siberian. In fact, not a lot about anything.'

'Can I ask how you came to meet him?' She gave a hint of a smile. 'I mean, did he break the law or something? I didn't think after he left Moscow he'd end up here, living with a policeman...'

'He's not.' I was brutally frank. 'He was, but he's gone.' I glanced at her again, trying to gauge her reaction. I realised I shouldn't drive her all the way up to the Chalet in expectation, and then disillusion her, that would have been criminal. But I wondered how she would react to this. Typically, as I was to learn, she hid her emotions well.

'And where has he gone to?' Her voice was matter of fact. 'Not to England? To find me there?' She examined her hands, and went on in the same quiet voice, so quiet that she was almost inaudible. 'I had a feeling he might try that, but when they told me at "Medina" that he was in custody here... Is it England?' She turned to me again, the moist eyes shining in the grey light reflecting off the snow. It was hard not to stare at that extraordinarily beautiful face, to absorb its every detail. She was absolutely stunning, even under those circumstances.

'I don't know. But I think I know someone who does.' Frédérique would know, I was almost sure she knew, and once Frédérique met Sigrid Sorensen, once she fully realised what the Suri Sect meant in flesh and blood, real torn flesh and raw blood, I was certain she would help me find Lakey and bring him back.

'I see. No. No I don't see.' She tried to scratch an itch with the bundle of bandages that was her hand, it was painful to watch. 'Would you?'

She turned her back to me, and I found myself in the ludicrous situation of steering with the left hand while locating the spot and industriously scratching away through the back of her track suit.

'Thank you, that's better.' She turned to face the windscreen again. 'I hadn't appreciated how inconvenient this could be.' She half-raised one hand. 'Oh, dear. Ben will think I'm terribly stupid, all of this just because... Never mind.' She compressed her lips and gave a toss of her head, the long gleaming hair tumbling over her shoulders and back. 'No, I really don't see, Mr. de Savigny.' The Swedish vowels were very clipped, pronouncing my name Savig-nee. 'You're taking me to your house, to meet a man who isn't there. I'm going with you to find a man I know isn't there. I don't think I see anything at all.'

For the rest of the journey to the Chalet I outlined the key events of the last seven days, ending up with my resignation that morning, and our chance meeting in the Admin block. She had blinked a bit when I got to Frédérique's part in the affair, I suppose that was natural, but what really puzzled her was his disappearance.

'If Ben had already gone, why did the Commissioner keep trying to phone you to come out and meet me?' We were driving past the spot where Dominique had died, and I didn't answer at once.

'He didn't know.' I was short. 'I only discovered yesterday that he'd gone.'

'He might be at this house he has, over in the Grisons, you think?' She sounded slightly desperate, and I didn't blame her. I shrugged. We had just passed Frédérique's place, and I had looked for the car as we swept past. It was not in the drive, and they had no garage. I didn't like the look of this.

'If only.' I muttered. 'That would make things so much easier. The one thing I am certain of is that he won't rest till he finds you.' I looked at her again. 'I can understand why, now.'

She blushed, and shyly allowed the long hair to cover her face.

'That was nice. You're very kind.' Again the childish speech. She had an odd way of talking. 'Is there any way we can find out? If he is in the Grisons?'

I said softly:

'We'll find a way. I promise, Miss Sorensen, we'll find a way. And now, after all these years, I can at last count on some real support, from Geneva police, and a legal expert.' I had just roped in Simona as well, which I think was what the Commissioner had intended by his final suggestion. 'Ah, here we are.' I turned the car into the drive and parked under the trees in front of the Chalet. I'd been half-hoping that Frédérique might... But there was still the possibility that she was up at Dominique's place.

We hurried through the blizzarding snow to the front door, and then we were inside, the old wooden room looking almost as shambolic as ever, and her feminine reaction to the mess I had made of Simona's re-organisation entirely in line with first Frédérique's and then Simona's herself.

'Ben was here? He lived here a whole week?' She looked around interestedly, but still with that same immobile face. 'Trust me to arrive just one day too late... Oh dear.' she said again, it was an expression she used frequently. 'Oh dear. I don't think...' She turned to me, her hair falling across her face, her hands held out together in front of her like a doll's. 'What am I going to do? I have no luggage, no money, no anything. And I was so hoping... When your Commissioner told me that Ben was here, and staying with you, and not under arrest or anything, it was like a dream come true. Now here I am and he's not.' She stopped talking then and stared intently around the room as if realising for the first time her predicament. And mine.

'There, there, Miss Sorensen.' I didn't normally talk like this, it was an unconscious response to her fragile beauty and her terrible hurt. Not just the hands, I was acutely aware she had been put through the full Suri indoctrination treatment. I was impressed by her self-control, her calm matter-of-factness. And it dawned on me that she was in shock, suffering acute reaction to Suri, and to ALBATROSS and whatever it had cost her to walk out of "Medina" and travel alone across Europe by train in search of her lover, only to find she had missed him by a few hours...

'I can't even get washed like this.' She had found a small wall mirror and was studying her face. 'And I'm filthy. Oh dear, what am I going to do?' she repeated, and the very inscrutability of her expression was more telling than any tears or excessive emotion could have been.

I took her up to the room that had been Charlotte's, it was clean if a bit musty, Mrs. de Almeida kept it ready for the impossible event that Charlotte might one day...

anyway, that's another story. She stared at the rumpled bedclothes, I hadn't touched them since Lakey had left. She knelt down by the pillow and looked up at me.

'Ben slept here?' Her voice was a whisper. I nodded, an unaccustomed lump in my throat. She buried her face in the pillow, and I heard her muttering something into the bedding, it sounded like 'Please come back.'

I left her there then to sort herself out as best she could, although the brushes, bottles and jars of skin cream that Mrs. de Almeida always had stocked there were of no use to her, with her hands in that state. I got the fire going and organised coffee, but when she came down again, she couldn't even hold a mug to drink from, and I had to help her sip the hot liquid like a child.

I don't know if it was then, or at the sight of her kneeling by the bed in Charlotte's room perhaps, that the idea of setting up a rehabilitation centre for "refugees" from ALBATROSS and similar sects first crossed my mind. It wasn't a clear-cut idea at the time, but there was an awesome rightness for a person who had turned her back on all that Suri represented now to be in Charlotte's room, probably to sleep there for several days. I fully intended to keep Sigrid Sorensen at the Chalet for as long as she wanted to stay, or until we found Lakey. Or both. I had found a surrogate daughter, and the fact that she didn't know I saw myself as a putative adoptive father never crossed my mind. I didn't know then that she was the offspring of a Swedish sailor and a Thai whore, conceived one violent night in the docks area of Malmö in 1959, and that the only family she had ever known had been exactly that, adoptive parents, the Sorensens.

'Thank you, Mister Savig-nee.' She sat very erect on the sofa in front of the log fire, her eyes on the faded enlargements on the wall. 'You're very kind. You don't know anything about me, yet you treat me as if you'd known me since I was a child. Is that your family?' She had a way of playing verbal hop-scotch, skipping from topic to topic as her mind moved. I said it was, and she got up then to examine Charlotte's picture with an intensity I failed to comprehend.

'She joined ALBATROSS, you said?' She turned to look at me, her cornflower-blue eyes moist, the whites of the eyes again prominent. 'Of her own free will?'

'Yes.' My mouth was dry. I was thinking of her hands. 'And yes. Of her own free will.' Had they done to that to my Charlotte? What had they done, actually, to Charlotte, that I had never heard of her again?

'I guess you're wondering whether I met her at "Medina" or anywhere?'

I hadn't thought of this, but now that she mentioned it... She continued:

'I didn't. But if I had, I wouldn't have known, if you see what I mean, known who she was.' She stared at the faded picture again. 'Oh dear. I think I shouldn't have spoken about her. Oh dear, I'm sorry.'

'It's all right.' I said. 'It was a long time ago. Let's talk about you, and the here and now.'

'Do we have to?' She gave a little grimace. 'I don't want to sound selfish, but I was thinking, hoping really, we might be able to talk later, when we've found Ben. Actions louder than words?' she quipped, her back very upright, someone straight out of a Victorian drawing-room, trying hard to be merry. I admired her for that. And for her straight talking.

'You're right. I'll call Frédérique.'

'Oh yes, I want to meet this Frédérique.' She paused, then went on in the same flat tone: 'Such a pity she couldn't have had more faith in you. Silly, silly person. Oh dear, what did she want to give him a car for? Was she in love with him?' She turned to me, her mouth strangely twisted, and her gaze downcast. 'Please tell me she wasn't.'

'She was as much in love with Ben Lakey as a sister is to a brother.' I was firm, we could do without the insidious green monster of jealousy raising its ugly head. 'I told you, she had a strange rapport with him from the start. But it had nothing to do with love. I think basically she was grateful.' I added. 'I told you about the way her sister died? The books and her mother? No love affair there.' I ended up firmly. 'I'll call her now.'

It was Madame Dantin who took the call, which was ominous, and my worst fears were immediately confirmed.

'She left last night, Paul.' Her voice was distraught and trembling, I guessed she had passed a beastly night alone, obsessed with the ghosts of her husband and her daughter, and she had missed Frédérique's company. 'She told me she would be gone for several days, and if you called, to give you a message.'

'Tell me.' I felt tired and drained, everything had gone wrong.

'She said to tell you it's a Hertz car, and to give you the number. Does that make sense?'

'Wait.' I got a pencil and paper. Everything had just gone right again. 'Go ahead.' I was conscious of Sigrid Sorensen's impassive eyes fixed on me.

Madame Dantin dictated the hire car number, and I asked her to give me Frédérique's car registration as well, and then on an off-chance whether she had taken her passport. She had to go and look for that, and I spent an anguished two minutes before she came back and said:

'No, her passport's in her room. Why, Paul, what's happening? Is it Benjamin Lakey? Has she... you don't think she's fallen in love with him, do you? They were very close the last few days.'

I didn't want to answer that question all over again, so I just said 'No, they weren't, and I don't think they will be.' Then came the all-important question. 'D'you know where she was heading? Did she say anything else?'

But she didn't know, and I was about to ring off when I heard the sound of a car in the drive outside. It seemed improbable in the extreme that this should be Frédérique, but I had a look. It wasn't, it was Simona's car. I rang off then, asking Madame Dantin to call me as soon as she had news of Frédérique. Whether it was my surprise at

Simona's arrival, or just plain stupidity I don't know, but it didn't occur to me to ask her to tell Frédérique that Sigrid Sorensen had turned up. I put down the telephone as Simona opened the front door, a suitcase on either side of her and snow dampening her fair hair.

'God, it's cold out there...' She stopped abruptly as she caught sight of Sigrid Sorensen on the sofa. 'Sorry.' She dumped the suitcases in the hallway, her eyes rapidly taking in Sigrid Sorensen's appearance, the bandaged hands, the grubby tracksuit. She went straight across and knelt down in front of her, looking past her to me. 'Not another of your waifs and strays, Paul? You really do have a...'

'Miss Sorensen.' I said formally. 'Ben Lakey's friend. But he's gone, and she's here. We were just...'

'Oh, no!' Simona squatted down and gently took the girl's swathed hands in her own. 'And this?' She indicated the bandages. 'This is...'

'Yes.' Sigrid Sorensen swept her long blond hair back with a single toss of the head. 'Yes, I'm afraid this is something I shouldn't have got into. I should have listened to Ben.'

'Gone?' Simona stared at me. 'When? When did he go? How did he...'

'Yesterday.' I took her coat; her perfume was arousing and there was a brief silence. Sigrid Sorensen stared at us, after all we were neither of us teenagers and I don't think she had expected such uninhibited passion at our age. I didn't care what she expected.

'Tell me.' She held me at arm's length and stared at me, reading my face. I think she intuitively guessed then what I had done, given in my notice and quit, for she went on before I could answer, 'No. Don't. I'll get something for us to eat...' She looked down at the shy girl on the sofa. 'Are you hungry?' she asked in English.

'Starving. I haven't eaten properly for... almost two days.' Her voice was calm, as if this were a common occurrence.

'Two days? Paul! How could you...' She dived into the kitchen, and there was the clatter of pots and pans and vegetable noises, and then the hiss of frying.

'That was the lady you told me about?' Sigrid Sorensen gestured I should sit down, an odd mannerism in my own home I thought. 'She's nice. I like her.' Again the childlike speech. 'About the telephone call?' I hadn't remembered that she didn't understand French and couldn't know that Frédérique was probably on her way after Lakey. I told her the good news first, that Frédérique had left me the number of Lakey's hire car, and that I could put out a police call as soon as I liked on the vehicle. And that I had her car number as well, and finally that she had not taken her passport, so the odds were that Lakey was still in Switzerland.

'But where?' she wanted to know. 'And do you still think she isn't in love with him? Why else would she go chasing after him?' And that was the bad news. I hadn't a clue where, I couldn't convince her that she wasn't and I couldn't explain why she had.

'That's settled, then.' Simona was feeding Sigrid Sorensen like baby, for she was quite incapable of holding anything. 'You'll stay here. And don't start talking about money and things being impossible again,' she reprimanded. 'I told you already, we can sort that out later, once Mr. Lakey is back.' She put down the spoon and lifted a glass for Sigrid to sip at.

'Thank you.' Sigrid Sorensen looked from Simona to me, and back again. There were tears now, for the first time tears of gratitude and embarrassment and relief. 'I'm sorry.' She bowed her head to let the long hair again cover her face, her emotion. Simona glanced at me across the table. We didn't need words then.

'First things first.' Her pragmatic side surfaced. She dried the tears from Sigrid Sorensen's cheeks with a serviette. 'As soon as we've finished this, I'll drive you down to Rolle. They have some very good shops in Rolle.' She was addressing the girl as if she were a child, it was somehow a natural and automatic response to Sigrid Sorensen's doll-like appearance. 'Get you some new clothes and things. Then back up here and a bath, I'll help you wash. Meanwhile Paul, I think, will not be idle?'

'The phone wires will be burning.' I agreed. 'But I was thinking. Ben Lakey told me in no uncertain terms what he thinks of the Swiss police. They put him in prison after that court case in '85.' I explained. 'He couldn't pay the... Anyway, I don't think it'd be very clever to put out an All-Stations alert on him, to have him picked up.' I was remembering Frédérique's angry words. "He won't do anything." I wondered. 'If they botched it, he might really disappear then. You think?' I turned to Sigrid Sorensen. 'You know him better than any of us.' She nodded.

'So what will you do?'

'A report-sighting call, I think. And then when we know where he is...'

'Do you think it will be today?' There was a pathetic eagerness about her suddenly, her eyes flicking from me to Simona and back again. She was almost at the end of her tether, I could see she was at breaking point, and I wanted more than anything else to say yes. But I couldn't, because I didn't think it would be. What could I say?

'Nothing's impossible.' Simona it was who found the right formula. 'But it might be a bit of a wait. Paul?'

I agreed it might, and with that they left for Rolle. I wondered as the car disappeared down the drive what on earth I would have done with Sigrid Sorensen if Simona Sentori had not suddenly taken it into her head the previous week to breeze into my life like a human whirlwind and transform my house and home so totally. Again that thought.

It was two hours before they returned, bringing half a dozen carrier bags and talking animatedly as they came into the house.

'Well?' Sigrid Sorensen came straight over to me, her eyes questioning. Simona tactfully busied herself in the kitchen. I led the Swedish girl to the sofa, and sat down beside her.

'Grisons.' I murmured. 'He's at his house in the Grisons...'

'Thank God.' Her eyes were moist. 'Oh, thank God. You're sure, you're not just saying this to... No, you wouldn't, no.' She leaned forward, reached out her two bandaged arms around me and hugged me close. Simona coughed gently from the kitchen doorway. Sigrid Sorensen jumped, her cheeks coloured violently and she released me. 'Oh dear. I'm sorry, was that wrong of me?'

'No.' Simona was laughing, there was an infectious pleasure in sharing her girlish happiness. 'Not at all. Come on then, Paul. Tell us about this masterly detective work.'

'It was child's play, really. A call to the *Contrôle des Habitants* in Müstair gave me his address. A second call to the local Gendarmerie, and the village constable drove out to have a look. In less than half an hour he called back. The Hertz hire car is parked in the drive to Lakey's farm. All we need now is to send a telegram, I gather his phone has been disconnected.' I turned to the smiling girl beside me. 'I thought you might like to do that bit.' I murmured.

'Oh yes.' Her eyes were bright. Ben Lakey was a lucky man to have a girl like this, I thought. More than lucky. 'Yes. But will you help me, I can't...' She giggled. 'I can't write anything.'

'I'll do it.' Simona offered, then, seeing the sudden apprehension on Sigrid Sorensen's face, 'What is it? Something the matter?'

'Well, yes.' The hair half-covering the face again, as always when she didn't want to show her emotions. 'This girl Frédérique somebody... Is her car there too? Did she go after him?' Simona glanced at me questioningly. I nodded.

'What's this?' She was gentle. 'You're surely not jealous? Believe me, Sigrid, there's no need.'

'How can you know that?' Her voice was flat, implacable. All the delight she had shown only moments ago had gone, replaced by a bitter insecurity. 'You don't understand. When we got off the train in Moscow, we weren't talking to one another. He thought I'd betrayed him. Because I stayed with the Maharaj Suri and the others. He didn't know that I couldn't help it, that I was... Oh dear.' The tears were there again, and I didn't know what to say, what to do to convince her. 'He thought I'd betrayed him, and that I didn't want to... Oh damn.' She broke down completely now and it was all Simona could do to keep her from losing the bandages, she was in a frenzy beyond her own control.

Again I found myself loathing Suri and all his so-called religious designs. How many Sigrid Sorensens and Charlottes did he want? Did he intend to go on driving person after person mad until there was nothing and nobody sane left in the world? Only days ago Ben Lakey himself had gone berserk and thrown things and yelled at me in that very room. Now it was his girl-friend. Simona looked at me and then at the phone.

I lifted the receiver and asked for Telegrams. There was no time left, no amount of careful wording would help now. I dictated a brief text, insisting he call Sigrid at my number, and asked for the telegram to be delivered immediately.

Simona didn't think he could possibly call for at least an hour, and with excellent psychology she suggested they pass the time with a hot bath and trying the new clothes. Sigrid Sorensen came across to me then and said:

'If he calls while I'm in the bath, please tell me. I must talk to him. I have to know, I mean, he has to know...' The emotion was welling again, and Simona had to help her, her eyes were swimming with tears.

Predictably Lakey called from Müstair Post Office only twenty minutes later, the Telegram Service was very efficient.

'How did you find me?' he wanted to know. He didn't really believe Sigrid was with us, suspecting me of some kind of trick to get him to show his hand.

'Never mind that.' I told him. 'Is Frédérique with you?' He wanted to know why, so I told him exactly why.

'She always was over-imaginative.' was all he said. 'Can I speak to her? And Paul... thanks for this. I can't...' I cut him short then and transferred the call to the bedroom extension. Simona came downstairs and we heard Sigrid Sorensen's excited voice distantly as she took up the receiver. The bedroom door closed.

Chapter Twenty-Two

'Heaven knows how I come to be musical.' Sigrid Sorensen replied modestly to Simona's question. 'In fact, I'd rate myself as mediocre. But it's fun... People say these things are often hereditary. I don't think that can be right in my case.' She blushed. 'My parents... Well, I was adopted, you see. And you're not supposed to know then who you are or where you come from. For years I didn't think that I ever would, know I mean. And when I eventually found out I wished I hadn't tried. But the Sorensens were not...' She stopped and reflected. 'Do you really want to know?' she asked Simona.

'Only if you want to tell us.' It was night, the snow was again blizzarding against the window panes in the way it had the previous night. But a very different atmosphere reigned now.

Ben Lakey was already on his way back from the Grisons, but with the weather conditions the worst the country had known for many years, he would have to make a long detour to avoid the blocked mountain passes. I didn't expect him before dawn, if then. He was leaving Frédérique at the farmhouse to get ahead there. I thought this was a pity, the sooner Sigrid Sorensen met Frédérique and knew what sort of person she was, the better for all concerned.

Meanwhile, we had settled down comfortably in front of the log fire to talk the night away. Sigrid was far too wound-up to be able to sleep while Lakey fought his way against the elements through the night. Also, she needed to work Suri and "Medina" out of her system. I had never met a refugee from ALBATROSS before, and we were feeling our way rather, not sure what was therapeutic and what dangerous.

'I suppose some children who are adopted don't find out that they are for years.' she went on. 'But when you look as different as I did from my parents, adoptive parents I mean, you find out very young that something is odd about you. Everyone's blond in Sweden, but my face didn't look like theirs... well, anyway. I must have been five or six when they told me but I think I knew before that. So I started wondering who I was and about my real parents much earlier than some people do. And Malmö was only a small town. They weren't very clever, the Social people I mean. There was no question of me never finding out who my parents were, half the town knew where I'd come from, the only child with blond hair and oriental eyes. Everyone knew except me.' She looked at Simona. 'Can I have a cigarette?' I hadn't known she smoked, in fact she did so only very rarely, and then only when stressed.

'How was that possible?' Simona was intrigued. The Swiss system of adoption is watertight to the point that often within a year of the adoption no-one has access to the circumstances any longer.

'My mother was a water-side prostitute from Thailand, and I understand not yet nineteen when I was born. That was in 1960. And my father was a Swedish sailor who was living with her, I think he was probably living off her too.' She blushed. 'God knows why they didn't try to have me aborted. I've often wondered about that, whether it meant that perhaps they actually were in love.'

I had never heard someone speak like this about themselves, and her directness was disconcerting.

'Anyway, apparently the authorities said a person like that shouldn't be in charge of a child, and the Sorensens were looking for a child to adopt. But they were rather old. I didn't realise that until a lot later, though.' Her eyes misted. 'I don't think they'd really thought it through. The years and years of keeping a child amused. Sorting out all the adolescent problems. In fact, they must have recognised their mistake quite soon after they took me in.'

'Why?' Simona probed gently.

'Why? Because the same year that they told me I wasn't their child, and I say, I was only six, they sent me away to a boarding school in Stockholm, a long way from Malmö. I remember it now, night after night, I would lie awake for hours, wondering about my real parents, making up little prayers to a God I didn't really know, asking Him to show me my daddy in a dream... God knows what he would have looked like if it had come true. Or my Thai mother.' She was silent a moment. 'It wasn't until years later that I found out who they really were.' she added. 'And by that time Malmö was a whole lot different from what it had been in 1960. I never actually met either of my real parents. So you see, I don't think any musical ability came from there.' She glanced at the faded enlargements on the wall with a wistful look. 'Oh, dear. I didn't mean to talk about myself quite so much. But it all ties in, you see. With the ALBATROSS business. When you don't know where you come from, and what makes you tick, it's very unnerving. You clutch at what looks like a straw before you know it's actually a nettle.'

'How did you come to be in Japan?' Simona tactfully changed direction. Sigrid Sorensen smiled at that.

'I had a job in a Travel Agency in Stockholm, well, I was a trainee, actually. The woman training me was Japanese, Megumi. We found we had something in common, she was a ski instructor in Winter, and I do ski jumping, as a Coach, I mean. Well, two years ago we spent the long winter holidays in Bavaria. She was a ski instructor, I trained ski jumping. It was really fun, like Chalet Girls, you know?' She looked at her drink and Simona helped her.

'But he went on: "You drink Bacardi and Coke. I was going to buy you one, but by the time my break came round, you'd gone." I hadn't a clue what he was talking about, but he got my preferred drink right. Well, we got talking, and the ship takes two whole days to reach Russia...' Her voice tailed off. Simona was looking emotional.

'That is quite the most romantic encounter I have ever heard!' She swallowed. 'Paul... more drinks?'

There was a pause while I went to fetch another bottle, but at that moment the phone rang, Ben had stopped at Buchs for food and wanted to talk to Sigrid. Simona and I left her alone in the living room to take the call, and when we came back several minutes later she was sitting staring into space with a quiet smile of pure contentment on her face.

'Would you like to hear about what happened on the *"Rossiya"*?' she asked. 'I'm afraid it's not at all romantic, though it was at first. But then... oh dear...' The hair fell across her face again to cover her emotions.

'Do you want to tell us?' Simona sounded as if she were unsure it was a good idea. The old problem, therapy or thunderbolt?

'If I don't tell someone I shall go mad.' It was said matter-of-factly. I opened a second bottle of Dole and stoked up the fire, and so at last we learned the full story of Ben Lakey's and Sigrid Sorensen's nightmare on Suri's Soviet 'ALBATROSSIYA'.

- - - - -

'Last November we both quit the Travel Agents, and Megumi – her family lives in a town called Niigata, near the Japanese Alps – she organised for us to spend the Winter up in the Japanese winter sports region. Even organised the coaching and all that, and a lot of Americans go there as a change from Colorado. And obviously I speak English.' She begged another cigarette but, unable to hold it, looked to Simona again for help. Just talking, talking about anything at all, had already helped the girl to regain a certain tranquillity.

'And yet you're back in... February, and by the Trans-Siberian. What happened?'

Sigrid Sorensen shrugged.

'That wasn't what we'd planned. We flew out on Aeroflot, via Moscow. Their prices are far cheaper than JAL, and with the Travel Agency perks, we only paid ten per cent of that. We were having a really good time there. Until three weeks ago.' She paused. 'We were at one of the prettiest little resorts in all of Japan, Hida Takayama, a jewel of a town, and superb winter sports. But not now there aren't.' Rather than repeat her question, Simona offered the cigarette for a few seconds, then looked at Sigrid questioningly.

'We were staying as Chalet girls high up on Mount Norikura. Skiing and jumping by day, duties in the evening. It was such fun! Of course, I'd never heard of Ben then, although we know now that I saw him once, down in Hida Takayama! There's a little café-bar there, with an Australian manager, and he was the bar pianist. Of all things. But I only went there once, and all I knew was that there was a British pianist playing bar music. He didn't sing, thank God!' She giggled.

As we had all night, it seemed unnecessary to push ahead to find out why she had left, but Simona was showing a hint of impatience to move forward.

'What happened three weeks ago?' she asked.

'There was a huge avalanche, on Mount Norikura. Thankfully, it was in the night, when there was no-one on the slopes, or ski jumping. Otherwise I might not be here... The upper part of the resort, and half of Hida Takayama, was wiped out. And the ski jump, of course. Well, my work permit was only for six months anyway, and for winter sports. Megumi took me to her parents' house in Niigata, but I couldn't stay there. Her family told me of the ferry from Takoaka to Nakhodka that connects with the "*Rossiya*", the Trans-Siberian, and I couldn't afford to fly home.'

'I'd always heard the Trans-Siberian went from Vladivostok?' I was puzzled.

'It used to, but that's all changed, it's a military town and naval base now, and no foreigners are even allowed into Vladivostok. It's Nakhodka for the train.' she insisted, then she started to giggle, not a nervous laugh, a genuine sense of humour revealed. 'I met Ben in Takoaka, queuing for the ship. He was behind me in line, and I heard this English voice say: "I've seen you before!" I turned round and I had no idea he was the pianist in Hida Takayama, and that he had to leave for the same reason as I did. Well, I thought he was just chatting me up... it happens...'

'Yes, I can imagine,' murmured Simona.